Deborah Sheldon is a professional w
Her latest releases, through several pu
horror novel *Contrition*, the dark fant
Little Stitches and Other Stories (win
Award "Best Collected Work 2017"), the dark literary collection *300 Degree Days and Other Stories*, the bio-horror novella *Thylacines*, and the monster-horror novel *Devil Dragon*. Her short fiction has appeared in many well-respected magazines such as *Quadrant*, *Island*, *Aurealis*, *SQ Mag*, and *Midnight Echo*. Her work has been shortlisted for numerous Aurealis Awards and Australian Shadows Awards, long-listed for a Bram Stoker Award, and included in "best of" anthologies. Other credits include TV scripts, feature articles, non-fiction books, stage plays, and award-winning medical writing.

Visit Deb at http://deborahsheldon.wordpress.com

Other IFWG Titles by Deborah Sheldon

Perfect Little Stitches and Other Stories
Dark Waters / Ronnie and Rita (two novellas)

Contrition

By Deborah Sheldon

This is a work of fiction. The events and characters portrayed herein are imaginary and are not intended to refer to specific places, events or living persons. The opinions expressed in this manuscript are solely the opinions of the author and do not necessarily represent the opinions of the publisher.

Contrition

All Rights Reserved

ISBN-13: 978-1-925759-52-5

Copyright ©2018 Deborah Sheldon
V1.0

This book may not be reproduced, transmitted, or stored in whole or in part by any means, including graphic, electronic, or mechanical without the express written consent of the publisher except in the case of brief quotations embodied in critical articles and reviews.

Printed in Palatino Linotype and Optima typefaces.

IFWG Publishing Australia
Melbourne

www.ifwgaustralia.com

For Allen and Harry

1

John Penrose got out of his car. The real estate agent, parked directly ahead, did not emerge. After a few moments, John walked up to the agent's Volkswagen Golf and stared through the windscreen. The little prick was lazing in the driver's seat, yapping on a mobile, in no hurry. John felt the familiar sting of humiliation. Like all real estate agents, this one did not give a shit because John wanted to rent instead of buy.

The winter breeze carried a chill. He stuck his hands into the pockets of his jeans and gazed about. The residential street had alternating eucalypts and bottle-brushes spaced along the nature strips. The houses looked rundown, each with a concrete driveway and flat-roof carport. It was a familiar scene. This suburb, some twenty-five kilometres east of Melbourne city, was blue-collar and falling into disrepair. And John should know, having rented around here for years.

He contemplated another cigarette. The agent was still on the phone. Why hadn't the little prick revealed the property's street number so that John could appraise it from the outside? Could it be the rendered house? The clinker-brick shithole with the palm tree out front? John resisted the urge to knock on the car window. Instead, he bit his lip and waited.

A dog barked. Traffic murmured in the distance. Magpies warbled. The area seemed quiet.

John's current home was next to a shopping precinct, which meant that it suffered from through-traffic at all hours. Meredith hated the hitching and whining noises that vehicles made while negotiating the speed humps. How many times had she raised a slat of the venetian blinds to glare at and curse the offending cars? When John was home from the factory, slumped in front of the TV, was it a dozen times a day? More than that? *Arsehole*, she would hiss at the window. *You inconsiderate arsehole.* Mostly, John tried not to care. He would drink his beers, steadily, one after the other, and ignore her. Once in a while, however, there was a program that interested him. Then he would tell her to ease up, that he was trying to hear the show. *To hell with you*, she would reply, turning her empty gaze upon him, her lifeless doll's eyes that made his flesh creep.

Yet she was not always like that.

Occasionally, she managed to bring herself back into the world, like a picture coming into focus. The saucy tilt of her chin, a slow chuckle, the way she tucked her hair behind one ear, these flashes of old and familiar gestures reminded him of days long past, when he had loved her and, more importantly, when she had loved him. It almost hurt. Then Meredith would submerge again, lost and bewildered.

John exhaled, concentrated on his assessment of the street. No speed humps. The nearest shop was at least a five-minute drive away. Maybe this rental property would be the right one. He had already viewed two others this morning. Both had been wrong for Meredith. He had known that as soon as he had walked in; as soon as he had seen that the bedrooms in each house shared a common wall. She could not abide a common wall.

"Mr Penrose?"

John turned. The agent stood on the footpath, grinning in a way that seemed disdainful rather than friendly. *The feeling is mutual, kid.* John bristled at the shiny suit and open-collared shirt, gelled hair and gauge earrings, clipped moustache and goatee, the snotty attitude. You're so young and stupid, John thought. Just wait until life starts kicking you around. But John needed a place to rent, and he needed to sign a lease today. No matter what, he must hold his tongue and smile, smile, *smile*.

"Mr Penrose, are you ready to see the property?"

Smiling, John nodded.

The little prick strutted across the road towards a cracked driveway. John followed. The weatherboard miner's cottage looked battered; hunkered into the ground. The gabled roof was tin. Two narrow windows flanked the door. The yard was hard-packed earth, a smattering of tall fescue and yellow dandelions.

Unexpectedly, nostalgia for the small Tasmanian town of Devonport squeezed at John's throat. Every house along his street had resembled this hovel in one way or another. He had lived in a cabin at a caravan park that overlooked Bass Strait, and had stayed there for six years, the longest he had ever resided at the same address. He could almost hear again the horn-blare of ships leaving the harbour. The ships had woken him once or twice every night as they had steamed towards the mainland, always saving him from bad dreams. No; from the same bad dream. Sometimes, he wished he were back there, sitting in a canvas deckchair on his porch, surveying the docks far below and the shimmering line where the sky met the sea, a beer in one hand, a cigarette in the other, alone and lonely, but safe. Safe from —

"Mr Penrose?"

John rubbed at a temple. "I'm sorry, what did you say?"

"That it's not an authentic miner's cottage. It was built in the seventies, I believe, originally as a two-bedroom property." The little prick approached the front door. "Back in the nineties, a previous owner added an extension; an extra bedroom with an en suite and separate exit. The owner-occupier used the extension to accommodate a boarder. Impressions?"

"I don't know yet. Let me inside."

The little prick turned the key and entered. The cottage exhaled a stale breath of dust, mildew, and neglect. The light was dim. John crossed the threshold and hesitated, waiting for his sight to adjust to the gloom. A hall lay directly ahead.

"Lounge is first left. Naturally, in this price range, there's no air conditioning."

"Naturally," John said, feeling the sting of humiliation again.

He trailed behind the little prick.

"Master bedroom, first right. Next left, bathroom, then kitchen. Yes, it's cramped, hardly any bench space. Put a chopping board over the sink: problem solved. Behind the kitchen, a separate laundry." The little prick gestured across the hall. "You've got a second bedroom over there."

Yes, that would be perfect for Meredith's hobby room, John thought. So far, in the dozen or so rental properties they had shared, she had never allowed him inside her hobby room. Not once. But, of course, he *had* gone inside, in every house and on many occasions, usually at night when she was asleep or out roaming. Curiosity can only be denied for so long. And besides, he had a right to know. He was paying the bills, wasn't he?

Next, they came to the closed door at the end of the hall.

"Here we have the extension." The little prick grabbed the handle and pushed.

John gave a small gasp. In contrast to the rest of the cottage, natural light flooded the room. A floor-to-ceiling window had a glass door to the back yard. John's heart galloped. *I could come and go as I please.* He peeped around the half-wall at the tiny en suite.

"This is fine," he said. "What about the back yard?"

Through the window lay a jumble of soil and weeds, a high timber fence greying and cracked with age.

The little prick sighed. "Yes, it's a bit of disaster."

They went out through the glass door. The extension turned out to be nothing but a skillion tacked on to the rear of the single-gabled cottage. Whoever had done the extension had botched the job, but John could not have cared less. As he tramped the yard, the earth gave beneath his boots, suggesting that it did not have too much clay in it. There were no trees in the yard either and no overhanging boughs from surrounding properties, which meant the grounds would enjoy full sun. John experienced a hiccup of excitement.

"This would be perfect for a vegie patch," he said.

"A vegie patch? Seriously? You're into that kind of thing?"

"You bet. Nothing tastes better than food you grow yourself."

"Well," the little prick said, with a polite laugh. "I'll take your word for it."

John looked straight up, a hand shielding his eyes. The clouds had cleared. The sun beat weakly on his face. "This is the one," he said.

"Are you sure? We've still got the two-storey unit."

"Sign me up for this place. When can I move in?"

"Oh, Mr Penrose, let's not get ahead of ourselves. I'll present your application to the owners. That's the best I can do, I'm afraid."

"No, it isn't. You can make the choice for them if you want."

"True, but only when one applicant is clearly better than the others."

The others? Jeez, as if this dump was in demand. John wanted to laugh.

Instead, giving his rehearsed and pleasant smile, he said, "Let the owner know I want to value-add to the property by improving the garden. Free of charge. Not just the vegie patch, mind you, but garden beds, here along the fence."

The little prick did not answer. John concentrated on the clucking of an unseen wattlebird and tried to hold his growing impatience in check. *Smile, smile, smile...* He could feel his fingers tingling. Soon they would start to tremble. He needed a drink.

The little prick said, "Sorry, but I'm still a touch bothered, to be honest."

And I'm bothered by your fucking stupid earrings, John thought, but do you hear me bitching? "I've got full-time employment," he said, "a good rental history, good credit. I'm not a risk."

"On paper, yes, but I've been in the business for three years now."

Wow, three years… John smiled and said, "Meaning?"

"Meaning I don't understand why a single man who lives alone would want a three-bedroom place, especially one with two bathrooms. Apart from the extra expense, there's the extra cleaning to take into consideration."

John lit a cigarette. Shit, his fingers were trembling. "I told you why already."

"And Mr Penrose, I told *you* already, our agency doesn't allow subletting. I want to make that point very clear."

"I'm not sub-letting. How many times do you need me to say it?"

The little prick made an exaggerated show of looking at his watch.

"Okay, I'll tell you the whole story, even though it's none of your business," John said, and blew a twin stream of cigarette smoke through his nostrils. "A young bloke like you wouldn't get it, and that's fine, you're at a different stage of life than me. But I'm nearly fifty. I've got a couple of grown kids, one of them married with a baby. They visit me from time to time. And when they do, I want to offer them more than just a blow-up mattress on the floor."

The little prick blushed. "Yes, those air beds can be uncomfortable."

"The extension is for my family. I won't have to clean it that often because most of the time it won't be used. Okay? There's the answer to your question about housekeeping. Not an issue."

"Right, yes, I see."

"I'll sleep in the main bedroom and use the second bedroom as my study. I'm doing a part-time university course. Shutting a door behind me once I've done my homework helps to clear the mind, right?"

Don't oversell it.

John dangled the cigarette from his lips and tried to look honest by widening his eyes. Meanwhile, his hands, stuffed into the pockets of his jeans, were clenched and sweating. Of course, he didn't actually *have* any children. In fact, he didn't have any family at all, not even a second cousin as far as he knew. He wasn't enrolled in any university course either, because he had dropped out of high school before the Year Twelve exams. But this tale had allayed the suspicions of every real estate agent he had encountered since living with Meredith. There was no reason why this agent would react any differently.

"Mr Penrose," the little prick said, "I apologise for casting aspersions."

"That's okay. No offence. I understand you have a job to do."

"Every day, we deal with terrible renters."

"I'll bet."

"Just last week, we sprang a couple that had sub-let their second bedroom, lounge and garage to three different families. Can you believe it?"

"Three families?" John tossed his cigarette butt. "Despicable."

"Two people on the lease, but eighteen people living in the place. My God, you should have seen the state of it. Now the owner has to replace the carpet, the tiles, repaint the walls..." He wrinkled his nose. "Oh, the stories I could tell. Some would make you sick to your stomach. My duty is first and foremost to the property owner."

"Yep, makes sense."

The little prick wandered towards the fence and gestured vaguely at the dirt. "So, you'd put garden beds here?"

"That's right." John walked over. "All the way along the boundary: raised garden beds, using sleepers. I'd put in clematis and foxglove in this section, maybe a few roses over there. A bit of Mexican sage and Snow White never goes astray."

The little prick laughed. "I've got no idea what you're talking about."

"Check out the place in a few months. You'll see what I'm talking about."

"A keen gardener, hey?"

"Very keen."

The little prick held out his hand. John took it. The relief lifted a heavy stone from his guts, and almost stopped his fingers from trembling. Almost.

"So, we're good?" John said.

"As gold. Is a twelve-month lease all right?" He dropped his hand and started towards the glass door of the extension. "Let's finalise things at the office."

"No worries."

They walked through the cottage without speaking.

Back in his car, John watched the little prick's Volkswagen Golf zoom off down the street. John turned the ignition key and glanced at the miner's cottage. It struck him, again, with powerful memories of Devonport. Every time the deafening blat of a ship's horn had shocked him awake, he would find that he had sweated through his sheets. Year-round, snow and ice from Antarctica, the very bottom of the world, shunted a cool wind over the isle of Tasmania, yet despite this chill, despite sleeping without blankets, John would sweat because of the dream.

Don't think about it.

He pulled away from the kerb, the tyres of his old Ford Falcon emitting a brief squeal. The real estate agency was only a few streets away. John would finish the paperwork, return to Meredith, and tell her the good news. Hopefully, she would be happy. And hopefully, they could move within days. Meredith had so antagonised their current neighbours that John feared the police might get involved. Just the thought parched his mouth.

No, stop, it would be okay.

He and Meredith could make a new start. The miner's cottage with its picture-perfect extension was an omen that everything would be all right from now on. The bad dreams—and maybe the bad times—could be laid to rest.

The front window of the real estate agency was covered in posters of houses for sale. Inside was an open space with desks, pot plants, and a sagging couch for clients who might have to wait. The place was deserted apart from the receptionist. She smiled at her colleague. By the time she flicked her gaze across John's face, most of her smile had worn off. The little prick went behind a desk, waved John into the opposite seat, and began searching through a stack of papers.

John wanted a drink. Very much.

To distract himself, he watched the receptionist.

Her fingernails were incredibly long, as curved as talons, and painted red. She typed with their tips. After a while, she stopped typing and tried to pick up a pen. It was like she wore mittens. She had to clumsily roll the pen along the counter and trap the implement between her palms. Christ, she had disabled herself with those ridiculous nails. How could she manage anything at all? Trying to wipe her arse after a crap, for instance, must be fraught with danger. The thought made John snigger. The receptionist froze, glared at him.

Chastened, John looked away.

The little prick was flicking through, and occasionally stopping to read, a stapled document of some kind. The wall-clock ticked interminably.

10.57 a.m.

No wonder John felt antsy. On his days off he began drinking at 10.45 a.m. sharp. This had been his habit for years. Why that particular time, he could no longer remember. He watched the clock.

10.58.

He pinched his upper lip between his thumb and forefinger. That sometimes helped. Maybe it was an acupressure point. Decades ago, back in high school, Meredith had told him about acupressure points. She had been an enthusiastic advocate of New Age bullshit, and used to talk about chakras, meridians, third eyes… She did not talk much about anything these days, apart from noisy cars and neighbourhood pets. She hated every kind of pet, but cats in particular. If she happened to spot a cat through one of the windows, she would bare her teeth and hiss.

The little prick tapped at his keyboard and paused to read whatever had come up on the computer screen.

11 a.m. Tick, tick, tick…

God almighty, what could be the hold-up?

Despite himself, John pictured a beer, the stubby cold enough for condensation to bead, cluster, and run down the bottle. The tantalising image made the thirst grow stronger. It ballooned up from his stomach, began to wither the mucous membranes in his oesophagus and sinuses, and spread throughout his mouth, desiccating his tongue. This was not an ordinary thirst. A gallon of water could not slake it. Only beer washed away the stricture in his throat, usually before he had finished the first stubby, sometimes on the first swig.

"Okay, Mr Penrose," the little prick said, offering a sheet of paper. "Here's the lease agreement. Twelve months, like we discussed. We need a month's rent in advance. The bond is the same amount as a month's rent. You'll get the bond back when you vacate, assuming everything's in good order."

"Yep, I've done this plenty of times. No need to explain."

"Humour me anyway. My boss goes off the deep end if I don't do my job." The little prick handed over a stapled sheaf of papers. "This is the condition report. Write down any other observations of damage that aren't mentioned."

"Sure."

"Some tenants like to take photographs as proof."

"Right. So, are we done?"

"Not quite."

The little prick perused more papers. John focused on the *clack clack clack* of talons on keys. Glancing at the receptionist, he was just in time to see her scratch at the corner of her mouth, delicately, with a single claw. Ouch. John would never let a woman with a crazy manicure like that anywhere near his block and tackle. Then he found himself wondering if she ever injured herself while masturbating. The thought was strangely arousing.

"Mr Penrose, you're a plate mounter for a printing company."

John looked around. "What?"

"You're a plate mounter."

"Right, yeah."

"What does that entail, exactly?"

He's playing with me; he knows I want to get out of here. John took a breath, let his arms hang, and silently vowed to sit in this chair all day if that's what it took.

He said, "I work for a company that prints food packaging."

"Food packaging?"

"The flexible kind: bread bags, packets for potato chips, biscuits, that sort of thing. Every print job has a set of plates. My job is to prepare them for the printer."

The receptionist paused her typing. John had a female audience. He sat up straight and pulled in his gut.

"There's a machine I use," he continued. "I put each plate on its table."

"Yes? Please, go on, Mr Penrose."

"The machine irons the plate onto the sleeve. I tape the edges of the plate so it doesn't lift up inside the press."

"Gosh. How fascinating. Isn't this fascinating, Lisa?"

In his peripheral vision, John saw the receptionist staring. Was she impressed? Hard to tell; he would have to look to find out. No, he decided, he would not look.

"You have a trade qualification for this?" the little prick said.

John hesitated. "I got on-site training."

"Ah. Which takes how long?"

About an hour, John thought. Instead, he said, "Well, that depends on the worker, their smarts and willingness to learn. I managed it in about a week."

"Really?" The little prick gave a slow smile. "An entire week?"

John again felt the sting of humiliation. *Clack clack clack* went the receptionist's nails. John leaned back into the chair and pinched at his upper lip.

"Your working hours," the little prick said. "I assume you're part-time?"

"Full-time."

"Ah, but today is Monday."

"Ah, that's correct, very good," John said, winking as if they were sharing a joke, trying his best to keep the edge out of his voice. "Today is definitely Monday. You're right on the money. But I work a twelve-hour shift every Wednesday, Thursday and Friday. Right now happens to be my weekend."

Frowning, the little prick held out a pen. "Signature on the dotted line."

John, fingers sweating, managed to scrawl his name.

Hopefully, Meredith would be happy about the new place. Whenever she was unhappy, she became difficult, unpredictable...feral. Sometimes he felt afraid of her. Shit, which was ridiculous considering her slight build. Merry probably weighed about the same as your average ten-year old, and John was tall and heavyset, so there was no reason for him to be frightened. No logical reason, anyway.

2

John left the real estate agency with keys to the cottage and wads of paperwork in his back pockets. His quivering hands and locked throat urged him home for a drink, but his empty stomach growled. He had not eaten since the previous night. There was next to nothing in the fridge or pantry. Momentarily, he was torn, struck by indecision on the footpath.

Other shoppers moved around him: swarms of tottering pensioners, women in sloppy tracksuit pants, unshaven men in jeans and bare feet, workers on their break wearing chemist whites, supermarket uniforms, or two-piece suits; everyone heading somewhere, except for John and a grizzled alcoholic slumped over a bench.

The sight of the alky—aged anywhere from fifty to seventy, it was hard to tell—gave John a sharp fright, like a poke in the ribs. The man's hair was matted, his face grimy, trousers piss-stained. If John got close enough, he would catch a whiff.

One of his rules came to mind: *You're an alky when you ditch meals for booze.*

And the bakery was just four shops away.

The doorway had plastic strips to keep out the flies. A dozen customers were ahead of him. John would have a long wait. He began to jiggle one leg, drumming the heel of his boot on the linoleum floor. The bakery was unpleasantly humid and smelled of yeast. The boy at the counter turned to the door that led to the ovens and called for someone to open the other register. A few seconds later, a bored-looking redhead walked through. Straight away, John remembered her name: Ginny.

So, she was still working here. Two (or three?) rental properties ago, he and Meredith had lived nearby. He had frequented this bakery all the time for a quick lunch. Ginny used to talk to him about the appalling state of the public toilet block situated in the midst of the carpark. *The council never cleans it*, she used to say. *It's a health hazard.* John would tsk-tsk and sympathise. *Someone ought to get a dunny brush and detergent*, she would add, bagging his order of pastries. He had thought about cleaning the block to impress her, but no, he had never done so, and then he had moved away.

His heart began to beat harder as his turn approached. Should he say hello? Ask if the toilet block was as filthy as ever? When she looked at him, he felt himself smile, a genuine smile this time.

"Yes, can I help you?" she said, with no flicker of recognition in her eyes.

Mumbling, John ordered his food. Ginny bagged the pastries, took his money.

"Yes, can I help you?" she said to the next customer in line.

On his way to the car, John stopped to take stock of his surroundings.

Nothing much in the shopping centre had changed. The continuity felt reassuring. Sectioned off with hoop bollards, a dozen parking spaces were now garden beds with shrubs and native grasses. The new landscaping offered a touch of much-needed class to the strip. Further along, the florist had become a two-dollar shop, the hardware store, a café. The latter had a hanging sign, hand-painted, *The Brunch Corner*. From the name alone, he could picture the menu: eggs any which way on sourdough, ham and cheese croissants, open sandwiches, soup, pasta of the day…

The breeze swung the sign on its hooks, gently.

Perhaps he could become a regular and strike up friendly relations with the waitresses. Even though tipping was not customary, John would be sure to tip, discreetly, a folded note pressed into a warm, grateful hand. It would make the waitresses happy. They would look forward to seeing him. They would know him by name. *Hi, John, great to see you*, they would say, and usher him to his private table, permanently reserved. *What can we get for you?*

Grey clouds raced overhead, shredding in the wind. Rain was coming. John hurried to his car, making sure to give the alky a wide berth.

"Hoi, you got a smoke, mate?" the alky called.

John did not look back. He got into his car, manoeuvred out of the carpark, and soon joined the traffic on the highway. The trip home would take around a quarter of an hour. The smell of pastries made him salivate. With one hand clenched hard around the steering wheel to stop his fingers from trembling, he scarfed down a sausage roll. Then, fuck it, he ate the other one. There were still a couple of pies left. And Meredith wouldn't care. When was the last time he had ever seen her eat?

The unit he shared with Meredith was one of three arranged side by side on the block. As always, John parked at the kerb. Their single carport held his trailer and a garden shed secured with a padlock. Before getting out of his car, John observed the windows of the other units. No curtains moved. Hopefully, he could sneak inside before somebody buttonholed him.

No such luck.

As his boots hit the driveway, the door of the first unit opened.

"Oh, John, there you are. Thank goodness. Can I have a word?"

Freezing mid-step, he arranged his face into a smile. Mrs Dwight tromped outside. She was an elderly, flabby woman, with a double chin so large it swung like a dewlap. No matter the weather, she always seemed to wear open-toed slippers and the same kind of shapeless cotton dress. Her eyes were red and watering as if she had been crying.

"Afternoon, Mrs Dwight," John said. "Looks like rain."

"Have you seen Angel?"

"Not yet. Like I told you, I'll let you know if I do. Okay?"

He took a step. Mrs Dwight put a hand on his elbow. He wanted to shove her away. Instead, he grinned, hard, and put his arm behind his back, clear of her touch.

She said, "Angel's a homebody. It's not like him to stay away."

"Cats are funny creatures, Mrs Dwight. Sometimes they wander."

"He's never gone missing before. It's been six days. I'm literally frantic. What on earth could have happened to him?"

John did not know for sure but had a damn good idea. An unpleasant one.

The headache was creeping up on him, the type that squeezed like a giant pair of hands. He rubbed at his temples. A single beer and the headache would vanish. He must get away from Mrs Dwight. Had he remembered to put more beers in the fridge? His memories of last night were fuzzy. If there were no cold beers he would drink them warm from his stash in the laundry and put a couple of six-packs in the freezer.

"I've called the pound," Mrs Dwight was saying, "and the local vets and the RSPCA, and nothing. I'm absolutely beside myself."

"Have you thought about putting up posters around the neighbourhood? Get a poster to me by tomorrow night, and I'll photocopy it at work. A dozen copies, okay? Two dozen, I'm happy to help. Don't worry. He'll turn up. Righto, see you later."

Again, he went to step away. Again, she grabbed his arm.

"What about your lady friend?" Mrs Dwight said.

He froze, his headache momentarily forgotten. "What lady friend?"

"You know, the blonde lady. Sometimes she looks out your front window."

He pursed his lips and shook his head. "I don't know who you mean."

Mrs Dwight began to stare at him, her eyes narrowing in disbelief or perhaps…suspicion? John glanced at his residence, expecting to see the venetian blinds pulled up and Meredith silhouetted there, white as chalk.

No, thank God. The venetians were down and closed.

"Oh," he said, snapping his fingers, "you're thinking of my cleaning woman."

"Cleaning woman?"

"Yeah. She comes over every now and then."

Mrs Dwight gave a hopeful smile. "Perhaps she might have seen Angel?"

"Nah. She's hardly ever here. In fact, she hasn't been around in weeks." He began to stride away. "Okay, see you later. Let me know about the poster, all right?"

Now, he just had to make it inside before the Kapoors in unit two spotted him.

For months, the Kapoors had been receiving anonymous notes in their letterbox. Mr Kapoor had shown them to John. The notes, handwritten on thick and creamy sheets, folded twice and delivered without envelopes, bore angry messages such as YOUR BIRDS ARE TOO NOISY!! A retired couple, the Kapoors owned a dozen budgerigars in a cage the size of a pantry cupboard. In fine weather, the Kapoors would wheel the cage into their back yard so the budgerigars could enjoy fresh air and sunshine. MAKE YOUR BIRDS SHUT UP!! The perpetrator must live nearby, Mr Kapoor had confided. Only close neighbours can hear such little chirps and whistles. And then, only last week, a note had been pushed under their front door. YOUR BIRDS WILL DIE!! Apparently, Mrs Kapoor was terrified. Apparently, Mrs

Kapoor wanted to call the police. And so, John had started calling real estate agents.

He made it past unit two. The Kapoors must be out.

At his own door, he hesitated. The handle felt cold. He put his ear to the jamb. No sounds. This was typical. Meredith never played music or watched TV. His teeth clicked as they came together. His stomach muscles tightened. Coming home always felt like this. He always had to take a moment to brace himself.

It reminded him of that one time in Devonport when he had finished his shift and returned to his cabin in the caravan park, tired and thirsty. Lifting his key to the door, he heard the screech of the cutlery drawer scraping along its wooden tracks. *Somebody is inside.* A zap of electricity shot through his limbs. He unlocked and threw open the door. A startled teenager gaped, empty-handed. John laughed. What had the kid expected to find? When the kid dashed for the door, John let him go. A quick search revealed nothing had been stolen. The kid, rifling through the cabin for Christ knows how long, had not found one single item worth stealing. And yet, that initial pop of fright, that fear of what lay beyond the door…

Viscerally, John felt it now.

With the key inside the lock, he steeled himself. Something caught his eye. Mrs Dwight stood on her porch, watching him, hands clasped and held tight against her chest. Shit. You know it's time to leave when neighbours start to watch you like that. With a jaunty wave at Mrs Dwight, he turned his key and went inside.

He leaned against the door to close it behind him. For a few moments, he could not see Meredith. He raked his gaze across the sofa, armchair, coffee table, as if she might be hiding, crouched, waiting to spring. His unease went up a notch. Perhaps she was in the hobby room, quiet and docile.

"Merry, I'm back," he called. "I've got news. Where are you?"

He took a step from the door.

Then he saw her.

Tension ebbed from his shoulders. Ever since they had begun living together, it had been this way: he needed to know her location before he could relax.

"Hey, did you hear me?" he said. "Meredith?"

A servery bench separated the lounge from the kitchen. She was standing at the sink, as motionless and stiff as a mannequin, arms by her sides, facing the window. The view consisted of a fence, some two metres away. Knowing Meredith, she had probably been standing like that for hours. Maybe the whole time he had been gone. He slung the greasy bag of cold pies onto the bench and went to the fridge.

Eight stubbies of Victoria Bitter.

Well, good enough for now. More could be put in the freezer.

He grabbed a stubby, twisted the cap, and took a long, long drink. Magic... There was no other word to describe the sensation. The bolus of beer released a familiar, tingling wave of relief as it slid down his oesophagus, easing the stricture in its wake, opening his throat like a blossoming flower.

"I've signed up for a new place," he said.

He finished the stubby and opened another. Thank Christ, his hands had stopped shaking. The headache let go of his temples and slid away. He finished the second stubby and reached for a third. He shut the fridge door. Since he was feeling better, he could drink at a more leisurely pace. He took a neoprene stubby holder from the top of the fridge and slid the bottle inside.

"Did you hear me?" he said, leaning on the draining board. "Merry?"

He regarded her profile. She was still beautiful: at least to him.

Meredith Berg-Olsen had a Danish father and a Swedish mother. This combination of Northern European genes had made her tall, slender, blonde, blue-eyed, with skin as white and clear as porcelain. In her late teens, Meredith Berg-Olsen had all the makings of a runway model. Now in her late forties, after everything she had been through—including horrors that John could only guess at—she looked bloodless instead of pale, skeletal instead of slender, more dead than alive.

"Can you hear me?" he said.

No, she wasn't looking at the fence. He followed her downcast gaze. On the windowsill lay the corpse of a fly, on its back, legs knitted together.

"Meredith," he said. "I've found us a new home."

Her head turned, slowly and mechanically, and her lashless eyes looked up. The blank expression told him she would likely not remember what he said, that he would need to remind her again later. The dark circles beneath her eyes resembled bruises. Her thin lips were chapped.

"You'll love it," he continued. "The place has three bedrooms. You've got the two at the front, side by side. Mine is at the back, separate with its own en suite. You'll have the main bathroom to yourself. How does that sound?"

John sucked on the stubby and waited.

After a while, Meredith blinked. Her gaze roamed over his face, lingering on the fleshy parts, the tip of his nose, his earlobes. Such close inspection made him edgy. He took a couple of plates from the cupboard.

"I bought us lunch, see?" he said. "Now here's my other bit of good news. You remember, a few years ago, that shopping centre with the bakery I liked?"

"The Swiss bakery?" she muttered, frowning.

"Yep, that one. From Saturday, it's going to be our shopping centre again. We're going back to an old stomping ground. Our house is built on its own block, so we won't be living cheek-by-jowl with the neighbours." He put a meat pie on each plate. "Speaking of which, Mrs Dwight asked me again about Angel."

A glitter passed over Meredith's eyes. She lifted a bony hand and raked fingers through her hair. The dry, colourless tufts sat out in a stiff halo.

"Angel the Siamese?" she said, and laughed, a hollow sound. "That fucking arsehole?"

John shrugged. "Aw, come on, he wasn't that bad."

"He used to shit in our yard."

"So what? I cleaned it up, not you."

Meredith stared again at the fly on the sill. "What did you tell Mrs Dwight?"

"That if she made up a 'missing cat' poster, I'd photocopy it for her."

Meredith's smile was a robotic twitch of the lips.

"And stop opening the front blinds," he said. "She's seen you."

"I don't care."

"We're moving on Saturday. Can you do me a favour? Don't write any more notes to the Kapoors."

"I'm not sure I can do that."

"Please," he said. "For me?"

"I want to take each bird and drown it."

"We'll be gone from here soon. Look, they want to call the cops."

"I would fill a pint glass with water," she intoned, her voice dreamy and soft. "One after another, I would put in a bird, head-first, and hold my hand over the top so it couldn't get out."

John's grip tightened on the stubby.

Meredith rested her fingernails on the strip of bench-top surrounding the sink and began to run them across the laminate in slow, meditative circles. For some reason, she always kept her nails long and in good condition. She allowed the rest of her to go to hell, but not her fingernails. It was a quirk that John did not like, another

17

reason why he always fitted a bolt to the inside of his bedroom door.

He finished his drink. "You can start packing if you like."

"I've started already. There's a box of things on my bed."

And it would be the same box of things, he knew. Trinkets from high school: text books, strips of photo-booth snapshots with girlfriends long forgotten, report cards, diaries cataloguing old crushes. It was the same box she carried from one rental place to another. He doubted she had ever unpacked it. Not even once.

"Eat your lunch," he said. "You might want to put it in the microwave."

Meredith picked up the plate and retired to her hobby room. John blew out a long, hard breath and ate a mouthful of meat pie. It was cold but he kept eating anyway. Tomorrow, if he happened to look in the kitchen bin, he would see Meredith's pie, intact, without a single bite taken from it.

3

A fter finishing lunch, John wiped his greasy fingers on his jeans and headed into Meredith's bedroom to retrieve her box of memorabilia.

The utilitarian room had a bed, side table, lamp, and nothing else. When they had first started living together, John had tried to give her the kind of bedroom he thought a woman might like: a mirror and dressing table, a silver brush and comb set, framed prints on the walls, a fussy valance. Meredith had hated it. She preferred to live like a nun who had taken a vow of poverty. No, he thought, as he carried the memorabilia box to the kitchen table, Meredith lived as if she were still institutionalised.

He grabbed another beer and sat down.

Yep, as he had guessed, it was the same box of junk that Meredith had somehow kept with her since high school.

Top of the pile happened to be her paperback copy of *Oliver Twist*. John smiled at the cover's anachronistic inclusion: preserved under a layer of transparent Contact adhesive, Meredith had pared and set amongst Fagin and his pickpockets a magazine clipping of Mark Hamill dressed as Luke Skywalker. In the still shot from the 1977 film, the actor, positioned next to the Artful Dodger, stared out from the book's cover, his youthful face eager and wide-eyed.

John put down the beer and picked up the book.

It felt cool and smooth. The yellowing pages smelled musty.

He opened the cover. The spine made a small cracking sound. *Meredith Berg-Olsen 7C* was written on the title page in a round, girlish hand. Year Seven had been...when? 1980. He quickly did the maths: thirty-six years ago, already.

Meredith, aged twelve, had loved Mark Hamill.

She had not been in John's class in Year Seven, but according to gossip, she constantly doodled the actor's name in her notebooks, replacing the dot over the 'i' in 'Hamill' with a love heart. Most of the boys fancied her, including John. How could they not? She was gorgeous. But Christ, so *aloof*. Some of the boys, aggravated by her ennui, her lack of reciprocal interest in them, tried to harass, tease or bully her. It never worked. She never cared. The boys had snickered amongst themselves anyway, claiming their hollow victories.

1980...

John saw Meredith for the first time on day one of high school.

Mum dropped him at the gate. He did not know a soul.

The hot February sun beat down on him. The stiff collar of his uniform shirt irritated his neck, the tie felt like a noose. Alone, wishing himself invisible or dead, John stood at the designated assembly area outside the gymnasium, stomach churning, palms sweating, and watched the other children chat, laugh and goof off in their groups, hating them all for their innate sense of belonging. Each group emanated an invisible force field. Just thinking about approaching anybody made his mouth go dry.

Across the quadrangle, he noticed a girl.

The sight of her fascinated him at once. Her platinum hair in a blunt bob, her rail-thin frame and pale legs, that regal aura of sophistication, the cool way she stood with one hand on her hip, everything about her, in fact, crawled into John's belly and started to burn. The singing in his blood did not make sense. His pre-pubescent cock stirred. He kept watching her. She never smiled. The other girls around her giggled and flounced and gazed, searching for an audience, but not her. She did not give a solitary goddamn. Falling in love felt like losing his breath.

And then a boy with blonde wiry hair stepped up to him.

Fearful, John moved away. No good. The boy stepped closer. Tall and thin, the boy did not look like a bully, yet you could never tell. The boy's eyes were sunken and ringed with dark circles as if he had not slept. John tensed.

"G'day," the boy said, with an upwards jerk of his chin. "Red or blue?"

"Huh?" John said.

"Winnie red or blue? If you want menthol, you're a poofter, and I can't stand poofters." The boy looked around, as if wary of being caught, and held apart the straps of his schoolbag to yawn open the zipper. Inside were packets of cigarettes with either red or blue designs.

Quickly, the boy gathered the straps and shouldered the bag. "Anyhow have a Winfield," he said, and winked.

John felt lost for words.

The boy said, "Two bucks a pack, fifteen cents per dart, so yeah, it's cheaper by the pack, no discounts, no credit." The boy waited, then gave an impatient sigh. "Come on, dopey. Wake up. You're a smoker, aren't you?"

John had never touched a cigarette. In lieu of a home-made lunch, however, Mum had given him a two-dollar note to use at the canteen.

"No worries," John said, reaching into his pocket. "Give me a pack of red."

The boy laughed. "I knew it."

"Knew what?"

"That you'd smoke reds, like me." Clapping a hand on John's shoulder, the boy said, "Pleased to meet ya. I'm Lyle Berg-Olsen."

"John Penrose."

"Johnno, hey?" Lyle shoved at him playfully. "Fucken hell, mate, we'd better be in the same class."

And they were. They became friends.

Best friends.

Lyle had a never-ending supply of cigarettes because he nicked them from his family's milk bar. John and Lyle spent every lunch-time sitting behind the pine trees that lined the oval, practising their smoke rings, trialling the different ways that a Real Man might hold a cigarette—cupped inside a curled hand, pinched between forefinger and thumb, dangled from one side of the mouth—while the other kids left them alone. Was it John's social awkwardness? Lyle's penchant for sarcasm and condescension? Probably both. So what? John did not want or need any other friends.

Soon after they became inseparable, John realised that Lyle's twin happened to be Meredith.

The sophisticated, mysterious, beautiful Meredith Berg-Olsen.

Whenever John visited their house, she appeared only in glimpses: a ghost on the stairs, a phantom leaving the kitchen, a vision crossing a window as he and Lyle shot hoops outside in the driveway. She ignored John at school too. Fair enough. As a dork, he had no right to expect her attention.

And then, out of nowhere, Meredith spoke to him.

It was in 1983, the summer of Year Ten at the close of final term. By that time, Meredith had long outgrown her infatuation with Mark Hamill. She was still willowy but had developed mesmerising curves.

John had changed too. After turning sixteen, he had grown to over six feet, his shoulders widening, his body becoming gangly, a smattering of hair and pimples sprouting on his chin. Like most other weekends, John was staying over at Lyle's place. On this particular night, they had watched *Mad Max* on video after everyone else had gone to bed. Their sleeping bags were side by side in the rumpus room. Lyle had begun snoring as soon as the lights turned out. But John could not sleep. At about two in the morning, he crept past Lyle and went to the back yard.

It was a warm night, full moon, the air sharp with the scent of a distant bushfire. He sat in a chair at the outdoor setting. Lighting a Winnie Red, he relaxed, listening to the shrill of nearby cicadas and the occasional rattle of leaves as possums leapt between trees. He was not sure what he would do over the summer holidays. Perhaps get a part-time job at Macca's and start saving for a car.

"Got a spare durry?"

Startled, John turned in his chair. Meredith stood by the open back door.

Barefoot, she wore a robe over baby-doll pyjamas, her hair mussed. He could not remember her ever looking at him before. A warm flush spread across his face. Self-conscious, naked except for footy shorts, he picked up and fumbled with the cigarette packet. Meredith crossed the patio towards him, eyes shining, as if his discomfort amused her.

He shook a few cigarettes to the front of the pack and offered the Winnies. She took one. But oh, not with her fingers, oh no; she leaned over from the waist, the pyjama top falling away slightly to reveal the hollows of perfect collarbones and a hint of small breasts, and took one of the cigarettes between her teeth.

His cock stiffened.

As she sat back in the nearest chair, she drowsily blinked, pale lashes fanning against pale skin. Unlike the other girls, Meredith shunned makeup. Against the whiteness of her hair and skin, her irises shone an intense shade of blue.

She met his gaze.

Pinned, he stared back. His stomach dropped away.

With a half-smile, she waggled the cigarette between her teeth at him.

"Oh, shit, sorry," John said, and blushed again.

Reaching out with the lighter, he lit the smoke for her.

How surreal. It felt like a movie moment. Any second now, she would toss the cigarette, take his face in her hands and kiss him. He would smell her and feel her tongue in his mouth. Taste her. She would murmur his name, press against him.

But none of that happened.

She drew on the cigarette, puckered her lips to blow out a thin stream of smoke, and said, "I fucking hate my brother. How come you like him so much?"

Now, snapping out of his reverie, John stood up from the kitchen table and threw Meredith's copy of *Oliver Twist* back in to the box. Luke Skywalker gazed earnestly past his shoulder. *I fucking hate my brother. How come you like him so much?* John reached for the stubby and knocked it over. Shit. Beer suds slopped onto the floor. He grabbed a tea towel and began to wipe up the mess.

How come you like him so much?

This was the problem with reminiscing, he thought, as he scrubbed the tiles. It leads you into deadfalls. He had to stop thinking about the past. Wasn't the recurring nightmare bad enough? Did he have to remind himself of Lyle when awake too?

"I heard a noise."

He glanced up. Meredith stood in the hallway, her face blank and drawn.

"It's nothing," he said. "I knocked over my beer."

She noticed the box on the table and approached. Tentatively, she reached out for *Oliver Twist*. With a slight frown, she rubbed at the cover with her long, manicured thumbnail. He took the book away from her and returned it to the box.

"I'll start packing today," he said. "No time like the present."

Dazed, Meredith raked fingers through her hair. "Packing? Are we moving?"

"Yeah, remember? Back near that bakery I used to like."

"The Swiss bakery?"

"Yep. We're moving this weekend. You've got a bathroom all to yourself. And no common walls, okay? I'm at the back of the house, you're at the front."

Unexpectedly, she clutched at his hand and smiled.

His heart gave a little hop.

Most of the time, Meredith's eyes were watery and faded. However, when she allowed herself a genuine smile, like now, her eyes lit up from within and became the blue of hydrangea petals, the sky on a warm day; the delicate lightness of a mill-pond in summer. John wanted to tell her these things but did not have the words.

"I'll like our new house, won't I?" she said.

"Yeah, course you will. You'll love it."

She dropped his hand and began to sort, absent-mindedly, through the box of memorabilia. John watched the churn of its contents: school reports; envelopes of photographs developed from rolls of film; birthday cards; a pair of knitted fingerless gloves (which she had worn every winter despite the frequent detentions for disobeying the uniform rules); school diaries. Meredith plucked out an envelope of photographs and opened the flap.

"Leave it," John said.

"Leave it?" She hesitated, and then slitted her eyes. "Fuck you."

"No, come on. What's done is done."

She took out the photographs. At first, she studied each one carefully. Sighing, John got himself another beer and sat at the kitchen table, waiting for her inevitable reaction. After a minute, she began flipping through the photographs, faster and faster.

"I don't recognise anybody," she said, voice rising. "Who are they?"

John held out his hand. "Stop. Give 'em here. Grab a chair and we'll go through them together. Okay?"

She obeyed. He recognised the photographs at once: their Year Eleven trip to Central Australia. A lump rose in his throat. His mouth twitched into a grim smile.

"What is it?" Meredith said. "What do you see?"

"You." He held up a photograph. "That's you, right there, sitting on the camel."

John had taken the snap with Meredith's camera. Just moments before John clicked the shutter, the camel had been sitting on the red dusty ground with its legs tucked under it, and Meredith had climbed into the seat with the help of the tour guide. The photograph captured the animal in its clumsy process of standing up. Its back legs were straight, its front legs still folded at the knees. Tipped forward on the seat, clinging to the seat's handrail and captured mid-shriek, was seventeen-year old Meredith, wearing jeans, white sneakers and a blue v-neck jumper. It had been cold in the Outback, despite the desert and clear skies, John remembered.

"That's me?" Meredith said, smiling uncertainly. "Are you sure?"

"Positive."

"But I look terrified. Why am I terrified?"

"I guess you were afraid of falling off."

She began to nod. "Yes. That's why. Yes, I was afraid of falling off."

John took the photograph from her. She let it slip from her fingers without resistance. Every time they prepared to move house, Meredith rediscovered this memorabilia box, and made him go through these photographs with her. She always picked the same packet too. Was she feigning her memory blanks? How else could she pick the same packet every single time? One look at her confused face, however, told him that her amnesia was genuine.

She held up another photograph.

"Who are these people?" she said.

With Uluru as a distant backdrop, three teenagers stood in the sparsely foliaged red dirt, linking arms: John, Meredith, and her brother Lyle.

John took a long drink of beer. This photo always hurt. Shit, how many stubbies had he consumed in the last hour? Four? Five? He had a harsh buzz going on.

With an unsteady forefinger, he pointed at the joyous, youthful faces and gave his usual answer: "That's me, you, and some bloke. I don't recall his name."

She put the group photograph on the table and began to flip through the other snaps. John stared down at Lyle's carefree and grinning face. Just over a year after that photo had been taken—

Resolutely, he put the stubby to his lips and drank.

John had moved house so many times, he had the routine down pat and could relocate within a day. His speed relied on eight rules, of which he felt quite proud:

1. Keep few possessions. Nobody needs books, records, CDs, DVDs, picture frames, knickknacks, vases, et cetera, nor the shelving units such clutter requires. Have the bare minimum of dinnerware and cutlery. Work uniform aside, a couple of pairs of jeans, a handful of shirts and a jumper will suffice.
2. Beds should have slat bases for easy disassembly.
3. Choose compact, light furniture. With a hand trolley and a few occy straps and nylon tie-downs, you can manhandle a small fridge by yourself. Ditto a two-seater sofa.
4. Pack larger items in the trailer, smaller items in the car.
5. Always use the ramps to load and unload the trailer to avoid injuring your back.
6. Before packing a single item, drive Meredith to the new house so she can prowl the empty rooms and touch every surface with her

hands and forehead. By the time you arrive with your first of four loads, she will have calmed down.

7. Unpack Meredith's bedroom furniture and belongings immediately to give her something to do while you're getting the rest of the stuff.
8. Instead of cleaning the old place, let the real estate agency keep your bond.

It was Saturday, first week of spring, with a cloudy sky but no rain. John steered the Falcon into the driveway of their new home, the faux miner's cottage, and braked. The trailer squeaked and groaned on its springs. He cut the engine and alighted. In this second trip, he had the lounge and kitchen furniture, pots and pans, boxes of random indoor stuff. Only two more trips to go—one for the shed and its contents—and he would be finished.

Jesus, what a relief.

Goodbye and good riddance to Mrs Dwight and her stupid cat that liked to shit everywhere. Piss off Mr and Mrs Kapoor, who could shove their bloody tweeting budgies and paranoia, their phone calls to the cops.

He glanced at the cottage. No sign of Meredith. The front had just two tiny windows so it was unlikely that neighbours would spot her. But she had a knack... Please don't make trouble, he thought. Let me stay put for a while. Sighing, he hauled the hand trolley from the trailer. The muscles in his lower back twinged. After tea, it would be good to have a long soak in a hot bath. However, his en suite only had a shower. Would Meredith object to him using her bathroom? It would depend on her mood. Sometimes, moving house exhilarated her. Other times, it made her anxious and fearful.

"Hello there!"

The cheery female voice startled him.

Breathless, he spun around.

Directly across the road, at the clinker-brick shithole with the palm tree out front, standing next to a red Toyota Corolla parked in the driveway, was a slim, middle-aged woman. She waved at him. Hesitantly, briefly, John raised his own hand. He had not heard the car pull up.

"Moving in?" the woman called.

He nodded. In case she missed the gesture, he added, "Yeah."

"Well, I hope you like it here. I'm Donna."

"John."

Donna wore desert boots, faded blue jeans with holes in the knees, a red-check flannelette shirt. Her straight brown hair was long and parted in the middle. From this distance, he could not tell the colour of her eyes, but she had a square face with rosy cheeks, and a broad smile that showed white, strong teeth. She looked country, like the kind of woman who might own a horse.

Uh-oh. She was still looking at him and smiling, as if waiting. What should he do next? Perhaps she expected him to be more forthcoming. *It seems to be a quiet area*, he could say. A remark about the weather might be more appropriate.

The passenger door of the Toyota opened and a child got out, a girl of around ten or twelve, wearing a netball skirt and her hair in a ponytail. The child scowled in John's direction and slouched towards the front door of the clinker-brick shithole.

Donna waved again. "Guess I'll see you round."

He nodded, but vigorously this time, so she couldn't miss it.

Donna and the child went inside. John watched their door for a couple of moments, then wrestled the hand trolley impatiently to one side, and undid the tie-down straps on the trailer. Flipping back the protective blankets, he glared at the cheap sofa and shitty coffee table with a fresh set of eyes: Donna's eyes.

His cheeks burned.

If Donna were peeking through the curtains right now, assessing his furniture, what would she surmise? That he was poor? On the dole? A cheapskate? Druggie?

A knocking sound drew his attention.

Barely visible through the lounge window of the cottage were Meredith's knuckles rapping on the glass. Cursing, John wheeled the trolley to the rear of the trailer. He dropped the tailgate, grappled the metal ramp into position, and strode up the ramp onto the bed of the trailer, hauling the trolley behind him, all the while biting his lip as he listened to the urgent *tap tap tap* of Meredith's bony knuckles. Shut up, he wanted to yell, as his back prickled with sweat. *Shut* the ever-loving fuck *up*.

Instead, he glared at the window and put his forefinger to his mouth. *SHH*.

The rapping stopped.

His hands were trembling. He lugged the fridge onto the trolley and scraped his wrist somehow, drawing blood. Shit. He paused to suck at the wound. If Donna were watching, what would she think? But she wouldn't be watching. John wasn't the kind of man that women liked to watch.

He closed his eyes. His throat felt parched. But another rule came to mind: *You're an alky when you drink and drive.* No, he had to hold on, wait it out. The breeze riffled his hair, slipped beneath the neck of his t-shirt, fanned across his chest. He inspected his wrist. The bleeding had stopped. Now, the cut was a red line along a jagged slash of skin. Slowly, deliberately, he secured the fridge to the trolley with occy straps. He took his time backing down the ramp to the driveway. Feigning a cavalier attitude, he whistled on his way to the front door.

The door opened. Meredith stood in the hallway, white and dishevelled.

"Get back," he said.

She obeyed. He looked over his shoulder. Had anyone seen her?

Once he got inside, he shut the door, and said, "You know better than that."

Meredith's eyes blazed. John steered around her, aiming for the kitchen. Meredith followed.

"Who was that woman?" she said.

"I've never seen her before."

"She told you her name is Donna."

"So what if she did?" He stopped the trolley and removed the straps. The cut on his wrist throbbed. "It's a neighbour being polite."

"You promised we wouldn't have to deal with any neighbours."

"Jesus Christ, all she said was hello."

He could hear Meredith panting. Meanwhile, he manoeuvred the fridge against the wall and plugged it in. The compressor started with a click and a steady hum. He had paid the electricity account on Monday, the same day he had signed the lease. The gas should be on by now too. Meredith still had not spoken. Duct tape held the fridge door closed. He peeled it off.

"Okay," he said, "at least the fridge works."

Still, not a word. He turned. Meredith's lips were tight and bloodless. John blew out an exasperated breath. "Look, I swear I don't know Donna."

Chin quivering, Meredith left the room, steadying herself by sliding her hands along the walls, as if she were drunk or pitching around on a boat. Strong emotions affected her balance. He did not know why and had never asked. His assumption was that, long ago, a medical treatment had fried her brain somehow.

At her bedroom door, Meredith hissed, "You better hope for Donna's sake she doesn't have a fucking pet."

Slam.

And silence.

John leaned against the bench. His headache was starting up again.

Donna's straight long hair and ready smile came to mind. He wished he had made small talk with her, had been quicker off the mark to respond. Chewing his lip, he contemplated the closed door of Meredith's bedroom. Right now, Meredith would most likely be lying face down on the bed, legs together and arms straight by her sides, stiff as a doll. The first time he had seen her in that unnatural position, he had panicked, assumed her to be dead or dying. He had turned her over to perform CPR. And Meredith's lashless eyes had snapped opened.

Yes, he thought, it would be awful if Donna had a pet.

Especially if it happened to be a cat.

4

John woke up the next morning with a thumping hangover that hurt all the way through to his eyeballs. The after-taste of last night's beer sat thick and sour on his tongue. God, he needed water. He sat up in bed, gingerly. His stomach gave a trembling little heave, but damned if he would vomit. Vomiting was not allowed. Vomiting was a sign of alcoholism.

When he opened his eyes, he didn't know where he was.

Frightened, he gaped at the unfamiliar surroundings for a moment, and then remembered moving house the previous day. His shoulders sagged in relief. Shit. Once, back in Devonport, he had woken up on a stranger's porch—sprawled over a weather-beaten couch that had stunk of wet dog—with a vague memory of singing a karaoke version of Rick Astley's 'Never gonna give you up' to a pub full of cheering faces. He had fled the couch, running until he had chanced upon a main road and could hail a passing taxi. Inexplicably, he was barefoot, his shirt buttoned askew, bottom lip split and a loosened tooth wobbling in his jaw. Yet he could not remember a goddamn thing. That blackout, one of his worst, had stopped him drinking for a few days.

John sat on the edge of the bed and smoked a cigarette. To settle his guts, he needed a big, greasy fry-up. The Brunch Corner café popped into mind. Yes, good idea, he'd visit the café for breakfast. With a full stomach and black coffee in his system, he could handle the supermarket. He put on his watch: 8.22 a.m.

Exiting his room, he paused, listening. No sounds of activity in the house.

"Merry?" he said.

No response. He took a few hesitant steps along the hallway, looking this way and that. The kitchen appeared empty, as did the lounge. The doors to Meredith's hobby room and bedroom were both closed. He hurried past.

On the veranda, he paused to inhale. The crisp, cool air smelled of daphne. Shielding his eyes with one hand, he gazed at the sky. Bright blue and dotted with round, fat clouds: perfect gardening weather. Tomorrow, he would go to Bunnings and get supplies to build his raised vegie patch. He would plant old favourites—tomato, capsicum—and try his hand at something new, like sweet corn or rhubarb.

Despite his lingering headache, he whistled as he strode to the carport. As he unlocked the Falcon, he glanced at the clinker-brick shithole across the road. The Toyota Corolla was gone. So Donna wasn't home. Where might she be? He pictured her in a paddock, murmuring kind and loving words while she brushed down a piebald horse, which nickered and whisked its tail. The image made him smile.

The drive to the shopping centre took five minutes.

At this early hour, the car park was mostly empty. John drove to the far end and got a spot in front of the café. On the footpath were a handful of tables, each one shaded with a square red umbrella and topped with an ashtray and a menu.

He took a seat, perused the meals on offer.

A young and stocky waitress came out, wearing a red apron, her bleached blonde hair in a bun. She took a pad and pen from her apron.

"Good morning, what can I get you?" she said.

"The full breakfast, and a long black, thanks."

"White or wholemeal for the toast?"

"White."

She stretched her face into a quick, professional grin and headed back inside.

John lit a cigarette. The only people walking the strip seemed to be old farts. Every bench was empty. He wondered about the alky he had seen on Monday outside the real estate agency. Where might the poor bastard be sleeping? The entrances to the public toilets were sealed off with locked iron gates.

"Oh hey, I thought it was you," a female voice said. "It's John, right?"

He looked around. The first thing he recognised was the long brown hair, parted in the middle. His heart tripped up. Donna's eyes were grey, the colour of polished river stones. She had freckles scattered over her broad, straight nose. And yes, her teeth were even and bright, as he had thought yesterday when she had waved at him. By Hollywood standards, it was a plain and unremarkable face, but the high colour of the cheeks, the warmth in the eyes, and the full lips made it very beautiful.

She touched a hand to her chest and said, "Donna. From across the road?"

"Yeah, of course, I remember," he said, trying to chuckle. She had caught him off guard. "What a coincidence," he continued. "You're here for breakfast too?"

Smirking, she held up a corner of her red apron and shook it.

"Oh, right, you work here?" he said.

"Three days a week, yeah: Sunday, Monday, Tuesday."

"Well," he said, lost for words. "Gee. It's a small world."

"Sure is. How are you settling in?"

"Oh, yeah, good," he said, nodding. "No worries."

He could not think of anything else to say. Stomach clenching, he drew quick and hard on his cigarette, and stared at the door to the café.

"What did you order?" she said.

"Uh, the full breakfast."

"Good choice. You'll love it. The chef makes the baked beans herself, can you believe it? She thinks canned beans taste like shit. You moved here with family?"

"Nah. By myself. To be honest, I've got no family within cooee."

"Aw, that's a shame. You know many people around here?"

He glanced up. Donna was looking at him with her head tipped to one side, as if considering…no, as if weighing him up. He sat straighter and pulled in his gut.

"I don't know a soul," he said, "apart from you."

She took a few strands of her long hair between her fingers and twirled them in a repetitive, practised manner, as if from habit. For some reason, the sight of it sent a flush of blood into John's cock. He could see her kneeling on a bed, in bra and panties, head tipped on one side as it was now, and twirling her hair just like that. He stared into her grey eyes for a few seconds too long. She stared back. A fluttering sensation passed through his solar plexus and into his groin.

"Why don't you drop over to my place tonight after tea?" she said. "Yeah?"

"Sure, why not? Bring some booze. We'll make a few house-warming toasts."

He took a punt. "Won't your husband mind?"

The sly cast to her grin indicated that she knew damn well he was fishing and didn't mind. "I'm divorced, actually."

33

"Oh. Sorry."

"Don't be. He was a right prick."

John laughed. "What time then?"

"Let's say...eight o'clock?"

"I'll be there with bells on."

The café door opened and the stout blonde waitress came out with John's coffee. As she placed it in front of him, she said to Donna, "What about your tables?"

"Yeah, I'm coming now."

Donna smiled at him, her grey eyes crinkling at the corners, and followed the stout waitress inside the café. John watched her every step.

He couldn't decide what to wear. Jeans, naturally, but what else? The wardrobe contained half a dozen shirts and t-shirts, all of them crap. When had he last gone clothes shopping? Two years ago? With increasing agitation, he slid the hangers back and forth along the rail, scrutinising the crumpled items with their baggy, scalloped necklines or curling lapels...no, no, no... Okay, what about this one?

The beige shirt looked the newest, simply because it was long-sleeved and he hardly wore it, preferring short sleeves. Good enough. A quick check of his watch: 7.41 p.m. Shit. He wrenched the shirt off the hanger and hurried to the laundry.

The iron had rust stains on its plate, which he scrubbed off with a bristle brush. He had been extremely careful all day with his drinking, pacing himself. The last thing he wanted was to show up hammered.

As he pressed the shirt, he heard footsteps behind him, and braced. He turned a little, so he could watch her in his peripheral vision.

"What are you doing?" Meredith said.

"What does it look like?"

She edged into the room. "Where are you going?"

"Out."

He glanced at her leggings: shabby. Since Meredith never left the house—at least, not in the daytime—he had to buy clothes for her. Every once in a long while, he'd visit Target for a bunch of tops, tracksuit pants, dresses, underwear, but everything had to be patterned or she wouldn't wear it. Perhaps block colours brought back memories of the years she had spent caged inside various wards. She never tried to coordinate the patterns so her tops and bottoms always clashed: stripes with polka dots, checks with paisley, differing floral prints.

"When are you coming home?" Meredith said.

"Later."

She pulled the iron's plug from the power point.

"Aw, shit, put it back," John said. "I haven't finished yet."

Glaring, she held the plug tight to her stomach.

That's when he noticed the blood. It jolted him. He stepped back. The laundry was a small room. Meredith blocked the doorway.

"Merry, there's blood all over you."

She failed to react.

"Did you leave the house last night?" he continued. "When I was asleep?"

(no, *drunk*)

The blood had dried in rivulets along both of her forearms, yet her hands were clean, as if she had washed them.

(*licked* them)

There were dark spatters on her windcheater. Twice a week, Tuesday and Saturday, John ran a load of washing, and sometimes, he had to pre-soak her clothes to remove bloodstains. For their first few months of living together, he had dismissed the stains as menstruation, and had not mentioned anything out of embarrassment. However, as time dragged on, he had become less sure. And now? Well, now he assumed she killed animals, but for what purpose, he didn't know and didn't like to think about.

"Stay home," Meredith said.

"I won't be long," he said, and pushed past her.

He checked his watch: 7.54 p.m. In the en suite he combed his hair; still a full head of it, thank Christ, but the black was turning silver, particularly around his sideburns. Back in the day, he'd been easy on the eye, so a few women had told him. At nearly fifty, his jaw-line was too soft, his lips too thin, nose and cheeks crisscrossed in thread veins. For a moment, he lost his nerve. Then he recalled the unmistakeable look that Donna had given him, and he put on his shirt. The sleeves were creased, but he could always roll them up.

As he started to fasten the buttons, Meredith appeared in the shaving mirror.

He spun around. "Hey," he said, "this is my part of the house."

She slitted her ice-blue eyes and drifted away. A few seconds later, he heard the click of her bedroom door closing. He leaned against the sink, blew out a breath. What would it be like to be free of Merry? As the pounding of his heart settled, he splashed on some aftershave.

"**G**ood to see you," Donna said, face flushed, a glass of white in one hand. "*Mi casa su casa,* or however it goes, right?"

John stepped over the threshold. The house smelled like lamb chops, and redgum smoke from a fireplace. He watched the twitch of Donna's hips in tight blue jeans as he followed her deeper inside. The tiled entrance hall led to the kitchen, an original 1970s build, white laminate with brown cupboards. The window framed scrubby grass, a barbecue, and queen-sized sheets revolving lazily on a Hills Hoist. Clean linen must be on her bed. That was a good sign.

Donna opened the refrigerator. Her movements were a little deliberate, a little expansive, as if she'd already had a few. "Pop your stubbies in here," she said.

"I'll grab one first."

"You want a glass?"

"It's already in a glass," he said, and they both laughed.

He followed her into the lounge. The room held a lit fireplace, prints on the walls, a bookcase with more photographs than books, two corduroy sofas arranged at right angles around a table, and a TV. He sat down. She took a seat on the other sofa.

Drumming his fingers on the armrest, he said, "Thanks for the invite."

"No worries. So how was breakfast at the café? Did you like the baked beans?"

He nodded. "Yeah, they were good."

"I prefer the canned ones, myself."

"All right," he said. "I confess: me too."

Smiling, Donna leaned back against the sofa. The posture lifted her breasts. She wore an orange top with a deep, round neckline that showed a glimpse of cleavage. John wanted to run a finger, no, his tongue, all the way down that cleft.

Oh shit, he'd been staring at her chest for too long.

"I like your necklace," he suggested.

She touched a hand to the base of her throat, just as she had this morning at the café (*Donna. From across the road?*), and said, "It's costume jewellery. Cassie bought it for me at her school's Mother's Day sale."

"Cassie's your daughter?"

"Oh, yeah, hang on a second." Donna sat up and yelled, "Cassandra!"

After a few seconds, John heard the slap of oversized slippers on tiles. The girl he had seen yesterday wearing the netball outfit walked into the lounge in a t-shirt and leggings. She gave him the death stare. He felt like he was back in high school.

"Cassie, this is our new neighbour. Say hello to John."

"Pleased to meet you," John said.

The girl said nothing.

Donna checked her wristwatch. "All right, into the shower, missy."

Sighing, the girl turned and slapped her moccasins out of the room.

"Kids," Donna said, and rolled her eyes. "You got any?"

"Yeah, two: all grown up." John trotted out his usual lie. "Sometimes, they stay with me. That's why I rent houses with spare bedrooms."

"Cool. Sons or daughters?"

John paused, and said, "Daughters."

"What are their names?"

He had never answered this question before. After taking a long swig from the stubby, he finally said, "Jane and...Susan."

"In honour of treasured aunts, I bet."

"You got it."

"How old are they?" she went on.

"Uh...both in their twenties."

"Married?"

"One of them is, yeah." He took a gulp of beer. The pulse was beating in his ears. *First impressions are everything*. If he didn't come across as sociable, friendly, easy to talk to, there would be no second invite. But, Jesus, what the hell could he say about his imaginary offspring? He added, "Susan's just had a baby, a little boy."

"Oh, wow! Congratulations!"

"Thanks. We're all pretty chuffed. They named him after me, as a matter of fact, but everyone calls him Jack."

"Aw, that's a lovely name for a boy. I prefer traditional names, don't you?"

"Yep."

"I mean, shit, some of the names at Cassie's school... What are parents thinking? There's a girl called 'Neveah', which is 'heaven' backwards, apparently, and another poor mite saddled with 'Shiraz', as in the wine. Can you believe it?"

He laughed.

Donna drained her glass. "Speaking of wine, another drink?"

"Cheers."

She went to the kitchen. The wood in the fireplace popped. It was a relief Donna liked to drink too. Once, he had tried to date a woman who reckoned she was allergic to alcohol. That relationship had fizzled within a couple of days.

"So tell me," Donna said, breezing into the lounge, "when does the bitchy teenage phase wear off? Cassie's just turned twelve, and it's started already."

Fuck. How in God's name would he know the answer to something like that? Donna passed him the stubby. His hands had begun to perspire. She sat down, sipped at her wine, and waited expectantly. His mind raced, his foot jiggled.

"Well," he said after a while, and took a drink. "I didn't see my daughters much when they were growing up. Me and their mum divorced when they were little."

Donna's eyes clouded. "Oh, now that's what I'm worried about with Cassie. With the travelling he has to do for work, she only gets to see him one weekend a month. That's not much, is it?"

"If he's a good enough dad, it ought to be."

She smiled, crinkled her nose. "Graeme a good dad? That's debateable."

"All she needs is some male role-models in her life, dependable and positive ones, like a loving uncle, and she'll be okay."

"Thanks." Donna gave him a long and tender gaze. "That's great advice."

They held eye contact. Should he make a move? Go over and sit next to her? It had been a while since his last woman. He wasn't sure if he was reading her right.

"So, what do you do for a living?" Donna said, breaking the moment.

"I'm a plate mounter at a printing company."

"Uh-huh. Nine to five?"

"No. Twelve-hour shifts every Wednesday, Thursday, and Friday."

"So you get four days off a week. Cool. You like your job?"

He shrugged. "It pays the bills. Look, this may sound like a weird question, but you wouldn't happen to own a horse, would you?"

"A horse?" She giggled. "Why, do you need one?"

"No, you just look like the kind of woman who'd be into horses."

"And what kind of woman is that?"

He shrugged again. "I don't know. Outdoorsy, I guess. Fit."

She got that look in her eye again. If she started twirling her hair, he would put down his stubby, move to her couch and take her in his arms.

"Shit, you're really pretty," he said.

"You're not so bad yourself, mister."

John put the stubby on the table. Before he could get up, he heard the slap of moccasins on the kitchen tiles. Instantly, Donna's coquettish aura switched off, and she checked her watch, frowning. Cassie appeared in the doorway, wearing pyjamas.

"That was quick," Donna said. "Did you even have a shower?"

"Yeah."

"So how come your hair's not wet?"

"Duh, because I didn't wash it. I washed it yesterday."

"All right, fine." With a harried expression, Donna clanked her glass onto the coffee table. "I won't be long," she said to John. "I'm off to tuck her in."

"No worries," he said. "Take your time. Goodnight, Cassie."

They left the room. He stared into the fireplace.

Something about Donna reminded him of Meredith; but the old Meredith, not the ghost he lived with now. The forthrightness, direct gaze, the self-confidence...

A knot of wood popped in the flames, and he remembered the bonfire party.

His high school had been located near a nature reserve with a creek running through it. This particular evening, the start of spring in Year Twelve, the boys congregated at the reserve and spent an hour or more collecting fallen branches, arranging them into a pile. The girls arrived later with the grog. After dark, the boys lit the fire. The wood crackled and snapped. Getting tipsy, fast, people started to pair off. John found himself with Meredith. They lay together in the grass, sharing a bottle of Vickers gin she had nicked from her parents' cabinet, swigging it neat. Dutch courage: that's what he hoped for. But Meredith made the first move. Running her fingers through his hair, she murmured, "You need a written invitation? Come on. Don't you want to kiss me, dopey?"

The scream of a police siren made everyone scramble to their feet. The cop car, lights flashing, turned off the road and bumped straight across the grass towards the bonfire. The kids scattered. Meredith grabbed John's hand. They ran with a bunch of others to a fence, which they scaled, dropping into someone's back yard. John started forward and fell through space. Icy water closed over his head. He surfaced, spluttering, tasting chlorine. The kids, including Meredith, were laughing, but holding their hands over their mouths to smother the sounds.

"Get out of my pool, dickhead," a boy called Darren (Darryl?) hissed. "Quick."

John hoisted himself onto the pebbled deck and, dripping, followed the others into a cabana. Everyone huddled together, giggling and shushing each other.

"Shut the fuck up," Darren/Darryl said. "If my old man finds you in here, I'm in deep shit."

The creaking of a door opening at the other end of the yard froze their throats.

"What's going on?" a deep voice called from the house. "Son, is that you?"

"Yeah, Dad, it's me," the kid yelled. "I'm having a smoke. Won't be long."

"Did you hop in the pool?"

Everyone huddled in the cabana, including Meredith and John, pressed hands against their lips to stifle laughter.

"Nah, why would I?" the kid yelled back. "It's too cold."

"I thought I heard a splash."

"Nah, there was no splash. Okay, Dad, I'll be there in a minute."

"Well, all right. Don't be long."

The door closed. They were safe. Everyone fell against each other in relief.

"All of youse, fuck off out of here, pronto," the kid said.

"But I don't understand," John said. "If your dad is cool enough to let you smoke, why would he care if you have some friends over?"

"Because I didn't ask the bastard first, that's why. Now fuck off and be quiet about it. Watch for the cops."

Darren/Darryl left the cabana first, climbed the stairs to the back door, and went inside the house. The other kids left in pairs. Meredith and John were last.

"You're shivering," she said, wrapping her arms about him. "Poor baby."

She kissed him, softly at first, chastely. Then she opened her mouth, and their tongues touched. His heart leapt. After all these years of loving her from afar, idolising her, John was kissing her; at last, at long last…

"Penny for your thoughts."

He glanced up. Donna strolled into the lounge. John took a drink of beer.

"You seemed a million miles away," she said, sitting, grabbing her wineglass.

"It's the magic of fireplaces, I guess. They kind of mesmerise you."

"I know, right? That's what I hate about summer: no cosy nights by the fire."

At the sound of slapping moccasins, Donna rolled her eyes and slammed down her wineglass. "Ugh, I swear to Christ..." she whispered.

He smiled. A moment of complicity passed between them. *Parenthood is so exhausting...* No different to anybody else, Donna had bought his lie too.

Cassie appeared in the doorway. John baulked. In her arms, she held a cat, a ginger tabby. Oh, shit. This was not good. This was not good at all.

"What are you doing up?" Donna said.

"I want Tiger in my room."

"No. Absolutely not. You know he'll jump on your bed."

"Please?" Cassie whined.

"No. I hate cat fur over the sheets."

"Please? I'll bring in his cushion."

Huffing, Donna glanced at John. He shrugged helplessly. She flung out her hands, and said, "Fine. Try to keep him on the cushion, not on the sheets, okay?"

Cassie hurried back through the kitchen, moccasins slapping.

"Did you hear me?" Donna called. "On his cushion!"

No answer.

Donna shook her head. "That stupid cat, I swear. Cassie always wants to cuddle him in bed like a teddy bear, and he lets her. I think he actually likes it. God help me when the bloody thing dies."

5

It was warm for a morning in early spring, twenty degrees already and sunny. Panting, sweat running into his eyes, John straightened up, took off his leather gloves and surveyed the construction of his soon-to-be vegetable patch.

A top job, even if he said so himself.

With a sledgehammer, he had pounded into the ground four galvanised iron corner-posts. Then, he had slid the treated pine sleepers down the slots of the posts, stacking them two sleepers high on each side, correcting any lean by eye.

He scrabbled in his shirt pocket for a cigarette. Both hands shook. Not from thirst, but from physical exertion. At least he'd got the measurements right. The sleepers had fit snugly within the posts.

He checked his watch—9.39 a.m.—still making good time.

Next would be a trip to the plant nursery for a cubic metre of dirt, a bag of chook shit, and seedlings. He would get a couple of capsicum plants, maybe some red onion. Sweet truss was his preference for tomato, but failing that, he'd settle for roma. Then he'd be home before beer o'clock: 10.45 a.m.

Might Donna appreciate a gift of homegrown tomatoes?

Yes, surely. Everybody loved organic stuff these days. Didn't they?

He could only hope the nursery had truss seedlings. A length of green vine sprouting plump fruit looked impressive; much more impressive than a plastic bag of romas that looked no different than the shit you bought from a supermarket. He imagined Donna's grateful smile, her hand pressed to the base of her throat in surprise and delight. *Oh John, for me? Why, these tomatoes are just too pretty to eat...*

But last night, despite the clean sheets on Donna's bed, she hadn't invited him to stay; in fact, had not even kissed him. He had left her place around eleven.

He mulled this over, drawing on his smoke.

Nearby, an adolescent magpie with grey feathers strutted amongst the grass and weeds of the back yard, occasionally stabbing its beak into the dirt to capture a worm, getting closer and closer.

"How come you're not scared of me?" John whispered.

The magpie stopped and regarded him for a moment with a red, glossy eye, and walked straight past, resuming the hunt. John flicked the cigarette butt over its head. The magpie didn't even flinch.

A respectable woman like Donna wouldn't screw him straight away—or anyone else for that matter—because she had her daughter, Cassie, to consider. This was John's dilemma. Somehow, he would have to win over the kid. He remembered the death stare Cassie had given him, and sighed. With the back of his arm, he wiped sweat from his face. The magpie broke into a trot, flapping its wings.

"This is for you."

John turned. Meredith stood with a glass of water outstretched in one hand.

"Holy shit," he said. "Don't creep up on me like that."

A flicker of a smile touched her lips. "Relax. It's only water."

"Well," he said, taking the glass. "I didn't hear you. Sing out next time."

As he drank, Meredith observed him with unblinking eyes. The sunlight played over her face. She looked as white as dough. The breeze shifted her lifeless hair, first this way and then the other. John held up the empty glass. She took it.

"What are you doing out here, anyway?" he said.

"Don't worry. The fences are high. Our neighbours won't notice me." She smiled again. "I've been watching you through the window. You looked hot. I thought you'd like a drink."

"Sure. Okay, thanks."

She approached the sleepers. "So you'll have tomatoes again."

"Fingers crossed, yeah, if I can get the kind I want."

"Will you offer any to that woman over the road?"

His skin crept into gooseflesh. It felt like she had been reading his mind. "You mean Donna?" he said at last. "Who knows? I haven't even thought about it yet."

"Yes. Donna. Will you offer any to Donna? Your new, flirty little friend?"

The breeze worried at Meredith's sleeveless smock, long and shapeless, rippling it about her bare legs. Each of her limbs bore a line of scars, regularly spaced, every scar a pair of crescents facing each other. The scars shone faint and silver in the daylight, like dozens of waxing and waning moons. John didn't like to see her scars. They made him queasy. It must have taken Meredith a lot of time, patience and determination to cut herself like that, so methodically, so precisely.

"Listen," he said. "I don't want you hurting any cats around here, all right?"

She gave him a slow blink, and arched an eyebrow, ever so slightly.

"I mean it," he continued. "You remember why we had to get out of the last place? The Kapoors were going to call the cops. Did you know that? About those notes you kept writing them. Merry, you have to leave other people's animals alone."

"Interesting. So, Donna has a cat."

He could feel the blood coming to his face.

"Okay, I'm off to the nursery," he said, striding past her.

He could sense Meredith's gaze boring into his back, but he wouldn't let himself turn around and check.

The plant nursery was all but deserted this early on a Monday morning. The elderly woman sitting behind the register had a buzz-cut of grey hair, a sour face, and bright red lipstick bleeding into her wrinkles.

"Cash or credit," she intoned, chewing on gum.

"I'd like to EFTPOS from my bank account," John said.

Grunting, she held out her hand for his card.

As she swiped it and thumbed buttons, John glanced across the countertop at tiny potted cacti; postcards; magnets featuring cartoon-style illustrations of fruit; and a stack of brochures for the Atlas Circus Royale. *Visit our wondrous kingdom!*

He took a brochure.

The colour photographs included a scantily-clad girl spinning hoops around her body while perched atop a glittering ball, and a fat clown in a bowtie grasping a fake bunch of flowers and mugging for the camera.

"Savings?" the old woman said, hovering her thumb over the device.

"Uh, yes thanks."

She offered the handset. John pressed the digits of his PIN. While waiting for the clearance, he scrutinised the brochure. *Fun for young and old!* The circus had set up on a vacant block not ten minutes from John's house. *Expect the unexpected!*

The register spat out a docket. The old woman handed it to him.

"Tell me something," John said.

She pursed her lips and glared with cold, hostile eyes.

"Do kids still like the circus these days?" he said.

Her bellow carried the scent of tobacco and peppermint gum. "Like it? Hey, they love it, mate. Lions, tigers, elephants: what's not to love?"

John tucked the brochure into his back pocket.

The tent reeked of hay and horse manure. Canned music blared. Spotlights swirled.

The Atlas Circus Royale did not have lions, tigers or elephants.

Instead, it had a dozen budgerigars that could ascend tiny ladders (*MAKE YOUR BIRDS SHUT UP!!*) and turn a miniature Ferris wheel (*YOUR BIRDS WILL DIE!!*), which elicited a half-hearted clap or an "aw" from the audience at every lame trick. Clowns blew whistles, squeezed air-horns, and threw buckets of water at each other that turned out to be—surprise—confetti. Listless ponies trotted the ring in feathered headgear, led by overweight women in silver sequinned bikinis. A couple of moustachioed idiots wearing frilly shirts juggled what looked like bowling pins.

Oh, dear God, for a beer. John pinched his upper lip, over and over.

About a couple of hundred people, mainly fat women with toddlers and squalling babies, were scattered around the tiered benches. Was anybody enjoying themselves? Hard to tell. The parents always seemed to be fussing with milk bottles, screaming at one of their tots, dragging a kid outside to the portable toilets, or doling out smacks. Mostly, the children appeared grizzly, tired and bored.

Jesus *Christ*.

Monday night, he had knocked on Donna's front door and asked if he could escort her and Cassie to the circus this weekend. *Oh yes,* Donna had said, *how terrific.*

And now, Saturday afternoon and ringside, occupying the most expensive seats in the house, they sat like a family, Cassie between John and Donna, and what an unmitigated fucking disaster it had turned out to be. The show-bags he had bought for Cassie lay ignored on the dirt floor, and now she was holding the untouched fairy floss by its stick, upside-down, tenuously between finger and thumb, as if waiting to drop it. He caught her eye by accident. With an imperious glare, she cut him dead with a slow, disdainful blink.

John wished he were anywhere else.

The clowns came out after every act. They kept hauling audience members into the ring to participate in dumb games. John hoped they wouldn't pick him. If they did, he decided, no way would he leave his seat. Fuck it, the whole audience could boo; he wouldn't leave his goddamned seat.

Donna turned to him and smiled.

"I'm sorry about all this," John said.

Donna said something, but he didn't get it. The music was too loud. She tried again, and again he didn't hear. Shit. He offered a wan smile and looked away.

No, stupid old woman at the plant nursery, *kids don't like the circus.* Kids like computer games, Facebook, and messing about on their mobile phones. The Atlas Circus Royale belonged to another era. John gazed around at the stands, at the children. Cassie was the oldest by about seven or eight goddamned years. No wonder she hated it. The blood burned in John's face.

If he'd had any chance with Donna, he'd blown it.

With a screech of tinny music, the clowns disappeared between the canvas curtains at the back of the ring. A new tune started up. Nothing happened. John checked his watch: 2.24 p.m. This must surely be one of the last acts. The music played on and on. The audience became restless. Talking noise got louder. The spotlights swirled. The tune stopped and then started over again from the beginning. 2.27 p.m. John's foot jiggled. What he'd do for a cold beer…

Cassie turned to him and said, "Is it over?"

"No, I don't think so."

She slumped in her seat and, with a flourish, dropped the fairy floss. Donna did not notice. John contemplated heading outside for a smoke.

With flailing arms, a man staggered through the curtains. He wore shorts, bare feet and a blue singlet, but had the green nylon wig typical of a clown. He stopped, squinted at the audience, and gathered himself, swaying. Oh, for the love of Christ…a drunken roadie, perhaps? John felt irked. This was too much, deserving of a refund. Why weren't the staff ushering this pissed dickhead backstage? Frankly, it was embarrassing. The man stumbled to the middle of the ring. The audience hushed.

The music ran out.

Donna gave John a quizzical glance, and he shrugged.

Cassie said, "Is this guy part of the show?"

"Maybe," John said. "Let's see."

"He's pissed, isn't he, Mum?"

Donna said, "Mind your language. But yeah, I think so."

A chubby woman in a sequinned bikini ran out with machetes, three in each hand. The drunk took the long knives. It seemed he was preparing to juggle them.

"For real?" Cassie said. "Oh my God, no way, he can't chuck those things around. He'll cut his fingers off."

John couldn't answer. He was too busy processing the sensation of *Déjà vu*; too preoccupied with a slow and dawning recognition of the man's posture, gait, and mannerisms; the shape of his nose, his face. John's mind reached into the dark depths of long years past, groped about, searching…

Noah?

Nick?

Nate?

Sudden knowledge flooded John in a hectic kind of panic.

Yes, *Nate*. This plastered and pathetic clown, this juggler, this *alky*, was from high school, from John's year level: Nate Rossi. The realisation hollowed out John's guts and pricked his eyes with unexpected tears. Nate Rossi had been smart, an A-student, but athletic and cool too, a perpetual love interest for the girls, the kind of bloke that John had envied, a bloke with the proverbial world at his feet. He had typically ignored John in the few classes they had shared. And who could have blamed him?

Nate threw the long knives into the air.

The audience, including John, collectively gasped in horror.

Cassie put both hands to her cheeks.

But something strange occurred; Nate turned into a well-practised automaton, juggling with speed and precision. How many thousands, no, tens of thousands of times had he performed these exact same actions? A couple of roadies held the curtains wide open, and the woman in the sequinned bikini pranced out, holding at arm's length a number of flaming sticks. With a grin and a curtsy for the audience, she turned to Nate and tossed a stick at him, then another, and another and another, until he had all the knives and all the flaming sticks whirling through the air in two smooth, unerring and mesmerising arcs.

When Nate's act ended, the applause went on and on, more from surprise and relief than anything else, in John's opinion.

"That was awesome!" Cassie said, her eyes shining.

The grotty caravan was dilapidated and small, one-berth. Hesitating, John turned to the decrepit woman who had led him here behind the circus tent, through the churned ground and mud, between the dozen other vans and trailers. She must have seen the indecision in his face because she smiled and nodded, bouncing dyed-red ringlets about her sagging neck.

"Yep, this is it," she said, pulling the coat tight about herself, and retreated with a dispirited wave.

Bracing, John stared at the caravan door. After the circus performance, he had driven Donna and Cassie home, and returned straight away, determined to find Nate. So he had found him. Now what?

John knocked on the door anyway.

No response.

He knocked again, harder this time. The caravan lurched on its retread tyres.

A petulant voice called, "That you, Claude? Hey, I fucken told you already, man, I'll get it to you by tomorrow, all right? Fuck. Give me a fucken chance."

John thought about walking to his car, letting go of the past.

Too late, the caravan door opened.

There stood Nate in singlet and shorts. The curly brown hair of his youth was a scattering of locks hanging from a balding scalp. The sight punched John in the gut.

"Who the fuck are you?" Nate said.

"Okay, hi, you may not remember me, but—"

"What do you want, mate? I've got no money. Fuck off."

John tried to smile. "You don't understand. We went to high school together."

Nate scratched at his ear. "Yeah?"

"John Penrose, Year Twelve geography? You and me had to do an assignment on South America."

Nate's brown eyes looked cloudy, bloodshot, confused. "South America?"

"Yeah, remember?" John grinned hopelessly. "Capybaras. We did this whole bit on capybaras, and the teacher—what was her name?— failed us because she thought we'd made it up. She'd never heard of the capybara. What an idiot."

Nate stared at him blankly.

John sighed. "I'm sorry to have disturbed you. I'll leave you to it."

"Hey mate, hang on, wait. You mean Mrs Van Fleet?"

John laughed. "That's right. Mrs Van Fleet."

"Oh man, yeah, what a stupid bitch. Who hasn't heard of the capybara? It's the biggest fucken rodent in the world." Nate grabbed John's hand and shook it hard, his palm rough and callused. "Well, come on in, you old bastard. Jeez, how long has it been? You like whisky? Sure you do."

John stepped inside.

The caravan smelled dank and sour, like unwashed laundry. An array of empty beer bottles, the large 750ml size, filled the tiny bench that surrounded the sink. The centre of the caravan held a laminate table and an L-shaped, built-in lounge consisting of upholstered foam rubber. Nate snatched up a discarded t-shirt and dusted a seat. Then he flung the t-shirt over his shoulder, where it landed on the double mattress, the bed sheets twisted into knots.

"Take a load off," Nate said. "You like your whisky neat? I don't have ice."

You're an alky if you drink and drive. But John pushed aside any reservations. "Okay," he said, "but just one shot. I've got my car with me."

Nate poured a couple of drinks into water glasses, gave one to John, and sat at the other end of the table. Grinning, he swallowed his drink and poured another.

"So," Nate said, turning his glass around and around on the table, his fingernails bitten to the quick. "You live around here?"

"Nope," John lied, "on the other side of the city, across the Westgate Bridge."

"No shit? What the fuck are you doing out this way?"

"A favour for a friend. I brought them and their kid here for the matinee."

"Ah, okay." Nate drowsily nodded his head. "What did you think of the show?"

"Yeah, it was good."

"The budgies suck, but."

"True." John looked at the glass in front of him, which was dirty, smudged with small flecks of...something...in the lip prints. Dried spit? Flakes of skin? His stomach gave a little churn. Pushing the glass away, he said, "What happened?"

Nate opened his eyes and blinked. "Huh? What do you mean?"

"I figured you'd end up as a lawyer or something."

"Oh, *that*." Nate spread his hands. "Shit happens, hey?"

"It sure does."

Nate laughed. "You manage a warehouse, don't you? Come on, Little Johnny Butt-Rose, you followed in your dad's footsteps, right? He gave you a job and you took over as manager when he retired."

John offered a tight smile. "Actually, he wasn't my real dad."

"Oh, yeah, I remember hearing about that stuff. You were adopted?"

"And it didn't work out. I left home and that was the end of it."

Nate raised his eyebrows. "No contact with any of the rellies?"

"Not a one."

After a moment, Nate raised his glass. "Well, here's to an uncomplicated life."

John raised his glass too, but didn't drink.

For a few minutes, they spoke of the circus. Nate was single, had been part of the troupe for years and, in his estimation, had travelled through eighty cities and towns across Australia at least twenty times over. Then, when John couldn't think of anything else to ask, they lapsed into an uncomfortable silence.

"See any of the old crew from high school?" Nate said at last.

John hesitated, and decided to keep lying. He shook his head.

"Me neither," Nate said. "You left before the end of Year Twelve, right? After Lyle Berg-Olsen disappeared. Sometime in November, wasn't it?"

"Sunday October 19th, 1985."

"Yeah, sometime around then. Love him or hate him, Lyle had personality. What a funny fucker! Remember his impersonations of the teachers?"

"Yeah, I remember."

"His piss-take on the principal always cracked me up." Nate's chuckle gave way to a sorrowful smile. "Aw, Jeez, his disappearance came as a shock, didn't it? Fucked us all up, hey? But Lyle being your best mate, shit, everybody understood why you dropped off the radar." Nate slurped his drink. "Where'd you go, anyway?"

"Devonport."

"Tasmania?" Nate sniggered. "You went to Tasmania?"

"Uh-huh."

"You're shitting me. What the fuck did you do down there?"

"I got off the boat," John said, "found a caravan park and booked a cabin." The mournful sound of blaring ship horns came back to him; how the ships in the harbour had woken him every night, saving him from the same nightmare about Lyle. The long drag of time made John feel old and weary. "I walked along the street," he continued, "went into the first business I found, a carpet factory, and asked for a job."

"Just like that?"

"Yep, just like that. The manager gave me a spot in the warehouse, driving the forklift. I was there for six years, until the factory closed down."

"Then what?"

"What else? I hopped on the car-ferry and came back to Melbourne."

John reached for his whisky glass, rubbed off the detritus, and drank. The spirit flared as hot as heartburn along his oesophagus.

Nate said, "Did the coppers ever find out what happened to Lyle?"

John shook his head.

"Bummer," Nate said, and winked. "Know what? I reckon he's over-seas."

"You mean in hiding?"

"Nah, man, just kicking back: taking it easy. He was an odd bastard, the sort that marched to his own drumbeat, or however the saying goes. It wouldn't surprise me if he was in Bali with a couple of wives and a whole tribe of kids."

John felt his eyes warm with unshed tears. "I like the sound of that."

"Can't you just picture him? Eating turtle every day, surfing, running some halfway house for travellers, speaking fluent fucken Balinese: don't you reckon?"

"Yeah," John said, and laughed. "That'd suit him down to the ground."

"Big boss on campus."

"Yep."

"That was Lyle: always showing off his stuff. Did you hear about the freaky shit that happened to his twin sister, Meredith?"

The breath caught in John's throat, cut off as if from a pair of determined thumbs. Nate, too hammered to notice, clattered the whisky bottle against each of their glasses to slop out a generous measure.

John shouldn't have come here. He should never have come here.

Nate continued, "After Lyle disappeared? Meredith lost her mind."

"I thought she had a nervous breakdown."

"Same thing."

John raised a finger. "Actually, no, it's not."

"Ah, split hairs if you want," Nate said, "but the fact is that once her brother disappeared, Meredith went fruit-loops and got sent to a psych ward. Rumour has it she'd tried to kill herself. Some say razor blades, others say a noose. I dunno."

John rested his elbows on the table and stared at the whisky. "Can I smoke?"

"Sure, why not? Spare a durry?"

John offered the pack.

Nate lit up, blew a stream of blue smoke, and said, "Anyhow, Meredith got bounced from one hospital to another. Nobody could help her. She just kept on wanting to die. And then this one day, something fucken weird happened to her."

John clenched his teeth. "Something weird...like what?"

"Screaming, and lots of carry-on," Nate said, tapping the ash from his smoke onto the floor. "It sounded like murder. The nurses burst into Meredith's room. This particular ward didn't have locks on the doors. What do you reckon they saw?"

John felt sick. "I don't know. What?"

"Bite marks."

John couldn't respond. A long and freezing shiver ran through his body.

Nate's eyes were wide and staring. "She was covered in blood. The nurses checked her. She had bite marks on both arms and both legs. Thirteen bites apiece."

John rubbed his hands over his temples, thinking of Merry's scars, her waxing and waning moon crescents. "Thirteen?" he said.

"Thirteen on each limb: four limbs by thirteen bites. You know what that comes to? Fifty-two. You see how freaky that is? Thirteen is a witch's number. Fifty-two is the weeks in a year. See the connection? It's some kind of supernatural shit. Meredith was making a pact with the devil."

"Did she bite herself?" John said. "Is that the theory? Meredith did it?"

Nate drank off the shot. "Yeah, she bit herself."

"How the hell do you know all of this?"

"My brother's girlfriend's cousin lived with a chick who was one of the psych nurses on the ward, that's how I know."

"A friend of a friend of a friend?" John sneered. "Chinese whispers. Bullshit."

"Hah, says you. Come on, you don't know shit either way."

The caravan felt hot and stuffy, airless. John said, voice rising, "Where's the proof? How could she bite the insides of her own elbows? That's a physical impossibility. You can't bite the insides of your own elbows."

"Who the fuck reckons she did that? Not me. I didn't say that."

Dizzy, John stood up, swaying a little. "I've got to go."

"Already? Come on, have another drink, one more."

John leaned against the door and it opened. His boots hit the mud and then he was running, running, running, dodging around trailers, heading back to the service road where his car was parked, tears blurring his vision.

"Hey, come back," Nate called, his slurred voice becoming fainter. "Hey, Little Johnny Butt-Rose, what's your fucken hurry, man? Come back. I can get us free popcorn and hot dogs. Come on back here. Penrose?"

6

As soon as he got home, John drank three stubbies, one after the other, and took the fourth to the kitchen table where he sat and nursed it, sipping, looking but not seeing out of the window. Beyond lay his vegie patch filled with rich, dark earth. He had protected each of his seedlings from the wind, cold nights and rodents with a *home-made* greenhouse: a plastic-wrapped cylinder of chicken wire pushed a few centimetres into the soil. The spindly trunks and tiny leaves would be safe.

But despite John's concentration on his vegie patch and its fragile life, the image of Nate's bloated and ruddy face kept leering.

Stop, that's not me, John thought, no, I'm not like him.

You're an alky when you drink hard liquor. And John didn't drink hard liquor. Just beer, only beer… And he had a good job, and he never missed a day, and he never went to work drunk. Not once, not ever.

He passed a trembling hand over his eyes.

Thirteen is a witch's number. Fifty-two is the weeks in a year… It's some kind of supernatural shit. Meredith was making a pact with the devil.

John smoked too many cigarettes in a row, until his lungs wheezed and he couldn't stomach any more. Now or not at all, he thought, and stood up, steadying himself against the table. His knees shook. At the closed door of the hobby room, he stood and listened. He could hear brittle clattering as Meredith sorted through her collection. The hairs rose on the back of his neck. He tapped on the door. The clattering noises stopped.

"Merry?" he said. "Can you come out here for a minute?"

"What for?"

"I need to talk to you."

He heard the soft closing of cardboard lids, the sliding of boxes along the hardwood floor. Meredith opened the door a crack and regarded him with one eye.

"Not here," John said. "Let's talk in the kitchen."

She nodded. He walked back along the hallway. Only then did she come out of the hobby room, closing the door behind her.

They sat opposite each other at the table. John wasn't sure how to start. He guzzled his beer. Meredith sat perfectly still, her blank gaze staring at nothing, back straight as a rod, immobile in a manner that always brought to mind the stillness of a reptile. Sometimes, when Meredith was unnaturally still like this, John's heart would race, for he imagined she might behave as a reptile and attack without warning.

"I saw Nate Rossi today," he said.

She didn't respond.

"Remember? He went to high school with us, in our year level, in fact."

"You saw him. So what?"

"He's an alky. He works in some shitty circus. He juggles stuff, like knives."

"I never cared about him. Neither did you."

"Well, as it turned out, we got chatting. Nate told me about something that happened to you in one of the hospitals."

Meredith was so still it appeared she had stopped breathing. John wanted to sip his beer, but her stillness had somehow paralysed him, pinned him in the chair.

Finally, she whispered, "Oh? And what did Nate tell you?"

"How you got your scars."

"And how did I get them?"

"He reckons you bit yourself on the arms and legs."

In the dead silence of the kitchen, faraway noises came to John's attention: the drone of a lawnmower, the honk of a car horn, a barking dog. As the seconds ticked on, it became so quiet in the room that he could hear the blood moving through his body, the pulse surging like a tide within his ears.

Then, by just an increment, Meredith cocked her head.

Her gaze slid to the wall behind him. Jolted, he had an awful feeling that somebody was standing there. He resisted the urge to turn and check. They were alone. The front and back doors were locked. Nonetheless, he half-expected to feel a pair of hands settle gently upon his shoulders.

Meredith said, "When he told you I'd bitten myself, what did you say?"

"That it was impossible to bite the inside of your own elbows."

Brightening, she locked eyes with him. For a moment, he glimpsed the young and sassy Meredith, and his paralysis loosened enough so that he could lift his beer and take a long, grateful drink. She rolled up her sleeves and lay her forearms on the table, palms up, so that the silvery half-moon scars were visible. He couldn't look at them. She smiled, but it seemed mirthless and sly.

"Who bit you, Merry?" he said.

In reply, she rolled one wrist, her hand making a dismissive gesture.

"Please," he said. "You must tell me."

"You've never asked before. Why now?"

He didn't know the answer.

No, wait, that wasn't true; he knew why, but in a formless, fathomless kind of way that couldn't be put into words. He needed to know because of three faces that wouldn't leave his mind: those of Donna, the teenage Meredith, and Lyle as he lay dying. Oh Jesus, he thought, I'm so fucking sorry for everything I've done. Against a flood of strong emotion, John clamped his jaw shut with an audible click of his teeth.

"Poor baby," Meredith said with a chuckle. "You look like you want to cry."

"Tell me. Please. Tell me what happened."

Her contemptuous expression melted away. She sat back in the chair and let out a long, weary sigh. John's guts clenched involuntarily.

"It was the nicest hospital," she began in a sing-song voice, as if reciting from a children's storybook. "It had bright yellow walls, and grounds with flowers and brick walkways, shady trees, benches where you could sit if you liked, with a nurse standing nearby, of course. There were always nurses standing nearby, with hypodermic syringes in their pockets, in case any one of us happened to flip their lid."

John froze.

Holy Christ...

How was she being so articulate?

As a rule, Meredith hardly talked. Some days, catatonic, she would not—could not—talk at all. Occasionally, she fell mute for weeks. And yet, here she was, having an actual conversation. In fact, she had just given the longest speech since they had begun living together, since he had found her sleeping in a suburban park, homeless and filthy, about eight years ago. Uncanny. And blood was colouring her cheeks. If he touched her face, the skin would be warm. She seemed to be coming back to life. John experienced a detached sensation throughout his body, a chill that felt more and more like fear the longer he looked at her.

"This hospital was keen on group therapy," she continued. "Every day, they made us sit in a circle and yabber about our problems, our preoccupations. I used to mention whatever came to mind at the time. That seemed to satisfy the shrinks."

A lighter and cigarettes lay on the table. She reached out, took a smoke from the pack and, pausing momentarily with the Bic flaring high, she lit it.

Transfixed, John could not tear his eyes away.

The last time he had seen her smoke they had both been eighteen, naked under a blanket, flushed and sweaty from lovemaking. They had shared the cigarette, passing it between them, tasting each other's lips on the filter, giggling, nervous and shy, embarrassed yet pleased. It had been the first and only time they had made love.

Meredith drew back on the cigarette and hesitated, as if unsure. Then, apparently satisfied, she relaxed and exhaled a thin stream of smoke through puckered lips, just like she used to do some thirty years ago. John's heart thudded.

"One day," she said, "we got a new patient. His name was Sebastian. He had scars on his arms and legs, like I do now. Such black hair and white skin, and the palest blue eyes you ever saw. As pale as pale could be; like the sun had been shining so hard and so long on his eyes that the colour had bleached out of them. He kept to himself. He never talked. At group therapy, he'd stare at the floor, or out the window. He liked to stare out of windows for hours and hours."

The same as you, John thought, and shivered.

"And he never ate," she said, showing her teeth.

"No food at all?"

"Not a single bite."

The same as you. "How come he didn't starve?" John said.

"Sebastian gave everybody the creeps, even the staff." Meredith took a drag of her cigarette. "Not me. I used to sit and talk to him."

"About what?"

"Dying. That if he wanted to die, we should figure out a way to do it together."

John nodded. "Did he ever answer you?"

"No. At least, not in words." She crushed the cigarette into the ashtray. "After group therapy one morning, he came to my room, held me down, and bit me, over and over, my left arm and then my right arm. At first, it was sexual, you know? I kept saying, oh yeah, keep going. When I'd had enough, I told him to stop, but he kept on biting along my right leg and then my left leg. You want to know the funny thing?"

A cold sensation sat in John's stomach, heavy as a lump of clay. He licked his dry lips and said, "Okay. What was the funny thing?"

"It didn't hurt until the very last bite: the fifty-second bite. Then all the bites hurt at once, and they hurt like hell. I screamed. Sebastian fled the room. The nurses freaked out at the sight of so much blood." She shrugged. "That's it. The nurses took me to the infirmary and patched me up."

John drank from the stubby, aware that his hand was shaking, and that perspiration dotted his hairline. "Why did Sebastian attack you?"

"I don't know."

"To murder you?"

She contemplated the ceiling. "To change me."

"Into what?"

"This." She smiled and pointed at herself. "Him."

"I don't understand."

She sighed. "After my wounds healed, I got discharged."

"To another hospital?"

"No, altogether, because I was cured: I didn't want to kill myself anymore." She regarded him, blinking her lashless eyes. "Instead, I wanted to kill other things. The doctors and nurses didn't know that, of course. I chose not to tell them."

"Other things? Like what? Animals? Like Mrs Dwight's cat, Angel?"

A faint smile crossed her lips. "I hated that fucking little fur-ball."

"Merry, what do you do to the animals after you kill them?"

The colour began to leave her face. "With nowhere else to go, I went back home. My parents didn't know what to do with me. Mother invited priests to visit with holy water. Dad kept locking me up, chaining me to the bed. So I ran away."

"How old were you?"

"I don't know."

"How long were you on the streets before I found you?"

"Oh, I can't remember." Her voice sounded weak. "What does it matter?"

John leaned over the table and took both of her hands in his.

Meredith looked faint, exhausted, as if the act of talking had drained the life out of her. The slackening of the muscles around her mouth

59

and the glazing of her eyes told him that a catatonic state was coming. She might not talk again for days. But there was one more thing he had to know. His breathing came so fast he felt dizzy.

"Listen, Merry," he said. "Nate told me something else: that you had your first nervous breakdown because your brother disappeared."

"My brother?" she murmured.

John had always blamed himself for destroying not only Lyle, but Meredith too, the only woman he had ever loved. Oh Christ...but he had to know for sure. After years of suffocating guilt and remorse, he had to hear it from Meredith, just in case...just in case... "It's not true," he insisted. "Is it? Tell me. Did you miss your brother so much you wanted to die?"

Her gaze went out of focus.

Damn, he'd lost her. She was gone for God knew how long, her mind adrift.

Then, as if swimming briefly to the surface, she said, "I died along with him."

John let go of her hands, fast, as if they burned, and drew back in the chair. "Who says he's dead? Nate reckons Lyle could be living in Bali."

Stiffly, Meredith stood from her chair and went over to the kitchen window. John watched her, barely able to breathe. After a while, she held her hands over the bench and began to draw her long, manicured nails in circles upon the laminate. The sound droned in and out, in and out, making John think of a stricken biplane whirling down, down, down in a death spiral.

"Stop that," he said. "Stop that right now."

She didn't react.

He leapt from the table, intent on dragging her from the bench to cease that terrible noise. Instead, he found himself putting his arms about her, and sobbing.

"God, I'm sorry," he said, "but I'm trying to make up for it, I really am. I'll take care of you forever, okay? I swear. Merry, I swear on your brother's name I'll always take care of you, and you'll never be locked up or homeless again, for as long as I live."

As he wept into her neck, her fingernails trailed on and on in monotonous revolutions over the laminate bench, around and around and around.

The knocking sounds wouldn't stop.

John opened his gummy eyes. Disoriented, he looked about. He was in his room, fully clothed and lying on his bed. Darkness had crept through the windows. Everything seemed grey and hazy. The digital clock read 6.22 p.m.

Sitting up made his head hurt.

Vaguely, he remembered having more and more beer, and then nothing. He was suspended in that no man's land between drunk and hung-over; still pissed yet suffering from a headache, queasy stomach, soured cotton-mouth.

The knocking sounds kept going.

Someone was at the front door. He waited for them to leave. They didn't.

Annoyed, he swung his legs out of bed and got up. The room tilted. Undigested beer slopped around in his gut. When he reached the hall, he turned on the light. The bulb shone too brightly.

Knock, knock, knock.

"Okay," he called, "for fuck's sake. I'm getting there, all right?"

He snatched opened the front door, squinting against the last rays of sunset, expecting a religious freak or some idiot wanting to know if he'd like to change electricity companies, but no—oh no—it was Donna.

Donna.

His stomach dropped. Panicked, he wondered how he must appear: dishevelled, bloodshot, and pissed. *You're an alky when people see you drunk.*

Donna, looking concerned, touched his arm. "Hey, it's okay."

"This isn't a good time." John glanced behind him. No sign of Meredith. She would be inside her hobby room, clawing through her goddamned collection.

"Is everything all right?" Donna said.

He had to salvage this situation. His mind raced. "I've had some bad news."

"Oh no, that's awful. Is there anything I can do?"

"No." John briefly closed his eyes. The beer made the ground pitch beneath his feet. He clutched the doorframe. "I've had a few too many. Let's just say goodnight."

"No, wait, hang on. I'd already planned on inviting you to dinner. Come over. There's a big pot of pasta on the stove. Cassie and I can't eat it by ourselves."

"But I'm drunk."

"So am I: a bottle of chardy and counting." She smiled, and it was gentle and kind. "You need to eat, right? I've made us mac and cheese, with a crap-tonne of bacon. You like bacon, don't you?"

It occurred to him that she didn't care if he was hammered. She was happy to see him, wanted to spend time with him. The shame and embarrassment began to retreat.

"And four cheeses," she continued, "mozzarella, cheddar, parmesan...I forget the last one. Gruyere? Well, maybe gruyere. It's all shredded in the same packet."

She laughed. He did too.

Such a beautiful woman.

What the hell. They were both pissed, weren't they?

Taking the keys off the hook, John closed the front door behind him. Together, they crossed to Donna's house, the clinker-brick shithole with the palm tree out front.

Cassie giggled, her mouth crammed with pasta. "Wow, I kept waiting for him to cut his arms off." She hurriedly swallowed, and added, "Or set himself on fire. How did he juggle those knives and flaming sticks? It was awesome."

Donna said, "You know, she's been talking about that one circus act non-stop."

"Have not," Cassie said, and blushed.

Grinning, John did his best to stay in the moment, to push aside the memories of his conversation with Nate Rossi. *Meredith lost her mind...* Shut up, shut up, shut up... *Once her brother disappeared, Meredith went fruit-loops...*

"They're professionals, honey," Donna said. "They do it all the time."

"Ugh, but still," Cassie said, and widened her eyes at John, as if she wanted him to be complicit with her, to join forces. "Am I right? When that clown first came out on the stage, I was like, whoa, he's pissed."

"Young lady," Donna said, "mind your language."

"Yeah, okay. But I was like, whoa, he'll get hurt."

Instead I got hurt, John thought.

He noticed Cassie staring at him, waiting for an answer. It dawned that, somehow, he was winning over the child, which would, in turn, win over the mother.

"Yeah, I thought he'd get hurt too," he said. "In fact, I had my hand on my phone, ready to call an ambulance. And he turned out to be an absolute bloody champion!"

Cassie burst out laughing. Donna joined in. John gazed around the dining table. God, they looked like a family, didn't they? An ordinary, suburban family enjoying a home-cooked meal together and it felt surreal, because he had never imagined himself in such a scenario.

Donna said, "I liked the ponies best."

Cassie rolled her eyes. "Ugh, that'd be right. They were *so* pathetic."

"Pathetic? They were not."

"Oh, Mum, they were lamer than the birds."

"No, they were cute. They had fat little bellies, and stumpy little legs." Donna gulped from her wineglass. "And their manes plaited with ribbons, now come on; you've got to admit that was cute."

John winked. "Hey, I told you, didn't I? You seemed like a horse fan."

Donna smiled. He liked the way she was looking at him right now. Goddamn, he liked it one hell of a lot. If only he could leave everything behind —

...*leave Meredith behind*...

—and start over. Start over like nothing bad had ever happened.

Donna was making coffee. He listened to the fridge door opening and closing, the clinking of a teaspoon. Cassie was in bed, the plates and cutlery stashed in the dishwasher, the curtains drawn against the night. John, sitting on a couch, stared at the fireplace. Now that he was alone, he couldn't stop thinking of Meredith (*I died along with him*) and of Lyle, and he scrubbed furiously at his temples with the heels of his palms. At the sound of Donna's footsteps, he composed himself.

She came in from the kitchen with two cups. As she handed one to him, she said, "If you want to talk about what's bothering you, I'm happy to lend an ear."

She sat on the other couch and tucked her legs beneath her. He let out a long, tired sigh. The wood in the fireplace popped and hissed.

"You can trust me," she said.

He tried to smile but it felt wrong, as if his mouth was twisting into a grimace.

"Besides," she continued, "my grandpa used to reckon that a trouble shared is a trouble halved."

"Not this one. This one I'm taking to the grave."

Yet Donna's face showed such compassion and tenderness that if he shut her out now, he feared she might never give him another chance.

It took him time to find the words.

"Have you ever done something so bad," he said, "that there's no way you can ever make it right?"

"I'm forty-five. There's a whole lifetime of stuff I regret."

"I don't mean everyday stuff. I mean something that keeps you awake at night, something that gives you nightmares for years, maybe until the day you die."

"No, I guess not," she said. "But we all make mistakes. Did you mean to do this thing, whatever it is?"

He shook his head, tears coming to his eyes.

"So, it was an accident," she said.

"I suppose you could call it that."

She put her cup on the table, got up, and sat next to him. "Then how can you blame yourself if you didn't mean to do it?"

Her cool fingers touched the back of his neck and caressed his hair. He closed his eyes against the tears, held his breath against the ache in his throat.

"You're not a bad man," she whispered.

"How do you know?"

A sudden weight hit the armrest. Startled, John looked about and stared right into the face of the ginger tabby.

"Relax," Donna said, "it's only Tiger."

"I thought he liked to stay in bed with Cassie."

"Normally, yeah, but cats are intuitive. They know when something's wrong."

"They do?"

"Sure. That's why Tiger's come to you. He wants to offer a little comfort."

Tiger crouched on the armrest as if readying to spring and then, instead, hopped delicately into John's lap. It kneaded at his legs. John felt the very tips of claws through the denim of his jeans. He thought of his previous neighbour, old Mrs Dwight, and her missing Siamese. *Angel's a homebody. It's not like him to stay away. It's been six days. I'm literally frantic…*

"Don't worry, he won't hurt you," Donna said. "He's as gentle as a lamb, aren't you, Tiger?"

She rubbed at the cat's ears. Tiger settled onto John's legs and closed its eyes as if enjoying the attention.

"You see?" Donna said. "Go on, give him a pat. It's all right."

Hesitantly, John laid his hand behind the cat's head. He could feel the nubs of shoulder blades. The fur was warm and soft, pleasant to touch. He stroked Tiger's back from head to tail, again and again. Faintly at first, the cat began to purr.

"Hey, how about that," John said, and smiled. "He sounds just like a lawnmower."

He glanced at Donna. She put a hand to his face and kissed him.

He entered the house and paused, alert now, his pulse thrumming. "Merry?" he whispered.

No response. No movement either.

The hall light was still on, as he had left it. Her bedroom and hobby room were both shut tight. Perhaps she was asleep. Quietly, John closed the front door, hung the keys on the hook, and started to creep along the hall towards his end of the house.

"Did you fuck her?"

He stopped dead. Fixed in the middle of the kitchen, standing stiffly at attention, was Meredith. God only knew how long she had been waiting there. He stared at her carefully. Her face was in shadow. He couldn't see her expression, couldn't guess her mood.

"Cat got your tongue?" Meredith said.

A chill ran over him. "It's late. Go to bed."

"Did you fuck her?"

"No."

"Did you want to?"

"Yes."

Meredith began to laugh. John strode to his room, shut the door and bolted it.

7

John thrashed aside the blankets and stared blindly at the ceiling as his heart continued to gallop. The sounds and images of the nightmare remained. *Lyle screams as soil and clods of grassy earth rain down on his face, smothering him, filling his mouth and nostrils, yet his screams go on and on and on, regardless,* John help me help me, *as John keeps digging the shovel into the earth, tossing the dirt over him.*

But that's not how it happened. So why did he always dream it that way?

God almighty...

John sat on the edge of the bed and switched on the lamp. He studied his open hands. The shovel had given him blisters, two straight lines of them across each palm, red and raw. It had taken a few days for the blisters to dry up. The callused skin had turned yellow and finally peeled away. No scars. Yet his hands should have been scarred, deserved to carry scars, from that day.

Did you mean to do this thing, whatever it is? So, it was an accident. Then how can you blame yourself if you didn't mean to do it?

Oh Donna, he thought, it was no accident.

I didn't mean for him to die, but it was no accident.

Sunday October 19th, 1985.

Eight o'clock in the morning on a hot and sunny day in the middle of a Melbourne spring. Eighteen-year old John was taking the old man's VB Commodore sedan to the countryside, with fishing tackle and a six-pack stashed in the boot. Don't get into a prang, the old man had said, and be back by dinnertime or cop a hiding.

'Out of Mind out of Sight' by The Models on the radio and John singing along—the lyrics having new meaning for him now that he was no longer a virgin—and smoking, his elbow resting on the open window, looking forward to a day of fishing instead of studying. He turned onto the main road, a three-lane dual carriageway. Brick and weatherboard houses sat behind grassy median strips and service lanes. People were out jogging, walking dogs, pushing prams, or lugging grocery bags.

What could Meredith be doing? Just the thought of her made him smile.

They had done the deed yesterday.

A man at last; John Keith Penrose had finally become a man.

Okay, he hadn't lasted too long, but she had enjoyed herself, right? And he'd get better at it. Practice makes perfect, Merry had said so herself, as they'd shared a smoke. The memory warmed him, stiffened his cock a little.

John flicked the cigarette butt out the window.

Up ahead, the traffic light turned red. He drew to a stop. Idly, he gazed about. Lyle happened to be strolling along the footpath, carrying his schoolbag. John would know that boofy blonde head and bouncing gait anywhere. He leaned on the horn. The driver in front put her arm out the window and gave him the forks.

"Get fucked, you dumb bitch," he yelled. "I'm not tooting at you."

She gave him a half-hearted wave.

Lyle had turned at the commotion. John tapped his horn again to get his attention. Lyle started to walk over. The light turned green. John put on his indicator and pulled into the service lane. Stretching his arm, he wound down the passenger side window. Lyle put his hands on the sill and looked into the car.

"Did you piss the bed?" John said. "Where are you going so early, ya bastard?"

"Aaron's place."

"Get in. I'll drive you there."

Frowning, Lyle dropped his gaze, as if he wasn't too keen on the offer.

"What's the matter?" John said.

With an exaggerated sigh, Lyle wrenched open the door, flung the schoolbag into the foot well and dropped into the passenger seat. John offered his pack of cigarettes. Lyle took a smoke without a word and lit it. Then he slammed the door and stared fixedly out the windscreen.

"Merry's got the car today, I take it?" John said.

Lyle tightened his lips.

"Shit, mate," John said, "what's up your arse?"

"Just get going."

John pulled out into traffic. "How come you're off to Aaron's?"

"We've got a science prac due tomorrow. Don't you have any homework?"

John made a derisive *pfft* sound. Who needed to bother with crap like English, maths and geography when there was money in plumbing? The old man, however, wanted John to get a job at the warehouse. Hah. Screw having the old man as a boss, and screw messing around with forklifts and inventories and getting fuck-all wages. John would finish out the HSC year—pass or fail, it didn't matter—and apply for a plumbing apprenticeship. Actually, he could have dropped out of school ages ago, but stayed to be with his mates. And with Meredith.

"I'm going fishing," John said. "Want to join me?"

"Dunno."

John glanced at him. His friend seemed distracted and pensive.

"Okay," John said, "I'll take you to Aaron's. Past the shops, isn't it?"

Lyle stabbed the cigarette into the ashtray. "Fuck it, let's go fishing."

"Sure?"

"Yeah, I'm sure."

"You want to drop in on Aaron first, tell him you're slacking off?"

Lyle shook his head. With a shrug, John decided to focus on the highway. The minutes ticked by. John watched the traffic, but kept sneaking the occasional peek at his friend, who remained stony-faced. How come he wasn't gabbing? Where were his funny stories, wise-cracks, laughter? The silence in the car became so uncomfortable that John found himself shifting about in his seat. It's me, he thought. I've fucked up and I think I know how.

"I'm going back to that really good spot for trout near Warburton," he said. "Remember? I found it a few months ago. The river will be jumping. We've had solid rain and then sunshine for a few days straight. Perfect conditions."

Lyle did not answer.

"And no arguments, I'm teaching you how to fish today," John continued. "You're not sitting on the bank and giving me shit. This time, you're an angler."

Still nothing.

"It's about an hour's drive," he went on. "Is that all right? We'll get there about nine or so, get in three or four hours of fishing, then head to the pub for a counter lunch. What do you reckon? I've got some beer in the back to keep us going."

Lyle kept staring out the window.

John bit at his lip. "Hey, what's wrong, mate?"

Lyle turned up the radio.

"Fine," John said. "Act like a prick, I couldn't give a shit."

He kept heading east. The further he drove, the lighter the traffic became.

The road dwindled to a single-lane dual carriageway without footpaths or kerbs, bordered by eucalypt forest and ferns, the occasional weatherboard house and gravel driveway. The air through the open window was becoming cooler. Up ahead, the hazy blue-green hills of the Yarra Ranges sat against a cloudless blue sky.

It was a calming, bewitching sight.

In his mind, John could already smell the clean, mentholated scent of the trees that lined the banks; hear the rush of the river, the water icy-cold from the mountains; see the darting of insects, the overhead flight of eastern rosellas and red-rumped parrots. The first cast was always the best. The rod was like an extension of your own arm, filled with nerves. You felt the weight of the lure spooling out on the line, the plunk of it hitting the surface. Once a trout bit down and began to fight, you could sense through the line and rod its every twist, pull and clench as surely as if you held the wriggling fish in your own hands.

"What's going on between you and my sister?"

John broke from his reverie. Lyle was glaring at him.

"Nothing," John said. "Why? What did she tell you?"

"Don't bullshit me."

John watched the road. "You're paranoid."

They lapsed into an uneasy hush. The trees whisked by, thick rows of them standing shoulder to shoulder, leaning their branches over the road. The line of scrappy bitumen continued to rise, fall and zigzag as it wended through the bush. There were no other cars.

Lyle said, "How come you always lie?"

"Huh?"

"You know what I'm talking about," Lyle said. "I understand lying to parents, teachers and shit, but to me? I thought we were best mates."

"We are. Jesus. What's got into you?"

Lyle crossed his arms. After a while, John saw the turn-off, and steered the car onto a gravel track. Stones ground beneath the tyres. The rear-view mirror showed a plume of red, boiling dust. The radio finally lost transmission. John killed it. He was acutely aware of Lyle, sitting only centimetres away, emanating such anger and hatred that it churned John's stomach.

He had never told Lyle about his love for Meredith.

In fact, he had never even hinted. God, just the thought of broaching the topic had always embarrassed him. And he had been pretty sure Lyle wouldn't want to hear it anyway. Who wants to hear that their sister is hot? So, no, John had not told him about kissing Meredith for the first time at the bonfire party a few weeks ago, or all the times since. He had not told him about Meredith inviting him over yesterday afternoon, since she would be alone—Lyle out playing an important basketball match, their parents in attendance—and had not told him of Meredith's request: *Bring condoms*. Because why in hell talk about sexual, intimate shit with a mate? What would be next, braiding each other's hair? Forget it. John's relationship with Merry was private. He would share the details with no one.

The track narrowed further. The ground became rockier. John had to slow down to negotiate the ruts. Still, Lyle had not spoken. Well, go fuck yourself, John thought. When he had spotted Lyle walking along the highway, he should have driven straight on by...too late now. He focused his attention on the track. The trees crowded in close. If he scraped paint off the Commodore, there'd be hell to pay.

Nonetheless, his mind wandered towards Meredith.

Towards yesterday afternoon.

The afternoon he had become a man.

The high flush of her cheeks, the shine in her eyes, the way she had squirmed, licked her lips and whispered, *Come on, what are you waiting for?* Both of them naked and lying missionary on her single bed, her legs around him, while a quartet of stuffed toys including a couple of worn teddy bears sat like an audience on the nearby dresser. John had experienced a moment of panic. His cock, although hard as iron, wasn't exactly sure where to go. He had begun to tentatively dab the head of it against her in the hope of locating the right spot. Merry chuckled—not with derision but with tenderness and affection—and had reached down and guided him inside her. The sensation was like no other. A revelation. Caught off-guard, he had murmured, *I love you*, and she had sobered, all of a sudden, and gazed into his eyes with such a desperate intensity that he had known, from that moment on, there would be no room in his heart for any other woman but Merry.

"Where the fuck are we going?"

John glanced at Lyle, who seemed angrier now than before. Much angrier.

"Keep your shirt on," John said. "In about a k, we'll reach another turn-off."

When they reached it, the road was barely more than a walking track. John nudged the car forward, with great concentration. Low-lying switches from gum trees slid along the Commodore, too slowly to damage the paintwork.

John heard the river before he could see it.

The clearing was barely large enough to park the car. John pulled the handbrake, switched off the ignition and alighted. Lyle remained in the passenger seat. Tough shit, John thought, as he opened the boot and hauled out the fishing gear, the little polystyrene esky filled with ice and beer cans.

As he walked towards the bank, he paused by the open driver's side window to say, "You coming or what?"

No answer.

Prick.

The river looked beautiful with the sun spangling off it, every wave and ripple shimmering like a jewel. John regretted bringing Lyle here. He should have kept this place to himself. Now it would be spoiled. Now, whenever he fished here, he would remember Lyle's shitty face and shitty attitude.

The bank sloped gently into a spread of grey stones that continued on into the water. Downstream lay the gnarled, twisted limbs of a felled gum tree. John sucked in a lungful of air, the scent so fresh, so cold, so much like a hit of pure oxygen it made his body tingle. Bird calls were everywhere: the chirp of fairy wrens, the raucous screech of cockatoos. Lyle got out of the car and slammed the door.

"Watch for snakes," John said. "I've seen a copperhead around here before."

He put down the gear, opened the esky and grabbed a can. As he cracked it, Lyle tackled him at full speed. They fell in a struggling tangle of limbs.

John hit the ground hard and got winded. A fist landed on his temple, another against his ear, another on his cheek. Jesus Christ, *Lyle was attacking him.* The unbelievable shock of it paralysed him for a few seconds. Then fury rose up from his belly. He grabbed hold of Lyle and threw him aside, with ease, since the skinny little bastard weighed next to nothing.

Lyle rolled away, panting, and stood up. John stood up too.

"What the fuck are you doing?" John shouted.

Lyle slitted his eyes and glared with malevolence.

When he attacked a second time, John met him with equal force. They did not fall to the ground but shoved and hit at each other.

John punched and felt the satisfying pop of Lyle's lips splitting open. Lyle retreated, gasping, pressing a hand to his bleeding mouth.

"Okay, hold your fucking horses," John said. "Tell me what this is about."

Cheeks blazing red, looking on the verge of tears, Lyle replied, "My sister."

Shit, John thought. Here it comes. No point avoiding it any more.

"What about her?" he said.

"You rooted my sister."

"So what if I did? What's it to you?"

Lyle blanched. "You fucking bastard."

"How am I a bastard? I love Merry, all right? There, I said it." John scanned the ground and picked up the beer can. There were still a couple of mouthfuls in it. He drank them and tossed the can at the esky. "You want to know something else?"

Lyle shook his head, slowly, as if stunned.

John continued anyway. "I reckon she loves me too. She's my girlfriend."

Lyle, eyes glittering, pressed the hem of his t-shirt to his bleeding mouth. Meanwhile, John opened a fresh beer and took a drink.

"Get over it, you dumb prick," he said. "Stop trying to mollycoddle her. She's eighteen years old, mate. She's old enough to vote, drink at a pub, drive a car, and certainly old enough to fuck. The age of consent is sixteen, remember?"

"You're a dog."

"Ah, for Christ's sake—"

"Only a dirty stinking dog would root his mate's sister. How long have you been sneaking around with her behind my back?"

John huffed out an exasperated sigh. "Listen, she was bound to lose her cherry sooner or later. Would you rather she'd lost it to a stranger? A one-night stand, a wham-bam-thank-you-ma'am kind of bloke? I even wore a condom. You don't have to worry. I'll treat her right."

Lyle seemed to regain his composure. Robotically, he strolled to the esky and helped himself to a beer. Once Lyle had consumed about half the can, John approached him with his hand out, ready to shake.

"Friends?" John said.

Lyle took another sip of beer, seeming to contemplate the churn of the river.

John refused to drop his hand. "Come on, mate."

Lyle continued to ignore him.

"The way I feel about her," John added, "we could be brothers-in-law one day."

That got Lyle's attention, quick smart, and he hurled the can into the river.

"Hey!" John said, as the can bobbed and twirled away in the current. "Don't pollute this place. You arsehole, don't you dare pollute this place."

"I gave her a lesson."

"You what?"

"That dirty whore." Lyle's mechanical twitch of a smile showed bloodied teeth. "When I found out what she'd done with you, I gave her a manners lesson."

"Nah, mate," John whispered. "You didn't hit her, did you?"

"Oh, you better believe it. I gave her a manners lesson she'll never forget."

"Tell me you didn't hit her."

Lyle began to laugh, a cruel and gloating bray.

The sounds of laughter, burbling river and bird calls faded. In their place, a loud buzzing started up in John's ears. The blood pounded in his head. Flowing out from his belly, the rage burned through his body, white hot, turning his vision into mist. Within a single moment, John was glowing with rage, incandescent with it, transformed, his mind scorched clean away. Like a baseball pitcher, he wound back his arm—as big as a tree trunk, solid as a rock—and smashed Lyle square in the jaw.

The impact lifted Lyle off his feet. Launched into the air, his eyes already rolled up inside his head, he landed full-length on the stones with a sickening crunch. John advanced.

I want to kill you.

But no, stop, breathe, step back. Dizzy, John dropped to his haunches. His face began to hurt where Lyle had first hit him. The little prick still hadn't moved.

"Get up," John ordered.

No response. Knocked out cold.

John stood on shaky legs and approached, hands doubled into fists.

No, I still want to kill you.

Shit.

There was only one thing to do: get away and calm down.

He jumped into the car, executed a clumsy ten-point turn in the clearing, and drove back the way he had come. Once on the bitumen, he decided to go to the pub. He would have a couple of drinks, clear his head. When he felt quiet again, he would return to the fishing spot. Lyle would be penitent by then, ready to shake hands.

The bartender, a fat bloke with a sweating bald head and a scrappy goatee, kept hovering nearby, keen to chat. At mid-morning, John was the sole customer.

"I've seen you before, haven't I?" the bartender said. "I'm good with faces."

John shrugged. "I like to fish around here."

"Trout?"

"That's the goal. But I'll take blackfish and eel if I can catch them."

The bartender winked. "My missus has an eel recipe. Know what she does?"

John thought of Lyle and if he'd be panicking yet, out there in that isolated spot by the river, all alone. "No, I don't know," he said. "What does she do?"

"Skins it, chops it, boils it, coats the pieces in flour and deep-fries it." The bartender lifted a shoulder and chortled. "Ah, nice enough, but sometimes it tastes a bit muddy. I guess it depends on the age of the eel, don't you reckon?"

"Could be."

"Like yabbies, ya gotta put 'em in clean water first, let 'em shit out the muck."

"You're right about that," John said, and drained the glass.

"One more for the road?"

John's anger had passed. Now he felt remorse. What if Lyle was afraid in the middle of nowhere? What if he had tried to walk to safety and instead got lost? "Nah," John said. "I'm good." He dropped a note on the counter.

"Well, best of luck with your fishing, son," the bartender said.

John exited the pub.

Grey-bellied clouds had formed. It looked like rain was on the way.

As he drove back to the river, John fretted about Merry, about Lyle, about how he could manage these apparently contradictory relationships. He loved Merry, but shit, he loved Lyle too. Did he really have to choose? How could he choose between his woman and his best mate? Oh Jesus, he thought. Can't I have both? My so-called family doesn't give a rat's arse about me, doesn't care if I live or die, so can't you cut me some slack? I'll never ask for more, I swear. Grant me this, and I swear...

Near to 11 a.m., he trundled the Commodore through the soft caress of eucalypt switches to the clearing. Where was Lyle? John cut the engine and got out. Nerves stirred in his belly. If that stupid prick had gone wandering through the bush—

But no, there he was.

The harsh reality took a moment to register.

When John had left, Lyle had been sprawled, unconscious, on his back. Now he was on his front, as still as a fallen tree, the back of his head bloodied and smashed. He must have roused and turned over, right before he had...(*oh no*)...before he had....*died...*?

Oh no, no, no...

That wasn't possible. Dead? No, he couldn't possibly be dead.

John approached.

"Lyle?" he whispered. "Mate, it's me. Are you right?"

God, there was so much blood on the river stones. John's heart skipped a dozen beats in a row. *No, he's alive, he's alive...* Kneeling down, John touched his friend's shoulder, which felt cool. The back of Lyle's head was a crumbled mash of soft, wet and red clots.

"Lyle!" he screamed, shaking him by the shoulder. "Wake up!"

Nothing...

Oh God, oh shit, oh God...

John rolled him onto his back. His face looked waxy and mottled, one eye half-open and unseeing. Desperately, John pressed his fingers, hard, repeatedly, into Lyle's throat, searching for the carotid artery. The skin was cold. There was no pulse.

Jesus Christ, there was no pulse.

Lyle is dead.

John rocked back on his haunches.

The air felt thin and empty. Black dots swam in his vision. His punch had dashed Lyle's skull against the river stones.

Lyle is dead.

For a time, John wept. Then a prickling sensation of dread crawled over him.

I'm a murderer.

No, no, no. Oh, Christ. He didn't want to go to prison. He couldn't go to prison. And yet, here was Lyle, dead at his feet. And John had killed him.

So now what?

Think. Goddamn it, he had to *think...*

What the fuck should he do now?

8

Gasping from exertion, retching, John hauled Lyle away from the river and back through the trees. He held Lyle by the ankles. It was awful watching the ruined head bump and bounce over the uneven ground, but if John held the body under the arms, he risked getting blood on his clothes.

Jesus, for such a skinny bastard, Lyle felt heavy now.

Dead weight...

Tears pricked at John's eyes.

The land rose in a slow gradient. He had to bury Lyle on high ground, well above the river. Generally, the Upper Yarra Dam prevented any flooding around here, but John had piss-poor luck. If he dug the grave too close, no doubt the next time the Yarra broke its banks the current would wash away the dirt, grab the corpse, float it downriver, and press it against bridge pilings where some bastard walking a dog would find it. No, Lyle's remains must never be found.

After a fifteen-minute struggle through the trees, John stopped and put down Lyle's feet. The shrubs and trees stood close together and the ground was a carpet of leaf litter. John hurried back down the hill to the car. His old man always carried a large plastic tub full of emergency items in the boot. John rummaged through the tub—first aid kit, torch with spare batteries, jumper cables, reflective triangle, duct tape, WD40—and as the seconds dragged by his stomach began to knot with tension.

Surely, the old man would have a shovel.

At the bottom of the tub, he found a canvas carryall. He grabbed it with shaking hands, unzipped it, and delved around, scraping his knuckles on the tools inside. Pinch bar, screwdrivers, tyre gauge... Sweat popped on his forehead. At last, thank Christ, he found what he was looking for: the collapsible steel shovel.

Oh fuck, it was *tiny*.

He unfolded the handle and locked it into place. The tool was only about half a metre long, the shovel blade no wider than a hand-span. Shit, he would be digging all day. Still, it was a million times better than nothing. He took Lyle's schoolbag and headed into the trees.

Scraping the ground over and over, he carefully piled the leaf litter some distance away. Then he got to work. At first, the red, volcanic soil gave easily beneath the shovel. As time passed and the hole got deeper, the dirt became more compacted, harder to shift, and tangled with roots. John removed his t-shirt. Soon, he was running with sweat. He tried to avoid looking at Lyle. Already, flies congregated on the nose and mouth, along the eyelids, upon the surface of the half-open eye. It made the bile roil in John's throat. Keep digging, he thought as he puffed and strained. Don't look; just dig.

An hour went by, then another.

God, he had to stop and rest.

He washed at the river and drank a couple of beers. Spotting the bloodied stones, he clawed them out of the mud and flung them into the water. He drank another beer and felt a little better. Lightheaded, but better. Even so, it took every ounce of self-discipline to walk back through the trees.

He didn't want to look at his friend.

Picking up the shovel, he recommenced digging. The muscles in his arms, shoulders and back ached terribly.

"It's your own fault, Lyle," he panted. "You shouldn't have hit her."

I gave her a manners lesson she'll never forget.

"And why did you attack me? I wouldn't have punched you otherwise. Understand? This is on you. So get fucked. You can go and get fucked."

Then John broke down, sobbing. Anguish took the strength out of his legs and he fell to his knees. Flies kept buzzing and flitting over the corpse in ever-increasing numbers. *Lyle is dead. And I killed him.* The horror rolled over John in such a powerful wave that it tore a scream from him and made him pull at his hair.

When he threw up, the thin dribble of vomit splashing into the grave brought him to his senses. No, he had to stay calm. He had to focus. Choking back the urge to scream and keep on screaming, John threw his desperate energies into digging.

By the close of the third hour, the grave was surely deep enough: about one metre, give or take. John let the shovel fall. Blisters and raw skin lined his palms. Grabbing Lyle by the ankles, he dragged him into the hole as the disturbed flies, buzzing, kept circling and landing, circling and landing.

Fuck. The grave was too short. John would have to manipulate the body to fit.

The thought of touching it, skin on skin, gave John the dry heaves.

Finally, steeling himself, he took hold of Lyle's head and tried to tuck the chin to the shoulder. Futile: the neck had stiffened. Rigor mortis? Already? John wrenched his hand away as if stung. Lyle's face had changed too. It seemed as if he were clenching his jaw, pulling back his lips in a grimace to show both rows of teeth.

John fought against dizziness. Working quickly, he gripped Lyle's feet, bent the knees and turned both legs at the hips, stuffing the legs into the hole. He shoved in the schoolbag next to the body and began shovelling dirt into the grave.

"I'm sorry," he gasped, "Jesus, I'm so fucking sorry, I didn't mean it, I didn't mean it, I swear to God, I didn't mean it..."

And he was crying again; crying like a kid, with fat tears rolling one after the other down his cheeks and his nose running with snot. He flung the dirt over the legs first, then the torso. Once the dirt reached the chest, he paused, suddenly afraid.

"Are you really dead?" he said. "Come on, mate. Are you dead?"

Kneeling down, he shook Lyle by the shoulder, pulled at both eyelids with his thumbs, pressed his fingers into the throat to find a pulse. Nothing, nothing...

Quit spooking yourself.

But when John picked up the shovelful of dirt and held it over the waxen face, the irrational feeling (*fear?*) that Lyle wasn't dead after all stayed his hand. Buried alive...wasn't that one of the worst ways to die? Frantically, John threw aside the shovel to check again the body's carotid arteries. No pulse. He was furious at himself now. There is no pulse, okay? *Lyle is dead.* Finish burying him.

Yet he couldn't do it with the shovel.

Weeping, John picked up handfuls of dirt and packed them gently around Lyle's head. When only Lyle's face showed, John covered the forehead, cheeks, eyes, and had to stop. He stared carefully at the nose and mouth.

Buried alive...

He grabbed the shovel. Looking into the trees, wheezing, guts churning, he flung the dirt into the grave until Lyle was gone. Then he leapt up and frantically shovelled the remainder of the dirt as fast as he could, his muscles burning and the breath rasping in and out of his parched throat. When the grave was full, he walked over it, tamping it down. Once the grave was as flat as he could make it, he scooped up the piled leaf litter by the shovelful and scattered the leaves over the bare ground.

Breathless, he stood back and surveyed his work.

You couldn't tell.

Honest to God, you could not tell.

The site looked no different from the land surrounding it.

"Don't haunt me," he whispered. Did he believe in ghosts? He wasn't sure. "Mate, you know it was an accident."

No answer, of course.

He picked up the shovel and his t-shirt, and staggered back to the river, to the esky with melted ice and one remaining beer, to the fishing rod, the tackle box, the gurgling of the current, the call of birds hidden in the trees, the old man's Commodore. Everything looked so normal.

John spent a long time washing the shovel.

When Lyle failed to return from Aaron's house that Sunday night, his parents reported him missing. The police quickly established that Lyle had never reached Aaron's house. The last sighting was of him walking the footpath alongside the highway, carrying his schoolbag, as reported by a neighbour who had waved at him while cycling past. Lyle had waved back. Sometime later, he had just…disappeared.

Over the next few days, the police interviewed everyone associated with Lyle.

They interviewed John at home.

The detective, a man named Barker, wore a green suit with his hair slicked back from his forehead. John showed Barker to the kitchen table and they both sat down. His adoptive parents were out on the patio, wanting no part of this. John couldn't meet the detective's eye. Instead, he stared at the table and kept his hands clutched in his lap, his blistered and raw-skinned hands. He felt sick inside.

"I understand this is tough for you," Barker said. "Lyle is your best friend?"

John nodded.

Barker opened a notebook, clicked a pen. "Can I start by asking you where you were on Sunday?"

"Fishing in Warburton."

"All day?"

"Most of it."

"Righto." Barker made a note. "Can anyone verify that?"

"Uh, the bartender at the Warburton pub: a bald bloke with a goatee beard. I was there sometime mid-morning for a couple of pots."

Barker made another note. "When did you last see Lyle?"

"At school on Friday."

"Did he seem to be acting differently in any way? Unusually happy, for instance? Maybe sad or angry? Anxious? Depressed, in your opinion?"

John shrugged.

"Was anything troubling him in particular?" Barker went on.

"I don't think so."

"Had he confided in you lately about problems? An issue with a mate or a girlfriend, perhaps? Is Lyle unhappy at home?"

"If he was upset about stuff, he didn't tell me about it."

"All right, that's fine. What about drugs? Does he take any drugs that you're aware of? Prescription meds? Dope? You can tell me, son. You won't get in strife, I give you my word. All I care about is finding Lyle."

John shook his head. "He smoked and drank. That's it."

Barker paused, closed the notepad. "You think he's dead?"

Startled, John looked up. The detective was watching him closely.

"Dead? Why would I think that?"

"Because you spoke about him in the past tense."

"I did?"

"Yeah," the detective said. "You did. Instead of saying, 'He smokes and drinks', you said, 'He smoked and drank', as if he were already dead."

"Well, shit... I didn't mean it that way."

Barker drummed his fingertips on the table. Then he tucked the notepad into his inside jacket pocket, clicked the pen and stashed it with the notepad. He smoothed a palm over his hair as if to check the gel was still holding. "Was Lyle mixed up in anything serious?" he said.

"Serious like what?"

"Crimes, gangs," Barker said. "Some type of illegal activity."

"Not that I know of."

"No enemies?"

"None."

81

"Lyle was expected at Aaron's place to finish a science project. Can you think of any reason why he wouldn't have gone to Aaron's place?"

Because he came fishing with me…

John gazed at the table's green swirling pattern. Despite himself, he could feel tears rising. "I don't know," he said.

"That's fine." Barker took out a business card and put it on the table between them. "If you think of any information that might be helpful, give me a call."

"Yeah, sure."

The detective stood up. John followed him to the door. They shook hands. Barker didn't seem to notice the raw skin and blisters on John's palm. So much for the sixth sense of police officers… John's stomach lurched, making him want to vomit. He watched Barker stride along the driveway to the unmarked cop car, get in, and speed away. John kept staring out at nothing.

The old man came in through the back door where he had been waiting on the patio, obviously spying through a window. He said, "Well? How did it go?"

John shut the front door.

"Have they got any ideas on what's happened to Lyle?" the old man said.

John trudged down the hall to his bedroom.

The Berg-Olsens wouldn't let him see Merry. They wouldn't let him talk to her on the phone either. She's not well, they kept saying. Please try again later.

It made a weird kind of sense, he finally decided. After all, how could he face her after killing her brother? Wouldn't she read his guilt in his body language, tone of voice, the touch of his hand? Even if he could have convinced her that Lyle's death had been an accident, what then?

She would have hated him.

And rightly so.

She would have told her parents, her friends. Somebody would have turned him in to the police. And he'd be languishing now in jail, with decades yet to go…

No, no, no.

Stop.

Choices had been made. It was too late to go back.

At a mere eighteen years of age, John had destroyed everything of value in his life. He wanted to sleep and never wake up. Depression flattened him. Lethargic, without the sufficient energy to suicide, he fantasised about car crashes, heart attacks, strokes, leukaemia, allergic reactions to peanuts, measles, violent home invasions, choking on a chicken bone...

He didn't return to school. Getting out of bed every morning proved to be impossible. He was so tired. The nightmare kept him awake half the night. Always the same dream: Lyle screaming and suffocating under dirt.

At first, John's parents were patient. For a couple of weeks, they indulged him, tiptoed around him. Then they got fed up; soon after that, mad as hell.

"You lazy sod," his mother yelled one day in early summer. "Get up!"

He obeyed. While she slammed around in the kitchen, making coffee and muttering under her breath, John dressed, packed a bag and quietly left. Hours later, he was stepping aboard the Spirit of Tasmania ferry, bound for Devonport, Tasmania.

Within a few days of arrival, he sent a postcard to his parents: *I'm living in Tassie and I'm fine.* Initially, he assumed they might try to find him via police or private investigators. But no, they hadn't. At first, their lack of interest hurt, sharply and deeply. After a few months, however, the freedom of this grimy little town and the mindlessness of his job at the carpet factory combined to give him the happiest time of his life. Well, perhaps *happy* overstated it.

More like content.

Yes, he'd been content in Devonport. Within walking distance of his cabin, twenty minutes along the same street, a pub full of wood and leather booths offered cheap fettuccini carbonara, rib-eye steak with mushroom sauce, chicken parmigiana, surf 'n' turf. Four nights per week, he frequented the pub. The remaining three dinners consisted of simple fare, on toast, he prepared at home—baked beans, eggs, sardines—to mirror his simple life, and he had eaten those meals on the veranda overlooking Bass Strait no matter what the weather. He enjoyed watching the ships. In summer, the sea glittered under a bright dome of blue sky. In winter, the horizon disappeared inside cloud, fog and rain. He preferred the view in winter; the ships moving in and out of the mist appeared and disappeared like ghostly apparitions.

If the carpet factory had not gone bust, he would no doubt still be there.

As if in a fugue state, he had lived the same weekly routine in

Devonport over and over and over, and it had calmed him, anaesthetised him. The same food, the same bullshit from the managers and co-workers at the factory, the same conversation from the Russian bloke who ran the corner supermarket who used to wink and say, "The eye can see it, but the tooth can't bite it" (which didn't mean anything until John had started to live with Meredith, until he realised that he was helpless against her), the same blare of ship-horns in the dead of night, the same terrible dream…

His cigarette had gone out.

Sitting on the bed, shivering, John dropped the butt into the ashtray.

Stop raking over the past, he thought. Lyle's been dead for thirty-one years.

Donna has the right attitude. *Did you mean to do this thing, whatever it is? So, it was an accident. Then how can you blame yourself if you didn't mean to do it?* From now on, he would try to his best to reframe the incident—

(*murder*)

—through Donna's perspective.

But, by God, he would always regret not telling the police the truth. Regret gnawed at his insides like an ulcer. Yes, it had been an accident. Stupidly, he had panicked and buried Lyle. By the time he had realised his error, it was too late. How could he have gone to the police and explained Lyle's death as an accident after spending hours upon hours carefully burying the corpse? Who would have believed him? Nobody: that's who.

Yet if he had told the truth…

Things may have turned out differently.

If Lyle had been given a proper burial, in a cemetery with a headstone, the Berg-Olsens would have got closure, at least. Perhaps Meredith would have dodged the death wish that had taken her into locked wards and, ultimately, into the hands of that monster, Sebastian, who had made her a monster in his own image. Perhaps John would have applied for that plumber's apprenticeship, found a woman to love who loved him back, married her and bought a house, had some children…

No, fuck it. *Stop.*

Trembling, he lit another cigarette.

How many more times would he fret over this exact same point? *What's done is done.*

You play the hand you're dealt, and all that bullshit.

A great fatigue swept through him. Gritting his teeth, he wiped a hand across his stubbled face and tried to throw off the dark mood.

What's done is done. He repeated it over and over in his mind, like a mantra.

He looked about the room. While he had been chain-smoking and torturing himself with memories, dawn had crept around the edges of his window. He dressed in yesterday's clothes, opened the curtains, and went into the back yard.

The air felt cold and crisp. At this time of the morning, everything looked washed out and grey. There were no sounds apart from the half-hearted clucking of wattlebirds, the cheerful whistling of a blackbird. John went to his vegie patch.

Crouching, he poked a finger into the black soil—*red, volcanic soil, easy to dig with an undersized shovel*—and found it too dry for his liking. Uncoiling the hose, he turned on the tap and sprayed a fine mist of water over the tomato and capsicum seedlings, moving the hose constantly from side to side so as not to pummel any of the tiny leaves.

This is what soil means to me now, he thought with great determination, nodding, biting at his lip. It is a medium in which to grow things. And he grew lots of wonderful things, each plant tended with such care and attention that it yielded large, healthy and brightly-coloured vegetables. He had never tasted better vegetables than the ones he grew himself. In a couple of months, when these spindly little seedlings would be waist-high and drooping under the weight of heavy, red fruit, he would give tomatoes to Donna by the kilogram.

His thoughts turned to last night's dinner after the circus, the unexpected breaking of the ice with Cassie, and the lingering kiss from Donna that held so much promise. He glanced at his watch. Donna would probably be in the shower by now, getting ready for her 7 a.m. Sunday shift at the café.

He longed to see her again.

It was too soon, but to hell with playing it cool. He would find some excuse for visiting her house later that day.

9

Donna finished work at 3 p.m. on Sundays, he recalled, so John gave her an hour's grace. He crossed the road with a bottle of chardonnay and knocked.

When she opened the door and saw him, her face lit up. Honest to God, she actually lit up. He grinned, could feel his eyes shining, his blood pumping.

I'm *in*, he marvelled. In like Flynn.

He lifted the paper bag. "A thank you present," he said, "for dinner last night."

Donna giggled. "And dinner was a thank you present for the circus. There was no need, but you're very sweet. Come on in."

He followed her to the kitchen. She was wearing tracksuit pants, t-shirt, bare feet, her hair pulled into a low ponytail. A half-empty glass of wine sat on the bench, and he put the bottle next to it.

"How was work?" he said.

She shrugged. "Oh, you know: same old same old." She took the bottle out of the bag and admired the label. "Gosh, this looks expensive."

John felt himself blush. "The sheila at the bottle-shop reckons it's very popular with chardonnay lovers. I wouldn't know. I don't drink the stuff myself."

"Well, I'm going to save it for a special occasion." Donna put the wine into the fridge and, with a flourish, took out a beer stubby. "Ta-dah. Look what I've got for you. Victoria Bitter is your tipple of choice, right?"

"Right."

A warm flush spread through him as he took the stubby. When was the last time anybody had done anything like this for him? Kept him in their thoughts while going about their business? Jesus, she must have gone to buy wine and decided to buy something for him too. He choked up, just a little, and swallowed hard.

Oblivious, Donna continued, "I'll make sure to stash a half-dozen from now on. Oh no, shit, I didn't get a stubby holder. They were right by the register too."

"No worries. It'll be down the hatch before it gets warm anyway."

They both laughed. Donna topped up her glass from a two-litre cardboard cask, almost to the brim, and walked through the kitchen into the lounge. John trailed behind. They took their customary seats; John on the couch facing the fireplace, Donna on the couch against the windows. He had been drinking slowly but steadily all day and felt relaxed, sociable; almost happy.

"How's the vegie patch coming along?" she said.

"Good. The plants are growing like Topsy. I had to stake them the other day."

A quick slapping of moccasins against tiles and Cassie hurried into the lounge. "Hey, John, I thought it was you," she said. "I heard your voice."

Damn, he was pleased the girl had sought him out to say hello. The way to a woman's heart was by making friends with her child, he knew that for sure. "I figured you'd have run away with the circus by now," he said. "Been practising your juggling?"

"Not really." Cassie meandered to the fireplace and leaned on the mantel. She stared at John, pensively sucking on her bottom lip. "Can I ask you something?"

A prickling of foreboding moved through him. "Sure."

"Oh, for the love of God," Donna said, clanking her wineglass onto the coffee table. "Honey, can't we give it a rest? I thought you had homework."

"I'm finished already."

"Then go and play on the computer or something, okay?"

"I will, Mum, just as soon as I ask John about it."

"Fine." Donna sighed. "Hurry up."

The child had dark circles under her eyes, as if she hadn't slept. John put the stubby on the coffee table and wiped his sweating palms along his jeans. Tiger strolled into the room, glanced around, and strolled back out again.

Cassie said, "It's a stupid question, I guess."

"Ask it anyway," he said.

"Do you believe in witches?"

His stomach fell. Donna was watching him, he could feel it; watching for his reaction. "Witches?" he said. "You mean warts, flying broomsticks and black cats?"

"Not exactly."

"Then what do you mean?"

But he knew. A crawl of adrenaline began to wend through his belly.

"I saw a witch last night," Cassie said.

"No," Donna said, "you were dreaming."

"Mum, I was not! I saw it, I really did."

"Saw what?" he said.

Cassie approached and sat on the edge of the coffee table. How young she looked, John realised; how vulnerable and small.

"I woke up because I heard something at my window; a kind of scratching, but not up-and-down. More like in a circle."

Meredith's long fingernails came to mind, how she liked to move them on laminate, around and around and around. He felt sick, as if the day's beer had collected and risen in a bitter tide to the back of his throat.

"I got out of bed and pulled aside the curtain." Tears came to her eyes and brimmed, trembling against her lower lids, threatening to spill.

"Come on, that's enough," Donna said. "We've talked about this, remember?"

"And I saw a witch."

"No, you had a dream," Donna said.

"Shut up, Mum, it wasn't a dream, I keep telling you."

"And I keep telling *you*—"

Quickly, John interjected, "What did the witch look like?"

Cassie edged closer along the coffee table. "Pale," she said. "But really pale, like she was dead."

"Oh, for God's *sake*—"

"With white hair and white skin and the boniest hands I've ever seen. She stopped clawing at my window..."

John said, "And then what happened?"

The girl's lower lip began to quiver.

Donna opened her arms. "Honey? You need a hug?"

But Cassie had not broken eye contact with John. "The witch bared her teeth and waggled her tongue like she wanted to eat me. And I screamed." The girl hiccupped on a sob. "I called for Mum."

"And when I came into your room," Donna said, slowly and deliberately, as if she had said these same words again and again, "you were tucked up in bed."

"That's because I jumped back under the covers!"

"And I turned on every light and looked through every window, and honey, there was nothing there, okay? Please believe me, there was nothing there." Donna, with an emphatic nod, gestured at John, and said, "It was a dream, right?"

He leaned back in the couch, sweating.

Trapped...

They were waiting for his verdict. If he sided with Cassie, he might alienate Donna. But if he sided with Donna, he would alienate Cassie which, in turn, would ruin his chances with Donna. A lose-lose situation.

Shit.

Resentment began to build within his chest and squeeze his heart. Fuck you, Meredith, he thought. You've poisoned my life once again.

Finally, he looked at Cassie and said, "Have you watched any horror movies lately? Read any scary books?"

She recoiled, insulted. "You don't believe me either."

"Oh, I believe you, no worries."

He heard Donna gasp. But Cassie smiled, tentatively, hopefully.

Encouraged, he went on, "Lots of things in this world don't make any sense. God knows things have happened to me that I can't explain. But I reckon I can explain what happened to you last night."

They both straightened up and stared expectantly at him.

"We've got lots of homeless people around here. What you saw wasn't a witch, but some poor old woman who's had a rough time of it: somebody's grandma."

"A grandma?" Cassie said. "Like an old lady burglar?"

"No, nothing bad like that. Maybe she's got nowhere to sleep and hasn't any money for food. Maybe she walks around at night and eats out of dog bowls."

"Dog bowls?" Cassie said. "Oh, that's awful. Wouldn't she have any family?"

John made a hushing motion with one hand. "It's all right," he said. "Homeless people look after themselves pretty good. They have their own community. And there are lots of places that help them out, like the Salvation Army. So put the experience out of your mind, okay?"

The girl's eyes shone with tears. This time, however, her emotion was not fear but compassion, he could tell; pity for the non-existent, vagrant grandmother. Unexpectedly, Cassie leapt up and flung her arms about him, just for a moment. Shocked, he felt the tender skin of her cheek, smelled the talcum powder scent of her body, and heard her breath at his ear, and then she pulled away. She looked relieved, almost joyful.

"Mum," she said, breathless and excited. "We should leave out food for the poor old lady: a picnic."

"Okay, we'll talk about it."

"Hey, whoa, hang on a second," John said. "Don't go trying to make friends with this grandma. Sometimes, people end up homeless because they're crazy, all right? Feel sorry for her, yeah, but don't trust her if you ever happen to see her again. Crazy people can do crazy things…like eat out of dog bowls. All right?"

Cassie sobered for a few seconds, quietly thinking.

"All right," she said. "Thanks for explaining things to me. I'll see you later."

He nodded. Cassie flashed a smile at her mother and raced from the room.

"I've seen people like that," Donna said, "hanging around the railway station. Druggies and drunks. Maybe I ought to call the cops."

"Nah, don't worry. Just keep your doors locked."

"I always do."

"To be honest," he said, lowering his voice, "I reckon she dreamt it all too."

And now Donna was gazing at him with amazement and…desire? Well, what do you know; lying had worked its magic, as always.

"Incredible," she said. "I've been trying to reassure her, getting nowhere, and you've fixed everything within thirty seconds."

Smiling, he gave a little *ah, it was nothing* shrug.

"I stupidly kept telling her it was a nightmare," Donna continued. "Thank you."

"No worries."

She sat next to him and put her hand on his thigh. There was no mistaking the signals. He kissed her, gently. She parted her lips. An electric jolt shot down his spine as their tongues touched.

She drew back. "I'm free from nine on Wednesday, as soon as I've dropped Cassie at school."

"I'm at work on Wednesdays."

"Oh, shit. You're Wednesday, Thursday, Friday, aren't you? And I'm Sunday, Monday, Tuesday at the café."

In reply, he kissed her. He liked the way she worked her tongue. It promised a certain skill. Blood suffused his cock. He trailed his fingers through her ponytail, the hair soft and thick, silky. Tenderly, he nuzzled at her neck.

"What about when Cassie's asleep?" he murmured.

"No. I'm too noisy."

Holy shit. His cock strained against the zip of his jeans. He clutched at one of her small breasts through the t-shirt and kneaded it. The nipple butted against his palm. She wasn't wearing a bra.

"When does she stay at her father's place?" he said.

"Not for a couple of weeks."

The slapping noise of moccasins on tile sprang them apart. Donna sat on the other couch and smoothed her hair. John picked up the stubby. Cassie appeared, her arms filled with Tiger, the cat looking fluffy and contented.

"I want to tell you something," Cassie said to John.

"Okay," he said.

"I liked the circus." She blushed. "Some of the acts were lame, but I had fun. There was good stuff in the show-bags too. Anyway, thanks for taking us."

"No worries."

Bashful, the girl scurried from the room.

"Hey, you've got yourself a fan." Dropping her voice, Donna added, "Just so you know, her father never takes her anywhere."

In like Flynn.

Donna sat next to him. They kissed again, and yet...

And yet his stomach churned as he recalled Cassie's wan and frightened face, her words: *And I saw a witch...really pale, like she was dead... She bared her teeth and waggled her tongue like she wanted to eat me...*

Donna rubbed her hand over his zip, but he was losing his hard-on.

"I should go," he said.

"You're right. We shouldn't torture ourselves. Hey, listen, I'll try to swap a shift tomorrow. We can spend the day together if you want. How does that sound?"

"Like music to my ears."

She followed him to the entrance hall and kissed him goodbye. As soon as she closed the door, John sprinted across the road towards the miner's cottage with its two myopic eyes for windows.

Panting, he threw open the door and slammed it behind him.

"Merry?"

No response. He scanned the surroundings. She must be in one of her rooms.

He went to the hobby room first and put his ear to the jamb, listening for the familiar clattering noises. Silence. He took a few steps to her bedroom and tapped on the closed door.

"Merry? Answer me. We've got to talk."

As he waited, he became aware that his heart still galloped and he couldn't catch his breath. It wasn't due to the brief run from Donna's place. No, this was fear. The tension in his shoulders, the quivering in his legs, the hesitation of his hand as he went to knock again. All of it: fear.

Never, in the eight years they had been living together, had Meredith deliberately shown her face to a neighbour.

Once or twice, a neighbour had spotted her through a window, but only by accident. Meredith would have been lifting the slat of a venetian blind to swear at something—a barking dog, a cooing pigeon, a car hitching over a speed hump—just as a neighbour happened to look. Meredith avoided people, would no more show anyone her face than go out dancing.

Until now.

He knocked again, more forcefully this time.

"We can talk in the kitchen," he said. "It's important."

She would be lying face down on the bed, he knew, legs straight and arms by her sides, as if at attention. How she didn't smother herself, with her nose and mouth pressed into the pillow, he had no idea. Did she sleep like that?

"Meredith, I mean it," he said. "Come out right now."

He knocked, hard, and put his ear to the jamb. Not a sound. It was as if her bedroom was empty. An awful thought occurred. Perhaps her bedroom *was* empty. Perhaps she had slipped outside and was even now across the road, slinking across Donna's yard, aiming to try the back door or find an unlocked window—but no; Meredith never left the house during the day. Except when she had brought him a glass of water while he'd been building the vegie patch. Oh, Christ.

"All right, that's it," he said. "I'm coming in."

He twisted the knob and began to push open the door.

It slammed shut with great force, rattling in its frame.

John staggered back. Goddamn… Meredith had been standing directly on the other side of the door this whole time, her face separated from his by nothing more than three and half centimetres of hollow-core Masonite and cardboard webbing. He brought a hand to his mouth. Just the suggestion of such close proximity made him queasy. There was something rat-like about her gaunt and pinched features, those yellowed teeth artificially elongated by receding gums.

"Please come out," he said to the door. "I've something to ask you. It's about our neighbours. Donna and her daughter. Will you please come out? Merry?"

After a moment, he strode to the kitchen. It was too early for dinner, just on 5.30 p.m., but fuck it, he had to do something with all this nervous energy.

She bared her teeth and waggled her tongue like she wanted to eat me.

He threw a few sausages into a fry pan, cracked in a couple of eggs, a halved tomato, and drank two stubbies one after the other, pouring them down his throat, while the whole mess of dinner crackled and spattered in butter on the stove. He opened another drink. What the fuck was he going to do about Meredith?

Well, he couldn't lock her inside the house.

He'd tried that before. Within a few months of finding her in the park and moving her into his apartment, he realised she didn't eat. At least, not the meals he prepared for her. So he had started taking more notice, had begun spying on her, in fact. Every night, she left the apartment a few minutes after midnight, and returned by five. He never followed her. The thought of encountering her in the dark gave him the heebie-jeebies. Around that time, he had started to realise the blood stains he occasionally found on her clothes weren't from menstruation after all. When the neighbours in the apartment building had got nosy—which hadn't taken long once pets started to disappear—he had moved her into a two-bedroom unit and decided to keep her inside at night. However, deadlocking the doors had failed. She had escaped through a window. He had then fitted deadlocks to the windows. Her solution had been elegant but simple: break a pane. And if he boarded up the windows, she would no doubt find an exit through the roof. Her night-time excursions could not be denied.

John finished the stubby and lined it up with the other empties; a baker's dozen so far today, not counting the one Donna had given him. He jabbed the tip of a knife into the sausages, over and over. Beads of liquefied fat began to ooze.

Nothing would stop Merry from prowling at night, he knew that.

But why frighten Cassie? Was Meredith trying to locate Tiger? Was she trying to figure out a way to kill the bloody cat?

"Merry," he yelled. "Dinner's up."

He put a sausage and half a tomato on one plate and piled the rest of the fry-up onto another. Even though she didn't eat regular food, he offered it to her anyway, one meal every day, in the hope she might take a few bites. It was a habit he couldn't shake. Christ, she probably had every nutritional deficiency under the sun: beriberi, scurvy, anaemia, that one that makes your bones thin and brittle…

He sat at the table with a knife and fork.

"Merry," he called, looking up from his plate.

He startled. She was already standing in the doorway.

"There you are," he said, and tried to smile. "Hungry?"

Her eyes were unfocused, her mouth hanging open with a thin line of spittle stretched between her chapped lips. John's stomach turned over.

Putting down his cutlery, he said, "Why did you tap on the neighbour's window last night?"

Meredith looked behind him as if somebody were standing there.

Undeterred, he continued, "You scared the shit out of Donna's little girl, and for what? Tell me why you tapped on the window and let that girl see you. Well? You've never bothered neighbours before. Are you going to tell me what's going on?"

She ran her hands through her dead tufts of white hair and slumped against the wall, as if the floor were tilting beneath her feet. This was a sign of stress. No doubt he had upset her with his questions. He was about to apologise when she suddenly put her back to the wall and glared at him.

Jesus, her eyes were blazing with fury, her teeth gnashing together. A hoarse growling noise was coming from deep in her throat.

Panicked, he jumped up from the table.

"What the fuck?" he gasped.

Grabbing her plate with its meagre dinner, she reeled and lurched from the kitchen, back along the hall to her hobby room. The door slammed.

John fumbled with the chair and sat down again.

Honest to God, he had thought she was going to attack him. Her moods were changing so fast, so unpredictably. Adrenaline surged through his veins, so intense he could almost hear it, like overhead power lines screaming in a strong wind. He ate quickly, mechanically, his mind racing. Throwing down his cutlery, he rummaged through the kitchen bin and pulled out a crumpled sheet of glossy paper. He smoothed it flat on the bench and hunched over it, reading the text.

Visit our wondrous kingdom!

Fun for young and old!
Expect the unexpected!

The Atlas Circus Royale only performed once on Sundays, at 11 a.m. Surely, Nate Rossi would be holed up inside his caravan, tying one on. John looked at his watch: 5.51 p.m. The bottle shop was open until eight. He had plenty of time to buy a conciliatory bottle of whisky before closing time.

The empty stubbies drew his eye.

You're an alky if you drink and drive.

Shit…

But he didn't feel especially pissed. On the other hand, his tolerance was high. And what if he encountered a booze bus? What then? He could lose his license.

Even so, he abandoned his dinner and hurried out to the car.

10

Nate opened the caravan door. John presented the whisky.

"Little Johnny Butt-rose, you beautiful old bastard," Nate said, eyes gleaming as he turned the bottle around in his hands. "If you weren't a bloke, I'd kiss ya."

"Look, it's nothing," John said. "I wanted to say sorry."

"Sorry?"

"For running off like I did."

Nate, looking blank, swayed in the doorway for a moment, and stepped back with a laugh and a careless wave of his hand. "Aw, fuck it, bygones and all that. Come on in, will ya? It's too cold to leave the bloody door open."

John stepped inside. The caravan looked and smelled exactly the same apart from a discarded pizza box by the sink, its smattering of withered pineapple pieces stuck fast to the cardboard by oil and yellow cheese. Nate shut the door. A small portable heater sat on the unmade bed, its element bright red, humming as it puffed out hot air.

"Sit down," Nate said. "I'll pour drinks. Smokes are on the table. Help yourself."

John sat. Nate's hands shook as he unscrewed the bottle cap. Trying to fill two water glasses in one unsteady pass, he spilt whisky over the bench, and actually leaned down to slurp up the drops.

"Waste not, want not," he said with a chuckle. "Am I right?"

John groped for a cigarette.

Nate put the drinks on the table. He was tanked, John realised, tanked to the gills. John felt depressed just looking at the poor alky bastard. Whenever he blinked, Nate's eyelids were out of sync; the left eye stayed closed for longer than the right. John lit his smoke and exhaled in a long sigh. Why had he bothered to come here? What help could Nate possibly offer? Another wrong decision... The story of my life, he thought morosely, and drew hard on the cigarette.

"Get stuck in, you old cock," Nate said. "For tomorrow we may die."

Nate raised his drink. After a moment, John raised his, and they touched glasses. Nate skolled his whisky in one mouthful and refilled his glass.

"Listen," John said. "Remember, we talked about Meredith Berg-Olsen."

"Yeah?"

"About how she bit herself fifty-two times; thirteen bites to each limb."

"Oh yeah, that's right. Fucken freaky, hey?"

John put on a smile. "You knew the psych nurse. What was her name?"

"Her name?" Nate looked puzzled.

"The nurse's name."

Nate put a forefinger to his temple and screwed up his face in a parody of deep thought. "Nup," he said. "Dunno, mate."

"Are you sure?"

"No, wait, it's coming back..." He slammed his palm onto the table. "Felicity. We called her Flick. Hey, what kind of name is Flick? Sounds like a fucken horse."

Fleetingly, Donna crossed John's mind. "And Flick's surname?"

"What do you take me for, a memory magician? I can't remember."

"Can you try?"

"Well, it was something Polish. Or Russian."

John tried another tack. "Your brother knew her, didn't he?"

"And rooted her a few times too, if I recall."

"Your brother would know her full name? Know where to find her?"

Nate pouted his lips obscenely as his hand wove the glass through the air, and with closed eyes, he took a deep, grateful swallow of whisky. John felt cold and ill. *Do I act like that when I'm pissed?* Just in case, he must never get pissed in front of Donna. Not once, not ever. Okay, yes, technically she had already seen him tipsy, but not *drunk* drunk...not hammered like Nate. But why worry? John wasn't an alky. Sure, he drank a lot but who doesn't? Besides, he didn't drink as much as he did in his younger days. Did he? No, probably not.

"This is important," John said. "Can you ask your brother about Flick?"

"My brother? Mate, I don't even know where the shithead lives."

A dead end. John sat back and rubbed his brow. He should have known. Did his luck run any other way? "Oh Jesus," he muttered, despite himself. "Oh, help me."

Nate perked up and leaned closer. "What's going on, Butt-rose?"

"Nothing."

"Mate, you can tell me."

John went to stand. "Thanks for the smoke. I'm off."

"You wanna know about Meredith, don't you? I've got some stories to tell, stories from Flick. That creepy stuff she told me, I'll always remember."

John sat down again.

Nate tapped the side of his nose and began to laugh, a wheezing gurgle that ended in a cough. "I told you about the bite marks."

"Yeah."

"All right, here's a doozy you won't forget." He tipped whisky into both glasses, a dribble in John's glass, and a lot more in his own. "Flick reckoned that Meredith changed after biting herself. Like chucking a u-ey; one minute she wanted to kill herself, the next she was different."

"Different how?"

"Like a whole new person. But hang on to your hat for this next bit, okay?"

Goosebumps prickled up the nape of John's neck. "Okay."

"Call me a bullshit artist, call me whatever, but this is what Flick told me, God's own truth. I swear it."

"Whatever you say, I'll believe you."

"Sweet," Nate said. "Well, this ward had pets: mice, birds, guinea pigs, hamsters, any animal that was easy to look after. It was therapy, right? Teaching the patients to care for something other than themselves, okay? Teaching those sad-sack motherfuckers how to love; how to feel again." He widened his eyes and grinned with relish, as if telling a ghost story around a campfire. "And this one day, a guinea pig went missing. Shit, I even remember its name: Peaches. Poor little Peaches went missing. Since you could only open its cage from the top, the bugger didn't climb out by itself. Somebody had to take it out. You follow?"

"Yeah, I follow. Get to the point."

"Calm your tits, I'm getting there. Right away, as soon as everybody knew Peaches had gone missing, Flick reckoned the culprit was Meredith."

"Was she right?"

"You betcha. Meredith's room got searched first. And they found Peaches. Oh yeah, they found Peaches, all right."

Stopping for effect, Nate leaned back in his chair, nodded once, and sucked on his whisky, his eyes never leaving John's face. John decided not to crack, not to ask. The seconds ticked on. Outside, somebody was singing; a reedy, ancient voice, the lyrics too faint to discern. It was probably one of the circus workers leaving their caravan to visit a portable toilet. Sweat gathered in John's hairline. His foot jittered against the floor. Nate kept smiling and sipping whisky, one eyelid starting to droop.

"Fine," John said. "The staff found Peaches."

"They sure did. You bet your arse they found that poor little bugger."

"Dead?"

"Worse."

"Hah." John crushed the cigarette and lit another. "What's worse than dead?"

Nate hunched forward. "Its bones were in the bathroom sink," he whispered, "bloody and raw, all chewed up. You follow?"

After a while, John nodded.

"Shit, I thought that'd floor ya," Nate said. "Maybe you don't get me. Okay, no worries, I'll be crystal clear: Meredith had eaten little Peaches."

John clenched his jaw. "Did they find the rest of its body?"

"Yeah, in a drawer of Meredith's dresser. But just the skin, right? Turned inside out; the fur on the inside. She'd ripped off the skin like a sock. Must have done it with her bare hands, too."

John felt himself blanch.

"Aw, I know, right?" Nate said. "Chuck-worthy. The patients weren't allowed any knives, razors, scissors, anything sharp. Flick reckoned the only way Meredith could have got started on skinning little Peaches was by using her teeth." He laughed and slapped a hand to his cheek. "Can you believe that shit? Meredith used her *teeth.*"

Yes, John could believe it.

"But that's not the worst part," Nate said.

"There's more?"

"Nobody ever found Peaches' innards. Heart, lungs, liver, intestines: gone."

For a time, John concentrated on his cigarette, on the hiss and crackle of the tobacco as it burned. *Nobody ever found Peaches' innards.* He had to ask. He didn't have a choice. "What was the theory?" he said. "About the guts?"

"Well, they gave Meredith's room a shakedown, looked out the window at the garden beds below, in all the bins on the ward, and found nothing."

"So? She could have flushed the guts down a dunny."

Nate shook his head and chuckled. "Nah, mate. That's not what happened."

"What are you trying to say? That Meredith ate them?"

"Damn fucken straight. But did she eat 'em while little Peaches was dead or still alive? Now that's the sixty-four-dollar question. An animal can live for a long while with its guts torn out. For hours, even days, if there's not much blood loss. You know what Flick told me? That for weeks afterwards, she had bad dreams about Peaches, about the poor little bugger squealing and kicking as Meredith chowed down on its innards straight through its belly, like eating a fucken apple."

John took a gulp of whisky. He felt lightheaded, detached, as if part of his conscious mind were floating outside of his body. Or perhaps he was just pissed.

"Did Flick question Meredith about it?"

"Course she did. They all did; the doctors and shrinks and whatnot. Meredith kept her trap shut, apparently. Never owned up to jack-shit." Nate gazed into the bottom of his glass, and mumbled, "I always wondered about that."

"About what?"

"Did Meredith kill the animals first? Or eat them alive?"

"Plural? You mean other animals in the hospital went missing?"

Nate slammed a fist onto the table. "All of 'em, mate! One after the fucken other, as fast as the staff could replace 'em, they'd go missing. Only Meredith was smarter about it after the Peaches episode and made sure not to leave any body parts behind. Still, everybody knew it was her."

John's throat felt tight and dry. He grabbed the bottle, poured himself a shot, and downed it, fast.

Nate said quietly, "Some people in this world like to eat animals while they're still alive. Gross, right? Take new-born mice, for instance. Hairless, pink, blind little things, so tiny you could fit one on a five-cent piece with room to spare. Well, there are people who think it's a fucken delicacy to take new-born mice and dip 'em in sauce, one at a time, and crunch-crunch-crunch 'em up in their mouths. It's as if the wriggling and the squeaking and the bleeding and the dying are part of the pleasure." He took a drink. "Makes me wonder if Meredith was that way inclined."

"You mean a sadist?"

"Nah, mate. What I'm talking about is a person who doesn't even register that other living things feel pain. In my mind, that's a person who's somehow less than human, somebody who's lost their humanity." Nate drained his glass. "Ah, listen to me, will ya? Tinpot philosopher. Shit, hey? But it's a fucked-up world."

"Oh God, it sure is."

They drank in silence for a while. Outside, the singing had stopped. Perhaps the person had returned to their caravan. Now there was only the swish of tyres on the nearby road, the occasional honk of a horn, the steady hum of the electric heater.

Finally, John said, "Did Flick ever mention another patient, a bloke by the name of Sebastian? He would've been on the same ward as Meredith."

"Sebastian? I dunno. Maybe."

"He had the same pattern of bite marks on his arms and legs."

Nate's bloodshot eyes bulged. "Aw, hang about, Butt-rose. You know more about this shit than you're letting on, don't you?"

"No," John lied. "Meredith's parents happened to mention him."

Nate screwed up his face. "Sebastian…it rings a bell. Sebastian… nah, I can't remember." He looked up and pointed a finger. "But I'll tell you something else. From time to time, once every few years, maybe, Flick had other patients like Meredith, ones with the same bite marks: fifty-two bites all up, thirteen on each limb. You couldn't let 'em near animals. If you did, they'd try to eat 'em. It gave Flick the willies. These people were like zombies, she reckoned."

John felt angry, hot and dizzy. "Zombies?"

"I know, right? Fucken freaky. The living dead."

"That's stupid. Ridiculous. There's no such thing."

"You know what we thought? Me and my shithead brother?"

"What?"

"These weirdos were members of the same cult, but with bite-mark scars instead of tattoos, you get me? Like a sign. Some kind of pagan shit that other members could recognise on sight, like witchcraft."

John gasped.

He recalled Cassie's drawn face…

And I saw a witch…really pale, like she was dead… She bared her teeth and waggled her tongue like she wanted to eat me…

"That's fucked," John said. "Black magic? Bullshit. That stuff doesn't exist. It must have been some kind of infection, something in the blood, passed along by an infected person's saliva."

"Like HIV?"

"Yeah, like that. It makes more sense than your dumb theories, doesn't it? Zombies? Witches? In the twenty-first century? Give me a break."

"Well, according to Flick, Meredith sure acted like a monster."

John sobered. "Listen," he said, gripping Nate by the wrist. "This is really fucking important. I need to talk to Flick. Understand? You have to contact your brother and find out where she is. Or if you don't want to talk to him, get me his number and I won't tell him who gave it to me. Okay, mate? This is urgent. Please."

As if stunned and confused, Nate gaped at him. He withdrew from John's grasp, crossed his arms, and narrowed his eyes. The look made John's heart jangle about. Christ. John helped himself to another shot of whisky. *You're an alky if you drink and drive...* Fuck off, he told himself. This is an emergency.

Nate began to nod, to smile.

John snapped, "What's so funny?"

"Little Johnny Butt-rose."

"Stop calling me that. I hated it in high school, and I hate it now."

"Poor little Johnny Butt-rose."

"Stop it. I'm warning you."

Nate chortled. "You loved her, didn't you?"

John didn't answer.

With a dismissive wave, Nate added, "Aw, come on, everybody in school knew you had the hots for Meredith. Isn't that why you're here? To find her? Well, you're too late. The world ground her up and spat her out. Didn't anybody tell you what happened to her in the end? She got turfed from the hospital and went to live with her parents. Then she ran away. That was ten, fifteen years ago. She's dead. A crazy bitch like that? Butt-rose, you know she's dead. What are you hanging on for?"

I don't know why. I don't know any more.

Exhausted, John closed his eyes. Outside, the wind picked up. The caravan shook and shuddered. He could hear snatches of an argument somewhere out there amongst the circus trailers, words carried by the wind—*cocksucker, you should have...I told you already...that's it, I've had enough of your*—and the banality took the strength from him.

Why not confide in Nate?

The drunkard wouldn't remember anyway. Why not tell the truth for once? John put his elbows on the table; put his head in his hands. When he opened his mouth, no words came out. Telling the truth didn't feel natural.

"Still hung up on her, huh?" Nate said.

"What?"

"Still hung up on Meredith?"

John shrugged helplessly.

"I don't blame you, mate," Nate said. "Meredith was sexy as all fuck back in the day, wasn't she? Better looking than Rachel, but she had that super-posh attitude, like she was better than everyone else, right? That gave some of the boys the shits, me included. Yeah, I preferred Rachel. Not a stunner, but a bloody good woman."

Dazed, John looked up. "Rachel?"

"Yeah, remember her? She was my bird for a while. We both ended up going to Melbourne Uni, me doing law, her doing some kind of writing crap. Wakey-wakey, Butt-rose. Rachel? Rachel Gilbert? The biggest Culture Club fan in high school? She idolised Boy George. The weirdo get-up she liked to wear back then, all the scarves and hair-ribbons, and whatnot. Remember?"

The girl with the black hat, the eyeliner... John offered a wan smile. "Rachel."

"We were together for a few years, actually. Things got pretty serious."

"What happened?"

"Aw, shit happened, that's what." Nate smirked as if he didn't care, but there was a pinched look about his eyes, a tightness to his lips. "We got to Uni and I turned into a party animal. She got uppity about it, always giving me a hard time for drinking and toking. Whatever. She dumped me for one of her lecturers. Can you believe that? Some balding fucker with a ponytail. Her Australian literature professor. Apparently, his take on 'Picnic at Hanging Rock' changed her whole outlook on life." Nate's sleepy eyes narrowed. "He sounded like a total wanker."

"A teacher rooting his student? Isn't that illegal?"

"Is it? Who knows? She was twenty-one or -two, something like that."

"Did she stay with him?"

"Aw, how the fuck should I know? It was so many years ago..." He gazed into the distance, his bleary eyes misting over for a moment. Then he drew heartily on his smoke and grinned. "And what about you?" he continued, focusing on John's hands. "No wedding ring, I see."

Automatically, John went to trot out the lie, now embellished thanks to Donna's prodding—*divorced when my two daughters were young, now I'm a grandfather and my grandson is named after me*—but, on impulse, changed his mind. For some reason, he didn't want to lie. Not this time. He didn't seem to have the stomach for it. The thought of confiding in someone, at long last, tightened his throat with an aching lump and he had a sudden, irrational urge to confess everything. Absolutely everything...

"Come on, Butt-rose. Out with it."

"Well, there's this woman," he said, and the truth felt awkward in his mouth, as lumpy as pebbles. "Donna. I've only just met her."

"What's she like?"

"Pretty." John smiled. "She's got long brown hair, great body, sweet personality. And these friendly, kind eyes that sparkle, you know what I mean?"

"Does she fancy you?"

"I think so. She's got this kid, a little girl—"

Nate raised both hands. "Uh-oh! Baggage."

"No, it's fine. Actually, the daughter, Cassie, is the whole reason why I came to the circus. I was trying to impress Donna by doing something for Cassie."

"Did it work?"

"Yep." John chuckled. "And Cassie's favourite act? Yours."

"No shit?"

"Honest to God. She couldn't stop talking about it."

Nate roared with laughter and poured out two shots. "You see?" he said, wiping his tearing eyes. "It's better to be a clown than a lawyer. Better to make other people happy than to make money for yourself, right? Ah, if only my family could hear this."

Nate's family... John pushed away the glass, feeling almost sober. "Your brother," he said. "I've got to find him. Damien, isn't it?"

"Good luck. There's about a million Rossi's in the phone book."

"Not that many with the initial 'D'."

Nate stubbed out his cigarette. "Yeah, but Damo always planned to Anglicise his name by deed poll. He reckoned wogs don't get the good job offers like skips."

"Anglicise it? To what?"

"Ross or Russ. Maybe Russell."

Dead end...*shit*. John rubbed at his eyes. "Okay, what's his job?"

"Accountant. And there's about a million of them, too." Nate sat forward, gripped John at the elbow, and said, "Forget about Meredith. She's ancient history. If you've got a chance at love, don't fuck it up. What's your girlfriend's name again?"

"Actually, she's not my girlfriend."

"What's her name?"

John felt himself blush. "Donna."

"Donna...isn't that a song?"

"I don't know."

"My folks liked Ritchie Valens." Nate let go of John's arm to take another drink, and his head wobbled on his neck. Slurring, pouting, he added, "I should've hung onto Rachel, probably even married her, finished my law degree, got into a practice. If I could do it over again, I would. There's a lot a man can do with his life if he's got the love of a good woman. My dad used to tell me that. I used to laugh at him, but I reckon he was right. Did your dad tell you the same?"

John thought of his adoptive father, sour-faced, hostile, the kind of bloke who had spent his whole life, when not at work, hunkered into his recliner and glaring at the TV. A man of few words. From habit, John effortlessly swept the memory aside.

"If you can't find your brother, what about Flick?"

"I told you," Nate said. "No fucken idea about her full name or where she is."

"Can you remember the hospital she worked at?"

Nate took another drink.

John stared at the table top. The laminate was chipped, scratched, crusted with food stains, covered in scorch marks from countless cigarettes laid on their sides and forgotten. The heater kept humming and the air was stuffy, sapped of oxygen.

"Another shot?" Nate said.

John stood. "I'd better go."

"Sorry I couldn't help you, mate. But I'm telling you, forget about Meredith, all right? Donna is your future. Donna and that kid. What was her name again?"

Pausing, his hand on the door, John looked back. Nate was staring at him intently, eyes red and watering, either from alcohol or memories, impossible to tell.

Oh God, I don't want to end up like you, John thought in a sudden and flaring terror. I want a life that means something. But I have to hurry, I'm nearly fifty. It's almost too late to start over. It's almost too late.

106

"Bye," he said, breathless. "I'll see you."

"Really? You will? You're gonna come back?"

John glanced around the caravan, at the black mould crawling out of the sink, the yellow smoke stains on the plywood ceiling and walls, the pizza box with its desiccating chunks of yesterday's pineapple. The bile roiling in his throat tasted a hell of a lot like panic. No, this place was a nightmare, the ghost of Christmas Future. He never wanted to see it again for as long as he lived.

As if reading John's mind, Nate scrabbled, trying to stand up. "You'll come back though, won't you, Butt-rose?" he said, staggering, grabbing the bench and table for support. "You'll bring your girlfriend, what's-her-name, and her kid for tea?"

"Sure, mate. Whatever."

"Yeah, sweet, but when? How about tomorrow? I'll order pizza."

"No worries." John opened the door. Fresh air hit him like the bracing shock of cold water. Anything he said now didn't matter. Nate was too pissed to ever recall it. "Keep on juggling. Take care of yourself, okay?"

"Will do. Thanks for the grog." Nate's voice became high and querulous. "Don't forget, Butt-rose. Tea-time here tomorrow, my shout. Okay?"

John stepped down into the soft earth and closed the door behind him. As he wended his way through the trailers, with the cold and distant stars glowing overhead, he heard again the disembodied and elderly voice singing, floating somewhere on the wind, the words indistinguishable; the tune forlorn, hopeless and flat.

11

What if he encountered a booze bus?

To make sure he didn't, John took nearly an hour to drive home. Each minute was agony. Like a mouse scared of a cat that may (or may not) be lurking in wait, he crept and hid, crept and hid, crawling the car along byways and through the tangled snarl of residential side streets. What if he lost his license? God, the thought popped beads of sweat. How would he get to work? Unless you wanted to travel straight to the city's CBD, Melbourne's public transport system didn't cut it. No doubt, he would have to take an insanely convoluted route, like a bus, then a train, a tram; lots of walking in between. His commute might be two hours each way. Fuck. And booze buses were everywhere. After drinking steadily throughout the whole day, he should never have driven to Nate's in the first place. And then all those whiskies on top of all those beers? God, he was such an *idiot*.

You're an alky if you drink and drive...

The idea occurred to him, gently, in a sidling and whispering way.

Perhaps he was already an alky.

No, he thought grimly, fingers tightening around the wheel. *You're an alky when you ditch meals for booze.* And he always made sure to have three meals a day.

Occasionally, those meals consisted of a piece of toast, a couple of Tim Tams.

He began to grind his teeth.

Yes, of course, there was the term *functioning alcoholic*, but wasn't that a contradiction? By definition, an alcoholic was somebody who could no longer function because of an over-arching dependence on booze. And John could function. He never skipped work because of a hangover. Never drank on a work day.

So, fine, he wasn't an alky.

But that insistent and soft inner voice kept needling. When he wasn't drinking, his hands shook. The shakes were a symptom of delirium tremens, were they not?

No, wait a minute. Hold on.

That poor bastard, Nate, was an alky. And that dero slumped on the bench outside the bakery, he was for goddamned sure an alky with his matted hair and clothes stinking of piss. Those two blokes were alkies, but not John. This stupid line of thinking was borne from anxiety—the fear of driving into a police trap, of being breathalysed, of losing his license—and nothing else. Everyone knew the .05 limit was only a bee's dick away from stone-cold sober. An old maid's gulp of sherry would register .05. The booze buses were nothing more than a devious way of squeezing more revenue from the already over-taxed Australian driver.

Perspiration drenched his shirt by the time John steered the car into the driveway. He turned off the engine and leaned his forehead against the wheel. When he got out of the car, his legs trembled. This felt like a small triumph. He told that accusatory voice inside his head: There, you see? I'm shaking *and* drunk so there goes the delirium tremens theory.

Across the road at the clinker-brick shithole, light glowed around the edges of what he knew to be the lounge room windows. He checked his watch: 9.08 p.m. Perhaps Donna and Cassie were watching TV. Or maybe just Donna; it was a school day tomorrow, after all. Had Donna managed to swap her Monday shift? He checked his phone. No messages. The let-down felt palpable. Fatigue swept over him.

Perhaps it was for the best. He was in no mood to make love to her anyway.

Nate's words came back: *Donna is your future. Donna and that kid.*

And then: *Did Meredith kill the animals first? Or eat them alive?*

Wiping at his eyes, John found tears on his lashes.

The myopic windows of the miner's cottage stared him down. He locked the car and trudged to the front door.

Please God, he thought, don't let Meredith be doing anything weird. Don't let her be standing like a mannequin in the middle of the kitchen or raking through her collection in the hobby room. Please let her be closed up inside her bedroom, quiet, maybe asleep. I can't stand it, he thought as he fitted the key into the lock. Momentarily, he rested his forehead against the front door. An errant sob clogged his throat. Please, he thought. Please.

He twisted the key.

The door creaked open.

His gaze darted about in the darkness. He groped for the hallway light and switched it on. Shadows disappeared. The flat and yellow radiance seemed expectant, hushed, like a held breath. He didn't much like it.

"Merry?"

Shutting the door, he cocked his head to listen.

No sounds.

Oh, for fuck's sake. What did Meredith *do* inside the house all day, for years and years on end? Stare at the goddamned walls? *Donna is your future. Donna and that kid.* But a man can't turn his back on his responsibilities. A man must try to atone for his sins, no matter how futile his attempts might be. And John had ruined so many lives. He should never forget that. Deliberately, he unclenched his hands, sighed, and put the keys on the hook.

Her voice sounded faint, confused. "John?"

He went into the lounge and turned on the overhead lights. Meredith, sitting stiff-backed on the couch, blinked at the sudden brightness.

"What are you doing here in the dark?" he said.

"Waiting."

"For what?"

"For you to come home."

He approached. Her hair stuck out in crazy tufts, as if she had been running her hands through it, over and over and over.

"Are you all right?" he said.

"Yes. Where have you been?"

He hesitated. "I went to see Nate Rossi."

"Again? Why?"

"I don't know. To catch up on old times."

"Did you talk about me?"

He shifted uncomfortably from one foot to the other. "Yeah," he finally said. "You came up in conversation."

"What did Nate tell you?"

"Nothing I didn't already know...high school stuff."

Her head turned, slowly and precisely, so that her gaze fell upon him. She smiled. Her lips stretched wide and bloodless. "Did he tell you about Peaches?"

John stared at her. She was very still. Unnaturally still. The notion that her ribcage wasn't moving, that she wasn't breathing, made his heart race. A half-minute passed when he couldn't speak. Her eyes during this long stretch of time stayed open, unblinking, reminding him of Lyle's dead eyes. He became aware of a faint smell of something ripe and mouldy, but he couldn't distinguish right now between reality and his fevered imagination, his nervous exhaustion.

"Tell me about Peaches," he whispered.

She laughed; a dry, brittle sound. Looking away towards the blank TV screen, she said, "You ought to know, Mr Green Thumb. Peaches are a fruit with fuzzy skin."

"Hey, don't play games."

"I will play," she said, "whatever kind of games I fucking well like."

Monday, and it had rained overnight but only lightly. The early morning sun had burned off the moisture. John ran the mower back and forth across the front yard. Long ago, maybe forty years back when the house had first been built, someone had planted a lawn of tall fescue. Little of it remained. Now thistle, dandelion and bindi eye choked what was left. Soon, perhaps tomorrow, John would go to Bunnings and buy some weed killer, seed, fertiliser, a sprinkler head for the hose. He would peg, in a zigzag pattern, a maze of twine and rags to help scare off hungry birds. With time and attention, this old miner's cottage would boast the best lawn in the street. He could imagine the grass, lush and thick, and felt proud already.

As he passed by the lounge room window, movement caught his eye. He stopped. Through the net curtain, he saw Meredith's face but just barely, a ghostly image. The hairs rose on his arms. She faded away. Logically, John knew she had merely stepped back from the window but his gooseflesh persisted. God, stop it, he had to get a *grip*. Talking with Nate had been a mistake.

Nate's bullshit about witches and zombies…and who's to say he was telling the truth about what that psych nurse, Flick, had said to him? The poor fucker's brain must be Swiss cheese from decades of heavy drinking. Maybe Flick had been making up stories, or at least embellishing them. And wouldn't he, John, know Meredith better than anybody? They'd lived together for eight years, after all. She wasn't a witch and she wasn't a zombie…

Was she?

Of course not; the idea was ludicrous.

But sometimes, the way she behaved, the way she looked…

Supernatural creatures did not exist in the real world. Merry was unwell, that's all; unwell both mentally and physically. He hated to admit it, but she had deteriorated since moving here. The old, nagging fear came back.

What would he do if she ever needed urgent medical attention?

If she fell, say, and broke a hip. He would have to take her to hospital. He couldn't just leave her...could he? No. But what would people think? She had been missing and "off the grid" for decades. The authorities would jump to terrible conclusions, assume she was his prisoner, that he abused her. No one would believe the truth; he had found her, rescued her. And even if they *did* believe him, they would badger him with insistent questions, wondering why on earth he had protected and sheltered and put up with such a nutcase for all these years. But he wouldn't be able to explain it to their satisfaction without confessing to Lyle's accident—

(*...murder...*)

—and he would never confess to that. Never, never, never.

John pushed the mower faster, panting and sweating.

For all he knew, Meredith's recent erratic behaviour flagged a mild stroke or a growing brain tumour. So how could he get her to a hospital?

God, if only she were mute. He could pretend he'd just found her on the street, a concerned citizen helping a random homeless woman— but she would talk.

If he took her to hospital, the police would track him down and lean on him. They would keep demanding to know his motive. Why he kept Meredith in secret, why he hid a crazy woman who happened to be the sister of Lyle Berg-Olsen, his best mate who had disappeared under mysterious circumstances thirty-odd years ago. How could John make them understand his obligation without divulging the truth? It seemed unlikely anyone in authority would see him as a Good Samaritan.

And as always when thinking these thoughts, John circled back to the same awful, heinous conclusion: if she ever got sick, really sick, he would have no choice but to dump her somewhere in the bush, somewhere isolated—

A sudden movement at the window startled a gasp out of him. Meredith again, scrabbling with the net curtains, glaring.

Shit.

Once in a while, it was as if she could read his mind.

Gritting his teeth, he shoved at the mower. He ought to be ashamed. A grown man acting like a scared little girl. Then he thought of Cassie's frightened eyes. *And I saw a witch…really pale, like she was dead… She bared her teeth and waggled her tongue like she wanted to eat me…* No, he thought uneasily, he might have every reason in the world to be afraid.

The toot of a horn made him jump.

The Toyota Corolla pulled into the driveway of the clinker-brick shithole. He glanced at his lounge room window. Nothing; Meredith was gone. He switched off the mower. Heart lifting, he hurried across the road as Donna got out of the car.

"You managed to swap your shift," he said on his approach.

"Yeah, didn't you get my text?"

"The last time I checked my phone was about nine last night."

"Oops. Sorry for texting so late."

"Nah, it's all good."

"So you're not busy today?"

He shook his head. "Even if I was…fuck it."

Donna shut the car door and smiled at him, looking up through her lashes, a faint blush on her cheeks. God, she was lovely. He wanted to take her face in his hands and kiss her, but he was covered in flecks of grass, weeds and dirt.

"I've dropped off Cassie," she said, "and I don't have to be anywhere until I pick her up at three-thirty. I bought a roast chicken and some salad for lunch. Still want to spend the day together?"

"Oh, you bet."

Their shared laughter sounded excited yet embarrassed, like a couple of flustered school kids.

"Let me finish mowing," he said, "and then I'll wash up. Give me a half-hour?"

"Okay," she said, with that coquettish look on her face again. "I'll be waiting."

Hopefully either nude or in lingerie, John thought, and winked.

She winked and laughed again, tossing back her long brown hair.

Heart flying, John raced across the street, roared the mower into life, and hurried and bumped it over the last few metres of yard. Without bothering to empty the catcher, he stowed the mower in the carport and hurried into the house. He didn't stop to check Meredith's whereabouts. In the shower, he washed fast and thoroughly with plenty of shampoo and soap, wanting to smell nice.

Too late, he remembered he should have first trimmed his pubic hair.

What if Donna wanted him to wear a condom? Now his pubes would snag.

Damn.

Indecision froze him.

If he trimmed after this shower, he'd need another shower to get rid of stray hairs. Already, Donna was probably waiting for him in bed, naked and wet, and his half-mast cock didn't want him to dilly-dally. Aw, so what about body hair? He kept lathering and then stopped. A shorter bush would also make his cock appear longer. His hand went to the taps, ready to turn them off... Hang on, where were the nail scissors? Could he even remember the last time he saw them? He wasn't about to use the giant pair of kitchen scissors for fear of cutting himself—

Oh, for Christ's sake, forget the bloody pubes.

John rinsed and turned off the taps.

For the first time, it occurred to him that he was nervous.

Yes, nervous.

He hadn't been with a woman for a long time.

Three years ago, give or take, he had visited a brothel. The bungalow had seemed homely from the outside. Inside, however, were red walls and red nylon curtains and dusty peacock feathers, with a cheap water fountain burbling in the waiting room and a cathode-tube TV showing porn on VCR. Contrary to expectations, his prostitute was middle-aged, puffy-faced, and distracted. She looked like someone's mum working the window of a school canteen. They went into a room with a bed. Her ordinariness threw him off and killed his erection. He didn't know how to behave. *What do you want, darlin'?* Her forced gaiety telegraphed so many disappointments: a shitty divorce, back pain, a problem child, bills to pay. He wanted to leave. Awkwardly, he decided on a hand job. She jerked him off quickly with expert skill, but he'd had to close his eyes against her indifference, against her faraway gaze as she had contemplated the framed Monet print on the wall.

And before that...

...a one-night stand at a party, some drunk and dark-haired woman. Angela? Angelica? A nose piercing, a sleeve tattoo; he couldn't remember her face. In the laundry, wedged between the washing machine and the closed door... She'd sucked him off, he recalled, making a strange little gargling noise every time she ducked her head—*urgh, urgh, urgh*—and there had been a basket of dirty clothes on the bench, Taylor Swift's "Today Was a Fairytale" blaring from the speakers in the back yard.

Before that, a few other wham-bams, but he'd been too pissed to remember many details. He'd rooted a few of them in the back seat of his car.

And before that, Cheryl, who had worked as a clerk at the same carpet factory in Devonport as John. She had been thirty-something with freckled skin and a halo of bright, curly red hair. They had fucked, perhaps, a couple of dozen times. *You don't love me*, she had accused that last time, sitting up in bed and sniffing back tears, attacking him with torrents of words, hours of words, while he had lain there, numb, trying to figure out why the argument had started in the first place. Finally, he had said, not knowing if it were true, just to shut her up, *All right, fine, I don't love you*, and Cheryl had got dressed and left. After that, he had entered the factory via the roller-door instead of the office because he couldn't bear to see her face and he felt empty inside. In retrospect, he figured he had loved her after all. Perhaps Cheryl should have been the woman he'd married. They should have bought a house together, had kids, John should have become a plumber, but oh, what was the point in rehashing every single goddamned mistake when life held so many? It was exhausting, to hell with it...

Before Cheryl, he had lost his virginity to Meredith.

Yet mixed in with that memory was Lyle's death the very next day. *That dirty whore. When I found out what she'd done with you, I gave her a manners lesson. Oh, you better believe it. I gave her a manners lesson she'll never forget...*

STOP.

Shivering, John leaned his palms against the shower tiles, heart racing.

Torture, this was torture, he had to stop torturing himself, over and over.

What's done is done.

Straightening up, he took a deep, steadying breath. Forget the past. He had something important to worry about right now. Could he remember how to make love? Surely, yes, like riding a bicycle, a man never forgets how to please a woman.

Stepping from the shower, John grabbed a towel and dried himself roughly. Don't think about it, he admonished. Once a man thinks too much about his erection, it fails to happen, especially if the man is middle-aged. John began to hum, a little tunelessly. *Don't think about it.*

He rolled deodorant in his armpits, sprinkled talcum powder on his balls. Just a little talc, mind you, and none on the cock in case Donna felt like going down.

Don't think about it.

Take your time, he reminded himself.

Foreplay, foreplay, foreplay: that's all a woman really wants.

And if his cock betrayed him, he still had fingers and a tongue, right?

He hummed and brushed his teeth and hummed and shaved his face and hummed and splashed aftershave and hummed and dressed and hummed and kept on humming as he combed his hair, precisely and methodically, humming and humming.

Striding along the hallway, he hesitated, turned back and went to the kitchen. From the fridge, he took a six-pack. The digital clock on the microwave read 9.53 a.m. A little early for beer o'clock, but that would depend on Donna. She seemed to enjoy her tipple. And maybe they'd both want a bracer or two beforehand.

He shut the fridge door. A surge of anxiety flooded through him as he remembered his paunch. He prodded it experimentally with his fingers, squeezing at the soft roll of fat. When was the last time a woman had seen him naked? Not the prostitute; he had merely opened his trousers. The one-night stands? Since he'd rooted most of them in cars, probably not. Oh no, *Cheryl*? But Cheryl had been...how many years ago? He quickly did the maths. Twenty-five years.

Was it a quarter of a century since he'd last stood naked before a woman?

Christ, a quarter *fucking* century?

"You're meant to be mowing the lawns."

John spun around. Meredith stood nearby, supporting herself with one hand on the kitchen bench. She wore a baggy grey t-shirt, the one with the London Tube logo and the words MIND THE GAP. An inside joke, apparently. He had never been to London. A long time ago, the t-shirt had been on sale at a local Kmart, and he had bought it for her. The sleeves almost reached her elbows. He could see her silvery scars along the inside of her forearms, crescent moons facing each other, one set after another, in a line to the wrist. Nate's words came back: *These weirdos were members of the same cult, but with bite-mark scars instead of tattoos... Like a sign. Some kind of pagan shit that other members could recognise on sight...*

"Morning," he said, and picked up the six-pack. "Well, I'm off."

"You're meant to be mowing the lawns."

He pulled his mouth into a semblance of a smile. "I'll be back around half-three. If you get hungry, there's lamb chops left over in the fridge."

"You're meant to be mowing the lawns."

"Don't worry. I'll finish the back yard before dinner."

He picked up the beers and headed down the hall towards the

front door. Meredith trailed behind, her footsteps stumbling. He could hear her dry palms rasping along the wall as she steadied herself. The sound gave him the willies.

Snatching the keys off the hook, he said, "Okay, see you soon."

"You're meant to be mowing the lawns."

His shoulders tightened. "What's with your sudden interest in gardening?"

Slowly, he turned and looked at her, scrutinising her, his breath held. Wan and blank-faced, she stared back with empty eyes, keeping herself motionless as if she, too, were holding her breath. She was still, so very still.

"Are you all right?" he said. "Merry, are you feeling okay?"

She whispered, "You're meant to be mowing the lawns."

Taking one hand off the wall, she reached out as if to touch him.

He ducked out of the house and slammed the door behind him. For a few seconds, he hesitated on the porch.

Get a grip.

He allowed the fresh air and the warm spring sunshine to flush away his pensive mood. The sight of the clinker-brick shithole pushed aside dark thoughts of Meredith. As he hurried up Donna's driveway, he started to wonder what she might be wearing. A negligee? Crotchless knickers? A silky dressing gown with bare skin underneath?

He knocked. The door opened almost immediately.

There stood Donna, dressed as she had been for the school run, in blue jeans and flannelette shirt. Damn, she looked sexy. He grinned.

"Come on in," she said, opening the door wider and stepping back. With a laugh, she added, "The water's fine."

12

He followed her into the kitchen.

"I don't normally start drinking this early," she said, "but *c'est la vie*, right?"

"What?"

Donna went to the refrigerator. "It's French. It means who the hell cares, or live life how you want, something like that." She took out a wine bottle and showed him the label. "*Voila*. See? I told you I'd keep it for a special occasion."

With a jolt, he recognised the chardonnay he had bought for her. He felt himself blush. So he qualified as a 'special occasion'. Shit, he could get used to this.

He took the bottle from her. "Allow me," he said, and unscrewed the cap.

"Why, thank you, kind sir."

She took a glass from a cupboard. He poured the wine. Then he took one of his beer stubbies and opened it. They each lifted their drink, ready to clink them in a toast, but their eyes met instead. For a few moments, they stared at each other. John wondered if his pupils were as dilated as hers. Probably, yes. He could smell her perfume, something musky like sandalwood. His fingertips tingled. He couldn't wait to put his hands on her. God, he could hardly wait.

"To us," Donna said, and touched her glass to his stubby.

"Yeah, sweet. To us."

They both took a sip.

When they lowered their drinks to the kitchen bench, his nerves came back in a rush. His mouth went dry. Should he make a move?

He had no fucking clue. It occurred to him he had no idea what to say, what to do, how to behave. Donna didn't appear to notice. She put the remainder of her bottle and his stubbies into the fridge.

"Come on," she said, picking up her glass. "Let's have a seat."

He trailed her to the lounge.

Tiger lay curled in a ball on the couch where John usually sat. A flurry of unwelcome images about poor little Peaches and Meredith's grisly hobby boxes whipped through John's mind. Uneasily, he sat down next to Tiger. The cat didn't even open its eyes. You dummy, John thought with a rise of irritation, Meredith could scoop you up and you wouldn't even have enough sense to jump free before—

"Tiger," Donna called. She made a few kissing noises, but the cat kept dozing. "Oh, push him onto the floor if he's a bother."

"No, there's enough room."

Donna sat on the other couch. There was a vase of flowers adorning the coffee table: lavender roses, yellow gerberas, and sprigs of white baby's-breath. He appreciated the romantic touch. If only the damned cat wasn't here. Tiger reminded him of Meredith. The cat twitched an ear, lifted an eyelid and closed it again.

"Do you keep Tiger inside at night?" John said.

"Yeah, mostly."

"Not always?"

"Well, sometimes he yowls and squalls to get out, so I let him. It means he can't come back inside, not without me getting up, and nuts to that idea. We don't have a cat-flap, you see. When we moved in, I asked the agent to ask the landlord for a cat-flap. No go. I offered to pay for it and everything, but the landlord didn't want to butcher any of his doors. Fair enough, I guess. It's his investment property."

"You're renting. Me too."

"Ugh, it's a pain, right? Graeme's dragging out the sale of our house, keeping tenants in there until the market hits the high or so he tells me. He won't drop the price. I can't buy without my half. I've got Cassie and she's only twelve. No full-time work for me until she's at least sixteen."

"And Graeme knows all of this?"

"Yep and doesn't give a damn."

John snorted. "That's pretty shitty."

"Tell me about it."

"Have you always been a waitress?"

She sipped her wine. "I used to work in a bank."

"What was that like?"

"About as boring as it sounds."

They both laughed. As if disturbed by the noise, Tiger moved around and stretched a leg. One paw came very near to John's thigh. John edged away.

"How long have you been divorced," he said, "if you don't mind me asking?"

"A few years."

John pulled at his earlobe, scratched at his temple. "No boyfriends?"

"None." She offered a shy, one-sided smile. "Not yet, anyway."

They gazed at each other. John's heel began to jitter against the floor.

Donna took a gulp of wine. "Gee, this is delicious, by the way. I normally drink the cheap stuff in casks. You can really tell the difference."

"Yeah?"

"Yeah, there's a real depth of flavour."

"I'm glad you like it," he said.

"I'm glad you gave it to me."

Again, the loaded eye contact. Again, the dry mouth and sudden blanking of John's mind. He made a rough calculation. Donna had been divorced for a few years, and her marriage must have been rocky prior to the separation. Maybe Graeme hadn't rooted her during their last few months together, give or take. And no boyfriends? Oh shit. No sex for maybe three, four years. That's a lot of pressure. A lot of expectation.

John's cock shrivelled into a nervous little nub.

When was the last time he had rooted a woman while sober? He ransacked his memory and came up with nothing that reassured him. Jesus, the house was so quiet. The only sounds were a faraway plane, the chittering of a parrot.

The cat arched its back and yawned.

John pointed his thumb at Tiger and said, "You should keep him in after dark."

"Not when he's yowling, no way. Haven't you got any animals at home?"

John hesitated, shook his head.

"Animals do what they want. You can't control them. Not really. Oh, they might come when you call or put out some food, but they stay wild on the inside."

John tried his best to grin. Donna, seeming to notice his discomfort, smiled pleasantly, eagerly, almost desperately. It made him feel awful. Damn you, Meredith, he thought. Stop haunting me, stop jinxing me—

"Is anything wrong?" Donna said.

"Nah, it's all good." He drained the stubby. "I need another drink. Top-up?"

"I'm right, thanks."

When he came back into the lounge, Donna said, "Tell me more about your job. What exactly does a plate mounter do?"

She was being polite, he could tell. Shit, he was fucking things up. He pushed all thoughts of Meredith from his mind and took a seat.

"The company prints flexible food packaging, like bread bags and chip packets," he said, and then it occurred to him, in surprise and delight, that Donna had remembered his occupation, and he relaxed, smiled. "Every job has a set of plates. It's my responsibility to get the plates ready for the printer."

"Wow, sounds tricky."

He paused, ready to trot out his familiar lie that taking the plates out of the machine and taping their edges was a skilled job that required intensive on-site training. Instead, he told the truth. "Nah, it's not tricky. In fact, a monkey could do it."

"Same for the café," Donna said, and raised her glass. "To honesty."

Their eye contact felt loaded with tension. Fuck this for a joke, John thought. He put his beer on the coffee table, got up and sat right next to her, thigh against thigh. He put an arm around her shoulders and pulled her close.

"John," she murmured, leaning into him. "John."

He stroked her hair, smoothing it back, fondling the silky strands. Then he kissed her. She opened her mouth and he felt her tongue.

When at last their kiss ended, Donna whispered, "Let's go to bed."

They stood up. Tiger woke, unfolded, and hopped onto the floor. Donna took John's hand and led him down the hallway. An open door at the far end glowed with sunshine. John glanced behind. A queasy sensation moved through him.

"Tiger's following us," he said.

"Don't mind him. When he doesn't sleep with Cassie, he sleeps with me."

John looked back again. Tiger was padding along, keeping pace.

"I don't want him in the room," John said.

She laughed. "What am I, some kind of freak? I don't want my cat watching us either."

They entered the bedroom. It had two windows looking out across a patchy, unkempt lawn. The mattress had a white doona cover and a dozen or more pillows of different sizes and colours. Why did women

like 'display' pillows? Donna pulled the curtains. The bedroom dimm-
ed. Tiger leapt onto the mattress, its yellow eyes regarding John without
blinking. It felt like an omen but of what, John didn't know.

Donna said, "Oh, piss off, Tiger. Go on, shoo."

She shoved the cat off the bed. After an awkward landing, Tiger
ambled down the hallway towards the kitchen. Donna closed the door.

"Ignore him," she said, and paused. "You know, I almost feel shy."

"Same."

Donna turned her back, unbuttoned her shirt, dropped it; unclipped
her bra, dropped it. John's cock sprang to life. Donna, cupping her
bare breasts to hide the nipples, turned to face him. Her cheeks were
reddened, her eyes wide.

"I don't know the etiquette," she said, "but I'm clear. No venereal
diseases."

"What? Oh, yeah, me neither."

"I'm wearing a cap."

John hesitated, unsure.

"A Dutch cap," she continued, "a diaphragm. You don't have to
worry about getting me pregnant. But if you want to wear a franger,
that's okay."

Shit, he hadn't brought any. "No," he said. "I trust you."

"I trust you too."

She lowered her hands. Her small breasts were the size and shape
of pears. Their generous pink nipples made him lick his lips. Quickly,
he unbuttoned his shirt.

"It's been a long time for me," she said. "I'm out of practice."

"Me, too."

Donna offered a timid smile. John took her in his arms. They kissed,
long and deep. Her breasts pressing against him turned his cock into an
iron rod. A scrabbling noise of claws at the door caught his attention,
and he sighed.

"Hey, look, I can't be thinking about your cat," he said.

"Think about my pussy instead."

Holy shit. John undid the button of her jeans and slid down the zip.
Kneeling, he shucked the denim to her ankles. She stepped out of the
legs.

"*Merci, monsieur,*" she murmured.

"You speak French?"

"No, not really. But I can swear in a few languages: French, German,
Italian, Greek. And I know a couple of nasty words in Polish."

"Does that mean you can talk dirty to me?" he said.

She giggled. "Well, I can cuss you out. What language would you prefer?"

"I don't know. Let's say Italian."

He kissed around her navel. She drew in a breath. He slid his hands up the backs of her bare thighs, softly kneaded her buttocks.

"*Figlio de puttana,*" she whispered, stroking her hands through his hair.

"What's that mean?"

"Son of a bitch."

He tugged at the elastic of her underwear, pulling them down. "What else?"

"*Na pas na gamithis,*" she said. "Oh no, wait, that's Greek."

"Meaning?"

"Go fuck yourself."

"No, I think I'll fuck you instead."

Donna was shaved clean. He licked gently, experimentally, at her cleft. She moved her feet to part her legs. Using his fingers, he spread her for a languorous lick. Gasping, she grabbed at his hair. The scratching sounds kept on and on from the other side of the door, but John didn't care any more about Tiger. There was only the taste of Donna, her heavy breathing, and nothing else.

They were sitting under the pergola in plastic striped chairs, drinking, John smoking. And it was the best-tasting goddamned cigarette he could remember. It had something to do with endorphins. A good root apparently enhances the effect of nicotine. And by Christ, Donna had been a good root. Her face was still flushed, hair tousled. Every time he brought the cigarette to his lips, he could smell her on his fingers. His cock stirred. Maybe he could get it up again in a little while. Not bad for an old codger nudging fifty.

"How long have you been a smoker?" Donna said.

For a moment, his mood soured as the unwelcome memory came back: Lyle showing off the packets of Winfield Red and Blue, asking for two dollars per pack. From long practice, John swept the image aside.

"Since the first day of high school."

"Wow. That's young. Ever tried to quit?"

He shook his head. "I hear the withdrawal is pretty rough."

"Everybody smoked at my school. The cool kids, anyway. I couldn't get the hang of it. The idea of breathing in smoke freaked me out."

"Yeah, you've got to work at it, I guess. The habit doesn't come naturally."

"Do you ever wish you hadn't started?"

"If I bothered to count up all my regrets, I'd never stop." He gazed around the yard. No trees, no flower beds; just a few scraggly bushes and an unpainted fence. "The landlord hasn't made much of an effort out here, has he?"

"Suits me. I pay a bloke thirty bucks to mow the grass whenever it gets too high, and that's the end of it. I don't have a green thumb like you. Housework is bad enough. I'd hate to be out here every weekend, pruning and weeding and all that shit."

"I'll mow your lawns from now on."

"What? Oh no, I couldn't ask that."

"You're not asking, I'm offering. It'll save you a few hundred bucks a year."

"No. Really? I mean, are you sure?"

"Positive," he said.

"Thanks. Money's pretty tight. That'd be great. I'll pay you in beer, okay?"

"Nah, you don't have to pay me in anything."

Her face softened, and she reached over the table to touch his wrist. "Has anyone ever told you that you're a sweetheart?"

He smiled. "I don't think so."

"Well, you are." She stood and picked up her wineglass. "Stay here and relax. I'll be back with lunch in a jiffy."

He watched her cross to the screen door, appreciating the sway of her hips, the fall of her long hair. Through the slats of the window's venetian blind, he could just make out her shadowed form as she moved between the fridge and bench, cupboards and sink. A warm, calm sensation suffused his body. They were an item now, he and Donna: a couple. He could take her to restaurants or the movies, buy her flowers, chocolates, do whatever boyfriends were meant to do.

Hang on, was she singing?

Stubbing out his cigarette, he paused, rapt.

Yes, Donna was singing, very softly, just to herself, a tune he recognised but couldn't name. So she was happy too.

He had made her happy.

Letting out a contented sigh, John leaned back, laced his fingers behind his head, and listened. This was the first time he had heard her sing...and there would be many more firsts to come: discovering her ticklish spots, her favourite TV shows, if she snored in her sleep.

Over the weeks and months—perhaps even years—she would reveal all kinds of small and wonderful things about herself.

A frenzied clawing sounded against the fly-wire mesh of the screen door.

Tiger.

Uneasy, John sat up in the chair.

"Go on, you dumb old cat," Donna said, opening the door for a moment. "Git."

Tiger strolled onto the patio's concrete slab. Donna closed the door. The cat met John's gaze and hesitated, perhaps deciding whether or not to approach and wind itself around his ankles. Swishing its tail, it sauntered away down the yard.

Fumbling at the cigarette pack, John lit a smoke.

Who the fuck was he kidding?

He wasn't able to have a relationship with Donna. What about Merry? How would he keep her a secret? Donna must never step foot inside the miner's cottage. What if she heard Merry scratching around behind a closed door, rattling through the contents of those hobby boxes? Even worse, what if Merry wandered out to join them in the lounge room? Donna would scream at the sight. And how could he possibly explain the presence of this witch, this zombie, with her crescent-shaped scars? Impossible. No, no, a relationship with Donna wouldn't work, couldn't work. Unless...and the notion came to him slowly, slyly, like a devil crouched on his shoulder, wheedling, needling, whispering—

"I hope you're hungry."

John startled. Donna shoved open the screen door with her hip. She held two plates, both piled high with roast chicken and salad. He stood up, took the plates from her and put them on the table.

"Terrific, looks great," he said.

"Thanks, but credit goes to the charcoal chicken shop at the mall."

She ducked back inside for her wine and came out with a freshened glass and another stubby for John. They smiled at each other as she sat down.

"Dig in," she said, and picked up her cutlery.

A mouthful of chicken woke up John's stomach. Jesus, he was famished. That's what an hour of good fucking can do to a man. He had performed, and well. Her moans and cries had testified to that. Just like riding a bicycle, a man never forgets how to ride a woman. And then a great, heavy sadness descended over him. This might be it, he thought. The only time he would ever share with Donna.

"Everything okay?" she said.

"Yeah, fine," he said, and smiled quickly. "Tell me, what do you get up to when you're not at work?"

"You mean hobbies?" She put down her knife and fork. "Well, I like to draw."

"Cartoons?"

"No, portraits of people. I took a life drawing class a few years ago and loved it. Mostly, I use Cassie as a model, but only her face and hands. I've got a friend who sometimes lets me draw her nude."

"Jeez. Nude? Sounds a bit sexy."

Donna laughed. "Oh, far from it. Drawing a person is about seeing and looking, paying attention to shapes and shadows and lines." She regarded him with a critical eye. "Actually, you'd make a great model."

He snorted. "Hah, don't bullshit me."

"You've got a great profile."

"Do I?"

"A straight nose, a strong jaw... And I'm used to drawing female faces, female bodies. You'd be a challenge. Would you consider posing for me? It'd be fun."

"Posing?" A deep, hot flush spread across his cheeks. "Uh, I dunno..."

"Come on, it's easy. You sit and don't move."

"In the buff?"

"Of course, in the buff." She giggled, touched his arm, briefly. "All right, no pressure. Just think about it, okay?"

"Okay. What do you draw with, pencils?"

"Yeah, though lately I've been getting into pastels. They make a hell of a mess. You end up with dust absolutely everywhere. I do my pastel pictures in the laundry and use drop sheets."

"Sounds like you need a studio."

"Oh, I need a lot of things," she said, and her gaze turned away for a moment, becoming sad and distant. She looked back at him and smiled. "And what about you?"

"Me?"

"I know you like gardening and growing vegies. What else?"

John took a mouthful of chicken and chewed on it for a while. At last, he said, "Nothing else, I guess."

"Oh, you've got to be interested in something."

He shrugged. "Day to day life can be pretty...time-consuming."

"What about footy?"

"Nah, I hate that shitty game."

"Good, same here. What about racing? You like Bathurst or Formula One?"

"I'll watch if it's on telly."

Donna gave him a mock frown. "You must have some kind of hobby. Woodwork? Fishing? Craft beers?" She laughed. "Soap carving?"

He rubbed at his chin. In a flash, the burble and swish of the Yarra River rushing over rocks had come back to him, the scent of eucalyptus, and the muscular pull of trout on the line. He swallowed hard, and said, "I used to like fishing."

"Sea or river?"

"River."

"My dad river-fished every weekend," she said. "When I was kid, Sunday night was fish night: Murray cod, perch, redfin; whatever he'd caught. Dad would cook the fillets on the barbie and Mum would make the salads. If he came home with crayfish, all of us kids would go *eww* and Mum would give us baked beans instead." Donna shook her head, eyes twinkling. "God, what I'd give for crayfish these days."

"You've got brothers and sisters?"

"One of each. My sister lives in the UK, but my brother's in Melbourne. You'd get along with him, I reckon. He's a straight-shooter too."

John put down his cutlery. "Is that how you see me? As an honest man?"

"Well, aren't you?"

He nodded and smiled. They ate their lunch, chatting between mouthfuls about this and that, but John had a cold tightness in his belly and a stinging behind the eyes. By the time they finished eating, he felt sick. He lit a cigarette and stared at the peeling paint on the overhead beams of the pergola, trying to gather himself together.

"Coffee?" Donna said.

"Sure, with a beer chaser."

Playfully, she patted his shoulder. She stacked the plates and went inside.

John drew back on the cigarette. The scraggly bushes in the back yard were camellia, hydrangea, and a bottle-brush…

Bottle-brush…

In his mind's eye, he saw the two-metre canopy of the bottle-brush in the park.

The park in Melbourne's outer-east. It had a lake, he remembered, and a cycling track, playground, barbecues for hire. Dusk, late

December, 2008. Parents rousting their children, packing up folding chairs, shaking out picnic rugs. John, forty-one years old, tipsy from the Christmas party at the paint factory. He had left his car at work and decided to walk back to his apartment. How long would it take? Half an hour? An hour? No idea. This was the first time he had gone home on foot.

As he approached the bottle-brush, he saw something underneath it, a shape in the shadows. He got closer. The shape revealed itself to be a person, rolled up in a ragged blanket, motionless as if asleep. Nearby, three plastic shopping bags filled to overflowing with bundled clothes. The person fidgeted, turned under the blanket.

Shit. John decided to hurry past, feign deafness, and keep his gaze straight ahead. Homeless people usually tried to bludge a smoke off him, and smokes were too expensive these days to give away, especially to strangers. He picked up his pace. His shoes crunched over the gravel path. The person threw back the blanket. It was a thin, frail woman. She propped up on an elbow and blinked at him with ice-blue eyes.

John stopped dead.

Oh, God.

No, it couldn't be…

In that awful, ghastly moment of recognition, his heart broke loose and dropped straight through his stomach.

The woman sat up and raked a hand through her white-blonde hair.

"John?" she said, and her voice sounded dry and husky, as if she hadn't used it in a long time. "John?"

"Merry?" he whispered. "Jesus Christ, is that you?"

A tentative smile twitched at the corners of her mouth. She held out both dirty hands to him, arms spread wide, as if for an embrace.

13

It felt like a punch to the solar plexus. John's breath shortened, as if winded.

The last time he'd seen Meredith Berg-Olsen was twenty-three years ago, when they had shared a cigarette after losing their virginity together. The day before her brother, Lyle, had...disappeared. A ringing noise started in John's ears. He dropped to his knees. Meredith went to touch him but he flinched away. At last, he found his voice.

"What are you doing here?" he said.

"Sleeping."

"No, I mean, how long have you been out here like this?"

"Not long. I think I got to the park yesterday."

John squeezed his eyes shut against the sting of tears. "No, I'm asking how long you've been like *this*," he said, flinging his arms in an all-encompassing gesture, taking in her dishevelled appearance, tattered blanket, split plastic bags of belongings.

Meredith stared at him vacantly.

He ran a hand over his face to wipe off the sudden drench of perspiration. For a few seconds, he concentrated on slowing his breathing, getting a grip. Even so, his stomach churned with nausea.

"Merry," he said. "Where's your home?"

She smiled. "Oh, I've got lots of homes."

He sat back on his heels and glanced about. By now, the park was almost deserted. Through the trees a few hundred metres away, he could just make out families as they fussed around their cars, buckling in kids and loading picnic baskets.

"Are you with anybody?" he said.

"Why would I be?"

"You're alone?"

"It's safer that way."

"Safer?" He rubbed at his temples. "What about your family? Your parents?"

Meredith shrugged, and regarded him pleasantly.

"My God," he said, choking up. "How long have you been homeless?"

"I don't know. What year is it?"

"Are you serious?"

She smiled.

Dizzy, he couldn't catch his breath.

In the few weeks after Lyle's disappearance, before John had moved to Devonport, he'd heard on the grapevine that Merry had gone to a psych ward. And why not? A missing sibling must be a terrible, suffocating kind of grief. And they had been twins, after all. Wasn't there supposed to be a special bond between twins? Yet, he had assumed her recovery. Over the years, whenever he had thought of her—which was often—he had always imagined her comfortable in a suburban lifestyle: brick veneer house, husband, two kids, dog, station wagon, part-time job, PTA meetings—the middle-class cliché, he realised now.

His vision blurred.

"Oh, John," Meredith whispered. "Are you crying?"

Her face broke into the smile he remembered, the radiant smile that crinkled the corners of her blue eyes. Yet her teeth were now long and yellow, like those of a rat. This is my fault, he thought, and the realisation that he had taken Meredith's life as well as Lyle's made him want to scream in horror. He clenched his teeth against the scream, holding it in, feeling hot and giddy, sickened, overwhelmed with self-loathing. If John had never been born, Lyle would still be alive, and Meredith—the sophisticated, intelligent, sexy, eighteen-year old Meredith—would have had gone on to enjoy all the riches of the adulthood she had deserved.

John had murdered them both. The two people he had loved most of all.

Exhausted, he hung his head.

"I know why you're crying," she said, and her familiar laugh tinkled, stabbing him through the chest. "You're happy to see me. Well, aren't you, John? Aren't you?"

Before he knew what he was doing, he leapt up, snatched the

blanket from her and flung it over his shoulder, grabbed the plastic shopping bags.

"Let's go," he said. "You're coming home with me."

Obediently, she clambered to her feet. Christ, she was thin. The grubby, shapeless cotton dress hung down to her bony ankles. Her face held a blank expression.

"Wait a minute," he said. "You sure you remember who I am?"

"Of course," she said, and looked up coquettishly through non-existent eyelashes. "You're my lover boy."

John's apartment was on the top floor of a three-storey building. The stairwell and landings were deserted. This close to Christmas, his neighbours must be on holidays or at break-up parties. He ushered Meredith inside and locked the door. She stopped in the centre of his living room and froze. John blushed. The place was messy, floors unmopped, the sink full of dishes. None of that could be helped.

"Take a seat," he said. "Relax."

Since there was no laundry in his four-room apartment, he kept the washing machine in the bathroom. He emptied Meredith's plastic bags into the machine's drum. Shit, her clothes were little more than rags. Amongst the clothes, he found a punch-card for a swimming pool centre, a train ticket, a Safeway receipt for soap, shampoo, feminine hygiene products. He put these papers aside. Heart thumping, he ran the washing machine with plenty of detergent.

When he came out to the living room, he found Meredith standing exactly where he had left her. He approached, took her arm, and led her to the kitchen table.

"Sit down," he said. "Please?"

She obeyed, her eyes staring vacantly.

Oh God, the realisation hit again that John had done this to her, ruined her mind, sent her mad, derailed her life. From the moment his knuckles had connected with Lyle's jaw, sending Lyle sprawling backwards and shattering his head against the river stones, John had sealed her fate.

"I'm sorry," he whispered. "Jesus, I'm so sorry."

She gazed straight ahead as if she hadn't heard.

He offered her a cigarette. She didn't take it. He gave her a coffee. She didn't drink it. He made her a toasted cheese sandwich. She didn't touch it. At a loss, John sat opposite her at the table. Her expression stayed unreadable, unfathomable.

"Do you know where you are?" he said.

She nodded. "At your flat."

"That's right. I'm washing your things. I don't have a dryer. Normally, I hang stuff on a rack and put it out on the balcony."

"Okay."

He bit at his thumbnail. "Do you always sleep rough?"

She shrugged.

He said, "You'd be better off at a shelter."

"Oh no, too many addicts. I don't like the fighting and yelling."

From his pocket, he took the papers he had found in her belongings and held them out to her. She took them and inspected them. He noticed marks on her forearms; silvery scars, a great many of them, and as fresh tears burned his eyes he wondered how many times she had tried to take her own life, this miserable, stunted life that he had given her.

"This is my ticket," she said, "to travel on the trains, back and forth, back and forth, so I can sleep without anyone bothering me. And this is for the public swimming pool. Twice a week, I go there to shower. And the supermarket...well, everybody has to buy things from the supermarket."

"How do you pay for all this?" he said, heart sinking, imagining the worst.

"I beg. In the city, you can make twenty, maybe thirty dollars a day."

John's lungs unclenched and allowed a full breath. "All right, that's it, enough. Merry, you don't have to beg any more. You don't have to sleep rough."

"Why not?"

He shook his head and closed his eyes. Hot tears spilled down his cheeks. He put his face in his hands and began to sob, hard, as if he would never stop.

"John, are you okay?"

He dropped his hands and opened his eyes. The moment of disorientation caused a flood of panicky adrenaline. No, wait, he was in Donna's back yard, sitting at the table beneath the pergola, Donna standing rigid at his side with a beer in one hand and a coffee mug in the other. She looked frightened, shocked. He had to steel himself.

"John," Donna repeated, "are you okay?"

"What?" he said, trying to quickly wipe away the tears, but his eyes were dry, his cheeks were dry. "What's the matter?"

She clattered the drinks onto the table in front of him and gripped his shoulder. "Fucking hell, you're white as a sheet."

"I'm fine," he said, pulling his mouth into a smile.

"You're not having a heart attack, are you?"

He sat up, adjusted his shirt, pulled at his collar. "Maybe it's an ulcer."

"Should I call an ambulance?"

"What? Nah, forget it. I'm fine now, honest."

Donna sat down and eyed him dubiously. "Have you really got an ulcer?"

"I don't think so. Actually, no, I haven't."

"My aunt died from a burst ulcer. No shit."

"Sorry. Look, I was kidding. Bad joke." He forced a chuckle. "There's nothing wrong with me. A touch of indigestion, that's all. Too much roast chicken."

"You sure you're okay?"

"I'm sure." John wiped the sweat from his upper lip and took a long drink of beer. "Right as rain."

He could feel her gaze on him. What must she be thinking? That he was some kind of lunatic? Thank Christ he hadn't started crying. But the memory had felt so real... He had to be more careful from now on, be sure to guard himself against making any more dangerous slips.

"You're mulling over that accident, aren't you?" she said.

He startled. "What do you mean?"

"That thing you blame yourself for, even though you didn't mean for it to happen. Whatever it is, you're thinking about that again, aren't you?"

Sighing, John nodded.

Donna rested her hand over his. The gesture brought a lump to his throat.

"I want you to know," she said, "your secret would be safe with me. If you ever need to talk, you can trust me. I promise, John. I promise."

He stared into her eyes. They weren't the cool blue of an ice sheet like Meredith's but a warm and rich grey, the colour of river stones under a summer sun, and the coincidence seemed like some kind of sign but whether good or bad, he couldn't say. He put his other hand over the top of hers. Donna smiled.

The small, joyous leap inside his chest took him by surprise.

Goddamn, he marvelled, as he smiled back through a veil of unshed tears. If he wasn't mistaken, this feeling might actually be love.

He couldn't believe it. John stared at the vegie patch and could not believe it.

Upon returning home from Donna's place at around 3.15 p.m., he had changed back into his old t-shirt and blue work trousers, emptied the clippings from the mower's catcher, and started mowing the back lawn. Whistling, preoccupied with thoughts of Donna, he had made two passes alongside the vegie patch before noticing its destruction and switching off the mower.

Fucking hell.

Incredulous, he shook his head.

His home-made greenhouses of chicken wire wrapped in plastic lay in a trampled pile by the fence. The tomato plants and capsicum plants had been wrenched from the soil and strewn for metres in every direction as if furiously, wildly flung, their brown and withered leaves telling him they were already dead. The wooden stakes were speared in a neat row along one edge of the vegie patch.

He dropped to his haunches and picked up the nearest seedling. It had been crushed and mashed, perhaps underfoot. He stroked and patted the shrivelled roots, gently crumbling away the soil, ranging his gaze across the devastation.

Something white caught his eye.

Nestled within the closest corner of the vegie patch was their jumbo box of iodised table salt. Dropping the seedling, he snatched up the box and shook it: empty. He scrutinised the dirt. Now he could see it; the tiny granules of salt, carefully and evenly sprinkled from one side of the vegie patch to the other. He trickled a handful of soil through his fingers. Nothing would grow here ever again. And then he spotted something much worse.

He recoiled, felt himself blanch.

No, uh-uh, no way. Right there in the middle of the patch, difficult to spot because it blended with the colour of the dirt, sat a big fat human turd.

A red mist descended over his vision. He began to grind his teeth.

That...

fucking...

bitch.

He burst through the back door at a run.

"Meredith!" he bellowed.

He made it halfway across the kitchen before he saw her, sitting at the table with a leg tucked beneath her, smoking one of his cigarettes. He hesitated, wary now, his heart knocking inside his throat. Gone was her familiar blank expression. With bright and clear eyes that seemed to mock him, she took a theatrical puff of the cigarette. Dragon-like, smoke poured from her nostrils. She laughed.

"How do you fancy my handiwork?" she said. "Not much by the looks of you."

"What the fuck is going on here? Why did you wreck my vegie patch?"

"It was time to make a statement."

He approached, breathing hard, his mind racing. The ashtray had two butts in it, neither of them his. So, she had been watching through the window the whole time he was mowing the back yard, waiting for him to notice.

"I can smell her, you know," Meredith said. "Every single note."

"What?"

"She's all over you. Perfume, shampoo, face cream, laundry detergent. And the smell of her muff, naturally. Was she a good fuck, John? Was she worth it?"

"Worth what? I don't even know what you're talking about."

Meredith made a dismissive gesture and dragged on the cigarette.

"For Christ's sake," he said, "you took a dump out there."

"I'm surprised you can't figure out why."

"Then explain it to me."

Her eyes flashed. "To show you what it feels like to be destroyed."

"Destroyed?" He felt the blood drain from his face. "I've done everything in my power to help you, Merry, to take care of you. You must know that."

Indicating a chair, she said, "Take a load off, dopey."

He sat down, bewildered and alarmed. Keeping her in his sights, he reached across the table, got a cigarette from the pack and lit it. Meredith stared at him with an arrogant tilt of her chin. Jesus, it felt like seeing a ghost.

"Where did you find my smokes?" he said.

"In your dresser, of course."

He tightened his jaw. "You're not supposed to go in my room."

"And you're not supposed to go in mine."

She arched an eyebrow. Her behaviour reminded him of her old self, but not quite. The performance was off somehow, in a way that he couldn't identify.

Smiling, she said, "Do you remember the first time I ever spoke to you?"

"Yeah."

"When was it? Tell me."

"December, Year Ten. Your house. I was sleeping over."

"That's right. You and Lyle had just watched *Mad Max*, the original." She tapped the ash from her cigarette and admired the burning red tip. "Let me tell you something. I liked you from the first day of Year Seven. You watched me as if you liked me too. Want to know why I ignored you for most of high school?"

Something painful twisted inside his chest. He nodded.

"Because you started hanging around with Lyle," she said. "I'd already endured twelve fucking years of sharing everything with him. Birthdays, clothes, presents. Every Christmas, our parents felt compelled to give us exactly the same fucking gifts. If he wanted a telescope, I got one too. If I wanted a camera, he got the exact same make and model." She offered a rueful smile. "I couldn't stand the thought of sharing John Penrose as well. But, hand on heart, I always liked you."

The pulse beat in his ears. He didn't know what to say.

With a sudden laugh, she stubbed out her cigarette and leaned forward, eyes sparkling. "Remember the first time we kissed?"

"What is this, twenty questions?"

"You don't remember."

"Sure, I do. Bonfire night down at the creek. You brought a bottle of gin."

"Vickers, from my mother's liquor cabinet. Lyle got the blame, poor sod. Yes, the bonfire night."

She ran a hand through her hair and down along her throat, licking her lips as if intoxicated by the memory. John's cock roused a little.

"And when we ran from the cops and jumped the fence into Darren Shaw's yard," she continued, "you walked straight into the pool. We kissed in the cabana. It smelled like chlorine. Or maybe that was you, drenched like a drowned rat." Her face clouded, and she sat back in the chair, pouting. "And now you smell like that whore."

John pinched at the bridge of his nose and stood up.

"Where are you going?" she said.

"I need a beer."

"Get one for me too."

Another first; he had never seen Meredith drink beer in the eight years they had lived together. When he took the stubbies from the fridge, he realised his hands were trembling. He was afraid, deathly afraid. No one else knew he was locked inside this house with Meredith. Not a soul in the world.

He crossed to the table, opened the beers and gave one to her.

"Cheers," Meredith said, holding out the bottle.

After a moment's pause, John reluctantly obliged, and clinked stubbies. He had a long drink and sat down.

"I've got questions of my own," he said. "You haven't been sandbagging? All these years, playing me for a fool? There doesn't seem to be much wrong with you."

Her chuckle sounded flippant. "Oh, there's plenty wrong with me."

"But not right now?"

She shrugged.

"Most of the time," he said, "you're on another planet. You can't talk, can't hear, don't react. How come? What's the matter with you?"

She waved a disdainful hand. "Some conditions are too difficult to explain."

"Give it a try."

Gazing at the window, she tapped her long fingernails in a rhythm against the stubby. John waited, breath held. After a time, the muscles of her jaws began to flex and stand out. Then she stared at him with a strained, anxious expression.

"It runs through me like a fever," she said.

He sat forward. "What does?"

"This…otherness. You know what it's like to have the flu? It's as if another living thing has taken control of your body. This thing makes you shiver, sweat, cough, ache, sneeze. You want to get out of bed, but you can't. You're possessed by a creature with a stronger will than your own." She took another cigarette. "That's the best way I can describe it."

"You're possessed?"

"I suppose I am. Occasionally, I've got the passion to fight it. Times like now."

Meredith lit the cigarette. They lapsed into silence. John listened to the nearby cawing of crows, music from a distant car stereo, the sounds of Meredith drawing on the cigarette and exhaling. He tried to swallow but didn't have enough spit.

"Merry," he said at last. "What are you possessed by?"

"Hah. You definitely wouldn't understand."

"Nate Rossi thinks you became a witch or a zombie."

"Is that right? Well, Nate always was a dickhead." When she met John's gaze, she startled. "Oh, I'm sorry. That was a question."

"Yeah, and I'm asking it point-blank. When you were in hospital and that other patient, Sebastian, attacked and bit you, he changed you, didn't he? Made you into something else." He hesitated. "Merry, are you still...human?"

She offered a wan smile. "Define human."

"People eat. Why don't I ever see you eat?"

"Because you wouldn't like it if you did."

He gripped the edge of the table. "You hunt at night, don't you? Like a cat."

"Like a cat," she replied, her voice rising, "like a huge, ginger tabby, fat from too many birds and mice. I've seen the whore's cat at night. It hunts rats in particular."

His body went cold. "Leave Tiger alone."

"Tiger?" Meredith relaxed into the chair. "Ugh, what an uninspired name."

"I'm asking you, as a favour, not to harm that cat."

"And I'm asking you, as a favour, to stay away from that whore."

He didn't—couldn't—reply. Sulking, Meredith crushed her cigarette into the ashtray and picked at her nails. John drained his stubby and got another from the fridge. He returned to the table.

"You haven't touched your beer," he said, standing over her.

"I don't feel like it now."

"Go ahead and drink. I want to see that you can."

"Oh, John," she said with a reproachful look. "Stop it, you're being gauche."

He dropped into the chair and worked on his beer. Out the window, sparrows fussed at the scattered remains of his seedlings. His temper flared.

"You still haven't told me why you ruined my vegie patch," he said.

"To show you how much I care."

"That doesn't make sense."

"Let's move," she said, eyes pleading, "far away, out in the country-side."

"What? And how am I going to get to work?"

"Just you and me. We could live on a farm."

"A farm?" He curled his lip.

"We'd be away from people, away from trouble and temptation."

"And who's going to look after a farm while I'm at work? You? When you're sleeping all goddamned day, or mucking around with your disgusting hobby boxes?" He shook his head. "I'm nearly fifty. My one skill is operating a forklift. Jobs aren't exactly falling out of the sky for blokes like me. And you're not earning any money."

"There's another way," she murmured.

John flinched. Head cocked, she was inspecting him intently, roving her stare across his nose, mouth, ears, the fleshy parts of his cheeks, like a raven deciding on its first peck.

"Give me your wrist," she said.

"Huh?"

Uncoiling her leg from beneath her, she put one palm on the table and leaned towards him, holding out her other hand, fingers grasping. He pushed back in his chair.

"We can both be free of this bullshit," she said, "all this tedious, nine-to-five suburban crap. Free to be wild, free to be ourselves, true to our instincts. Give me your wrist." She smiled. "I won't hurt you. It doesn't hurt. Not until the last bite."

John leapt from the chair, overturning it, dropping his beer.

"Christ," he said, "you want to *bite* me?"

Her eyes glittered. "Come with me, John."

"Thirteen times on each limb," he said, backing out of the room. "Then what, I become like you? Fuck that. You stay away from me."

Meredith slumped in the chair and gazed out the window.

John hurried to his bedroom and locked himself in. He put his ear to the door and listened. Could he hear any movement? The rustle of her clothes, the sound of her bare feet padding across the floorboards? Nothing, he could hear nothing. When her voice came directly from the other side of the door, he staggered back.

"John, please," she cried. "Don't you love me anymore?"

14

At 9.30 a.m. on a Tuesday, the mall's car park was almost full. John found a spot by the supermarket, cut the engine, and got out. The cool breeze made him zip up his jacket. Shoppers thronged the footpath. The grizzled old alky was in his usual place, slouched on the bench near the real estate agency. John hurried past, striding towards the far end of the mall, his gaze fixed on the sign for The Brunch Corner café. After a restless sleep filled with nightmares, he wanted—no, needed—to see Donna. The dream, that terrible dream…

Don't think about it.

He walked faster, knocked into a delivery driver exiting the green grocer. Brushing off the man's apology, John jogged the last few metres to the café. He ignored the outside tables. Donna worked the inside tables, he remembered. Pushing open the glass door, he paused to look around.

Polished timber floors, pine tables and chairs, a red leather banquette along one wall, and terrible acoustics; the racket from music and the conversation of two dozen or so customers rattled at his eardrums. The service bar and kitchen were located at the rear. He could see four wait-staff.

Where was Donna?

A panicky chill moved through him. He should have called her first. Maybe she was home sick. Maybe Cassie had taken ill. Or maybe something awful had happened to Tiger. As John reached into his pocket for his phone, the kitchen door swung open and there she was, resplendent in her red apron, her shining brown hair tied in a low ponytail. He could breathe again. Relieved, he stepped inside and allowed the door to close behind him.

Donna hadn't seen him yet. She carried two plates of food. He watched her approach a table, smile and chat, put the plates in front of a couple of old biddies who smiled in return, bobbing their blue-rinse heads. John lifted his hand. Donna saw him and her eyes lit up. I love you, he thought. It's only been a few days, but I love you.

She hurried over, grinning, and touched his arm.

"What are you doing here?" she whispered, blushing. "Don't kiss me or anything, the boss is watching."

"Which one's the boss?"

"The woman making the cappuccinos."

"I'll be sure to tell her what a fabulous waitress you are."

"Sweet," she said, and laughed. "You really want a table?"

"Yeah, but only in your section."

"You'd better leave a good tip. Follow me."

She directed him to a table in the back corner.

Sitting, he said, "Full breakfast with white toast, thanks, and a long black."

"No worries." She took a pen and notepad from her apron pocket. "Want a glass of fruit juice?"

"Sure, why not. Give me whatever you reckon."

"I'll get you the cranberry."

"Cranberry?" He chuckled. "What the hell does that even taste like?"

"Yummy," she said, and winked. "Trust me."

She scribbled in her notepad and left the table, heading first to the bar and then to the kitchen. He watched her every move and gesture. She walked lightly and on the balls of her feet like a dancer. With each step, her long ponytail swung like a glossy pendulum. Yesterday in bed, when she had ridden him, moaning, her loose hair had whisked across his chest every time she leaned forward to kiss him. A bell sounded and she disappeared through the door into the kitchen. Pensive, John bit at a thumbnail. So now what?

Meredith hates Donna.

Donna has no idea that Meredith exists.

How could he reconcile these two women in his life and keep them both? He didn't want to choose. Why should he have to choose? Last night, in between bad dreams, lying awake and grinding his teeth, he had contemplated this dilemma over and over. He still didn't know what to do. As far as he could tell, it boiled down to either doing his duty or following his heart. Shit, if only he had someone to confide in;

a friend. But the only friend he had ever had was dead. Visions from the nightmare reared up, Lyle screaming and suffocating under a steady rain of dirt from John's shovel…

Don't think about it.

A sudden noise startled him. John opened his eyes. Donna had put a coffee cup in front of him.

"You feeling all right?" she said.

He showed her a big grin. "You bet. In fact, I'm tip-top. Just tired from a marathon session I had yesterday with a certain pretty lady."

She laughed, colour rising in her cheeks. "Okay, Romeo, I'll get your juice."

They didn't have time to talk. The Brunch Corner café was too busy. Donna had a smile and a few words for every customer; a joke here, a giggle there. What a woman, he thought as he ate his breakfast. What a beautiful, special woman.

Meredith's words came back. *I'm asking you, as a favour, to stay away from that whore.* Or else…what? What would Merry do?

Donna began to gather his plate, serviette, cutlery and cups.

"My compliments to the chef," he said. "Honest. Great stuff."

"I'll let her know. And how was the cranberry juice?"

"Actually, I liked it."

"See? I'm trustworthy." She hesitated, sobering. "By the way, I saw Cassie's witch last night."

John took a sharp breath. "Where?"

"Outside my bedroom window."

"What time?"

"I don't know, around two o'clock. It happened exactly like Cassie described: the scratching at the window, the white face, the waggling tongue."

"What'd you do?"

"Told her to fuck off," she said, straightening up and taking the dishes in both hands. "I'm a grown woman, mate, not a little girl."

The breakfast roiled in John's throat. He couldn't talk, couldn't breathe. Donna had already moved away from his table and through the kitchen door. Tension tightened his body into a spring. Nauseated, he put his face in his hands and rubbed hard at both temples.

I'm asking you, as a favour, to stay away from that whore.

He scrabbled for his wallet. Jesus, he had to get out of there before Donna returned, before she could see his face, how sick he must look. For a $25 breakfast, he left a $10 tip. He bumped into a chair on his way out and didn't turn back to apologise. When he got outside, the cool morning air hit him like a bracer. He jogged along the footpath towards his parked car.

Meredith had some explaining to do.

And he wouldn't accept her blind, deaf and dumb routine, either. He would take her by the shoulders and shake the living piss out of her if that's what it took to get her talking. Did she really think he'd allow her to stalk Donna and Cassie? This campaign of harassment had to stop. All of Merry's bullshit had to stop.

"Hey, you there," said a gruff voice. "Spare a durry?"

Oh, for fuck's sake… The alky, sprawled on the bench, extended an arm, dirty palm upturned. John was about to jog by.

Until he saw the scars.

He stumbled and froze.

The alky's coat sleeve had ridden up. On the inside of his forearm were scars, regularly spaced, each one a pair of crescents facing each other like waxing and waning moons. John couldn't breathe. The alky watched him carefully, intently, without blinking; his eyes such a light blue they appeared almost white, his dilated pupils a pair of black holes. After a time, the alky dropped his arm to his side and began to tap his fingers on the bench seat. His nails were clean, manicured and sharp.

"Who are you?" John whispered.

The alky's pleasant smile showed long, yellowed teeth. "You know who I am."

Desperately, John looked around. Shoppers walked the footpath, going about their business, ignoring them as if they were both invisible. John had the vertiginous feeling that the alky could stab him, slash his throat, chew off his face, and no one would notice. He stared at the man's thick mane of salt-and-pepper hair, his sallow face, his penetrating eyes, and knew. Christ almighty, he knew.

"Sebastian," John said.

As if bored, the alky sighed and briefly closed his eyes to shrug.

"Hang on," John continued. "I first saw you the day I viewed the miner's cottage, the day I signed the lease. How did you know I was going to move into this neighbourhood?"

"Oh, don't get yourself in a lather. I'm not psychic. It's coincidence. I happen to move around quite a bit to stay in contact with my associates."

"Your associates? You mean Meredith? And who else?"

"Good gracious, you're dumber than I thought."

"What's going on?" John said, his voice rising and cracking. "What are you?"

Sebastian began to laugh. "Come now, give me a cigarette and be on your way." As he extended his arm once more, the scars glinted silver in the sunshine.

John broke into a run. A gaggle of middle-aged women tutted and scolded as he pushed through them. He jumped into his car, gunned the engine, backed out and fled the mall, tyres squealing, heart thumping, his stomach in his throat.

Nate, he had to see Nate.

This time, he would tell Nate everything, the whole sordid, heinous saga, yes, even the circumstances of Lyle's death, even that. And about Meredith and how he had been harbouring her, looking after her in secret these past eight years, and how she was…changing, somehow, changing for the worse so fast in just a few days…and that he was scared of her and what she might do, what she might be planning to do to Tiger, perhaps, or to Cassie, to Donna… And he would tell Nate about Sebastian.

Holy shit: *Sebastian.*

John's heart gave a mule kick to his ribs.

What did Sebastian mean about his 'associates'? How many others were like Meredith? How many had the bastard attacked and bitten over the years? And come to think of it, who had bitten Sebastian? Maybe Nate was right. Maybe the scars were part of an initiation ritual into a cult that killed and ate animals raw—but for what purpose? Some kind of religious devotion? They could be Satanists. But did such people exist? John had read, somewhere, long ago, that despite police investigations into satanic cults, no hard evidence had ever been found. Or was he remembering a specific case? Surely, if people could worship gods, it was also possible to worship devils. John's hands shook on the steering wheel. God, he needed a drink. He needed a drink so bad. His throat was drying out, withering, closing over—

Shit!

John slammed his foot on the brake. The car fishtailed. The tyres gripped the road and stopped just in time. He blew out a shuddering breath. He had narrowly avoided hitting the stationary vehicle in front. The light was red, for Christ's sake, *red,* he had to pay attention to the road, had to focus on the traffic.

Fumbling, he lit a cigarette. He cracked the window and glanced about at the other cars. The driver of the coupe in the next lane was glaring at him and shaking her head. She must have seen his near-miss.

Well, she could go and get fucked. He noticed her hand on the steering wheel, her long fingernails. Quickly, feeling a wave of panic, he looked away. What if she were one of *them*? Maybe the cult members were everywhere. Maybe some of them were shadowing him right now. Maybe they had been shadowing him for a long time, ever since he had found Meredith homeless in the park and taken her back to his apartment.

The light turned green.

John drew on the cigarette. Gently, he put his foot on the accelerator. He had to cool down, concentrate on driving. The circus wasn't far. Ten minutes away, tops. They had pitched their tent and parked their caravans in a giant paddock at a major intersection, a paddock that was no doubt already earmarked by the council to be subdivided one day into hundreds of townhouses, crammed in cheek by jowl. Dozens of such developments were springing up all over the outer-eastern Melbourne suburbs. The typical Aussie home on a big block was going the way of the dinosaur.

Stubbing out his cigarette, John lit another. See? He was calm now. He was thinking sane, rational thoughts. Everything would be okay. He would talk this whole thing through with Nate, and in the telling, might experience an epiphany. Speaking the truth would remove the blinkers from his eyes, he was sure of that. After confessing, he'd know exactly what to do and how to do it.

Even so, the thirst for beer felt urgent, maddening. He pinched his upper lip between forefinger and thumb, hoping that 'activating' the acupressure point might help, but doing so reminded him too much of Meredith explaining acupressure points to him in high school, and he dropped his hand back to the steering wheel.

He turned at the next set of lights. The posted limit was eighty kilometres per hour, but he nudged the speedo closer to ninety, moving from lane to lane, overtaking at every opportunity.

Not long now. In a few moments, he would see the orange and yellow stripes of the Big Top. Any moment now...any moment...

His mouth dried out as he steered into the service lane alongside the paddock. Behind the wire fence, the paddock stretched into the distance, wide, flat and empty. *Empty.* The circus had gone. Sometime overnight, they had packed up their tent and their mobile homes and gone. Nate Rossi was gone.

Pulling over, John cut the engine and got out. The cool wind nipped at his nose and ears. Lightheaded, he walked across the footpath to the wire fence. He could see where the circus had been. The earth was churned into muddy ruts.

Now, what had been the bloody name of the circus?

He had thrown away the brochure, put the recycle bin on the nature strip for the garbos on Sunday night, and the rubbish had been taken yesterday morning. But there was always Google, right? He felt a lifting of hope that didn't last long. Why bother to find the circus at all? The caravans and semi-trailers were probably headed for Sydney or Adelaide, and if he chased them, what was his plan? Abandon Donna and Cassie to an unknown fate while trying to get some kind of sense out of Nate Rossi? Forget it. Nate was a drunk, not a guru.

Too late, too late...

John had had a chance to confess his sins and had missed it.

A great tiredness washed over him. He put his fingers though the cyclone fencing and hung his head. God, if only he'd never spotted Meredith sleeping rough in the park. If only he'd never hit Lyle. If only he'd never pulled over when Lyle had been walking to Aaron's place to do that stupid assignment. If only John had never slept with Meredith and angered Lyle in the first place. Yet there was no way back.

And only one way forward.

Galvanised, John hurried to his car, started it, and fanged the stretch of service lane until it met the intersection. He turned, sped fast, watching the road closely, overtaking, weaving in and out of traffic.

In less than six minutes, he reached the mall.

He parked three rows back from the shops and found he couldn't get out of the car. A suffocating dread had drained his strength. From this distance, he couldn't get a line of sight to the park bench. Was Sebastian still there? John squeezed his hands into fists and hit at his thighs, once, twice, three times, psyching himself. Then he jumped out and ran through the car park.

The bench was empty.

Thank Christ.

John shoved open the door to the real estate agency. The only person was the receptionist, typing at a computer. She paused to look him up and down.

"Yes?" she said. "May I help you?"

John gaped at her fingernails; long talons painted blood red. The first time he had seen those nails, he had wondered if she ever injured herself while masturbating. Now, he wondered if she used those nails like ten little scalpels to stab at animals, to peel off their skins and fur.

If she had scars, John couldn't see them. Her shirt had long sleeves cuffed at the wrists.

The receptionist pushed back in her chair and frowned. "Can I help you?"

"Yeah," he said, and pointed at a desk. "I need to see the young bloke who normally sits there."

"You mean Ryan?"

"I dunno. The bloke with the goatee and the earrings."

"That's Ryan. He's getting coffee. Take a seat, he won't be long."

She went back to her typing, using the very tips of her talons. *Clack, clack, clack.* Sweating, John sat in the sagging couch by the window. He glanced at the wall clock: 10.36 a.m. Almost beer o'clock. No wonder his hands were shaking. His foot began to jitter against the floorboards. The receptionist cut her eyes at him. He gave what he hoped was an apologetic smile and crossed his legs. The urge to bite his nails made him sit on his hands.

"Where's the alky?" he said.

The receptionist turned with an irritated air. "I'm sorry?"

"The old bloke who sits on the bench. Where'd he go?"

"No idea."

"Does he sit there every day?"

"I wouldn't know. They don't pay me to stare out the window."

"Okay. Sorry to bother you."

She sniffed and began typing again. *Clack, clack, clack.*

The door opened. John leapt up. The little prick with the shiny suit, gelled hair and gauge earrings startled and took a step back.

"Ryan," the receptionist said, "this gentleman would like to see you."

The little prick recovered and waved John towards a desk. "Not a problem. Have a seat over here, would you?" He held a takeaway coffee cup and wore too much aftershave.

They both sat down on opposite sides of the desk. Ryan smiled at him, eyebrows raised, expectant. He doesn't recognise me, John thought.

"I rented a property off you a couple of weeks ago," John said. "The imitation miner's cottage."

"Oh, that's right. The three-bedroom place. You're doing a university degree and use one room for your studies, the other for visiting family, correct?"

"Correct. John Penrose."

"How can I help you, Mr Penrose?"

"I need to break my lease."

The little prick hesitated, laughed, and took a sip of coffee. "Let me get your paperwork," he said, tapping at the keyboard and rolling the mouse. "Give me a sec. Ah, here you are: John Penrose." The little prick pursed his lips. "You signed the lease August twenty-ninth, two weeks ago yesterday."

"That's right."

"A twelve-month lease."

"Yep," John said.

"And now you want to move out?"

"As soon as possible."

"Would you like to tell me why?"

"Is there any law that says I have to?"

The little prick's smile turned brittle. "Well, no, not really, but out of common decency... I'm sure the landlord would appreciate knowing what the matter was. For future reference, you understand."

A plausible excuse? John had not thought that far ahead. He would have to wing it. Putting on an earnest face, he began, "Family emergency, I'm afraid."

The little prick raised his eyebrows again.

John continued, "My daughter has...blown the discs in her lower back, and she needs help to look after the baby. She lives on the other side of the city, you see."

"I see. That's terrible news. I'm sorry to hear it."

"Thank you. So how do we go about breaking the lease?"

"Well, first I need it in writing."

"Have you got a pen?"

The little prick smiled. "Wait, Mr Penrose. Have you ever broken a lease before? It can be very expensive."

"I don't care about the money."

"Okay, if you say so." He started to count on his fingers. "One: you'll be charged a re-letting fee, which is two weeks' rent."

"Fair enough."

"Hold on, I'm not finished yet. Two: you'll have to bear the costs of advertising. Three: you must keep paying the rent until a new tenant takes possession of the house or until your twelve-month lease runs out, whichever comes first."

John sat back in his chair. "Shit."

"Exactly. Do you still want to break your lease?"

I could do a runner, John thought. No, he couldn't—they had all his personal details on file. He rubbed at his temple but stopped when he realised his hand was shaking. "Tell me something," he said. "How long has that alky been hanging around the park bench out there?"

"You mean Seb?"

A chill ran down John's back. "You know his name."

"Oh, everyone knows old Seb. He's harmless enough. I don't know how long he's been here. He pre-dates me, and I've had this job for almost three years."

That meant Sebastian had told the truth. *I'm not psychic. It's coincidence. I happen to move around quite a bit to stay in contact with my associates.* Perhaps John was panicking over nothing. And if the landlord didn't find another tenant, asap, John would be up shit creek in a barbed wire canoe. He couldn't afford to pay rent on two properties. He was being rash, acting paranoid. But no, no, he thought, Meredith is becoming unstable. She wrecked the vegie patch, even took a shit on it. And she's stalking Cassie and Donna, might be planning to kill and eat Tiger—

"Mr Penrose?"

John glanced up. "Yeah," he said, "I want to break the lease. Right now."

15

Upon returning home, John went straight to the fridge. He downed a stubby within seconds, opened another, and shut the fridge door. There was no sign of Meredith. He walked to her bedroom. Instead of listening or knocking, he turned the handle and barged straight in. She was lying face down on the bed, arms by her sides, face buried in the pillow. John's stomach felt a churn of revulsion.

"Merry, we have to talk."

No response.

"Stop playing dead and roll over."

No response.

John took a sip of beer. "Guess who I ran into today? Sebastian."

She turned her face to look at him.

"Hah," he said. "I figured that bit of news would wake you up."

She arranged herself to sit on the edge of the bed. If she had been sleeping, it didn't show. She looked alert and wary; her eyes bright and opened wide, unblinking.

"You met Sebastian?" she said.

"That's right."

"Where?" she said.

"Up at the mall."

"What did he say?"

"Not much. He tried to bludge a smoke off me."

"That'd be right." She picked at her nails. "Did he mention me?"

"Not by name. He told me he moves around a lot so he can keep in touch with his 'associates', as he called them. I guess you're one of his associates, right?"

Reluctantly, she nodded.

"You meet up with him at night? When you go wandering?"

She gave a little shrug. "Sometimes."

John stared at her in the t-shirt and shorts, at her stick-thin arms and legs, at the half-moon scars. How on earth had he mistaken those bite marks for razor cuts? If you looked closely enough, you could almost distinguish the individual teeth—incisors, premolars, molars—despite each scar forming a near-solid line. Jesus, how *hard* had Sebastian bitten her? Hard enough to almost rip out a chunk of flesh, that's how hard. And fifty-two times, no less. Jesus, how didn't that hurt? How didn't it hurt her until the fifty-second bite?

"Talk," he said. "Explain to me what's going on."

In a defeated gesture, her shoulder raised and dropped again.

"How many others are like you?" he said. "Tell me."

She didn't react.

Anger clamped John's teeth and tightened his grip on the stubby. "You'd better answer me," he said, "because I've had all I can take of your bullshit."

She leapt to her feet, startling him, her eyes flashing.

"And I've had all I can take of yours," she said, and shoved past him.

He followed her into the kitchen. She took a cigarette from the packet on the counter and lit it. He watched her drag on the smoke, one breath after another without stopping, exhaling through her nostrils, until she had burned the cigarette down to the butt. Somehow, she didn't seem to get dizzy. She threw the butt into the sink and raked both hands through the white tufts of her hair, over and over. Some of the tufts stayed upright, leaning at crazy angles. John kept watching her, carefully.

"When you found me in the park," she said, "why did you bring me home?"

"Shit, I'd have thought that was obvious: to take care of you."

"And why did you want to take care of me?"

He shifted uncomfortably, swallowed a sip of beer. "I felt sorry for you."

"Sorry?" She lit another cigarette. "You felt sorry for me?"

"Well, yeah, but not just that."

"Then what else?"

He chewed at his lip and mumbled, "We loved each other once."

"Ugh, how maudlin." She gave a mocking laugh. "You took me in for old time's sake? Is that it?"

"I suppose, yeah."

"Are you sure there's no other reason?"

Spooked, he met her gaze. Her eyes were flinty.

"I don't know what you mean," he said.

"Oh, we're always talking in circles. It drives me fucking mad." She mashed the cigarette into the ashtray. "All right, I'm telling you straight. Keep away from Donna. Keep away or you'll be sorry. I'll make you both sorry. Do you understand?"

Anger rose in him like a tide. Meredith's eyes widened in surprise. Slowly, deliberately, he put the stubby on the counter and grabbed her by the shoulders. Squeezing hard, he felt her bones through her thin flesh, the creak of her joints as he lifted her onto her tiptoes. Impossibly, her chalk-white skin appeared to blanch.

"Don't go near that house ever again," he said. "Got it?"

For a moment, Meredith's lips trembled. Then her eyes narrowed, her lips pulled back over long, yellow teeth, and she hissed like a cat. John threw her away from him. She fell against the counter and waggled her tongue.

"What the hell are you?" he shouted.

He bolted from the kitchen to the hobby room and flung open the door. She yowled in dismay and tottered after him, her bare feet shuffling over the tiles. He hauled out a cardboard box at random from the nearest bookshelf. When she reached the doorway, he hurled the lid at her and upended the box. A cascade of bones clattered to the floorboards, scattering and skittering like jumping jacks in every direction. They were vertebrae, small enough to come from cats or possums. My God, the first time he had peeked inside her hobby box—just the one box back then, eight years ago when she had started living in his apartment—he had recoiled in horror, put his hands to his mouth, feeling queasy, frightened. Now, he felt nothing but contempt.

"No, stop," Meredith said, and dropped to her knees. "They're mine."

As she scrabbled for the vertebrae, trying to gather them up inside the scoop of her baggy t-shirt, John upended another box. A rain of tiny skulls, the beaked skulls of birds as delicate as china cups, spilled across the floor.

"Stop it, stop it," she said. "You'll break them. Don't break them."

"Or what?" he said. "What happens if they break?"

He brought down his boot, savagely, and smashed some half-dozen skulls underfoot. Meredith screamed in anguish and ripped at her hair. He opened another box. Long bones this time. From what

155

animal and whether from front legs or back legs, he couldn't tell. He tipped them over her head and tossed the box aside.

"How do you get them so clean?"

"Stop, please stop," she wailed.

"There's not a scrap of meat left on any of them. You eat the animals raw. Then you boil their bones, don't you? You wait for me to go to work and you take the skeletons and boil them on the stove, right?"

"Yes, yes, I boil them."

"In the big silver pot?"

"Yes, in the big silver pot," she said, whimpering, hands clenched in her hair as she surveyed the disarray. "Stop it, John, please."

He grabbed another box. "If I stop, will you talk?"

She hesitated.

He took off the lid.

"Yes, yes," she sobbed, "I'll talk, I promise, just stop. Please stop."

She started crying in earnest. The red mist of anger left him. He put the box back on the shelf. Panting, his heart rate slowed, and his senses returned. Shame tasted bitter in his mouth. Weeping, Meredith groped blindly at the bones. He knelt down and arranged the three empty boxes in a row in front of her.

"I'll help you," he said.

She grabbed him by the wrist. "No," she whispered. "Don't touch them."

"Why? What happens if I touch them?"

She shook her head, sobbing.

Apart from the bookshelves, the room held no other furniture. John scooted backwards and leaned against a wall. Wiping at tears, sniffing back snot, Meredith began to refill the boxes. He watched. She would pick up a bone, inspect it for damage, polish it on the hem of her t-shirt, and place it with great care into a box.

"All right, Merry," he said. "I'm going to ask you questions and you're going to answer them. Let's start from the top. Do you ever eat normal food?"

"No."

"You only eat animals?"

"Yes."

"Animals that you hunt and catch at night?"

"Yes."

"What kind of animals?"

"Name it. Rats, mice, birds, foxes—"

"Foxes? Wait a minute, don't they attack you? Fight back?"

She paused to rub a tiny skull, like that of a sparrow, against her cheek. "No," she said. "They're too afraid."

"Too afraid? Of you?"

"Yes."

"Is that because they somehow know you're not... That you're not..."

"Human? Yes. They know. They can smell it."

A slow prickle of gooseflesh crawled along John's neck and arms. "Okay, now we're getting somewhere," he said. "If you're not human, then what are you?"

She shrugged indifferently.

"A vampire?" he said.

She rolled her eyes. "That's pathetic, John, even for you. I don't give two shits about garlic, crucifixes or sunshine, and I certainly don't sleep in a fucking coffin."

"Hey, don't crack the shits, just answer my questions."

"I'm answering them, aren't I?" Scowling, she buffed at a long bone.

"How often do you meet up with the others? With Sebastian?"

"I don't know. It depends. Sometimes I hunt by myself."

"When you're in a group, do you ever travel by car?"

She rolled her eyes again. "What for? Animals are everywhere."

"You always hunt on foot?"

"Yes."

He waited. "Well, come on," he said. "Tell me how you do it."

She sighed, put the bone inside a box, and sat back with her hands on her thighs. "I can see perfectly in the dark: movement, silhouettes and outlines, even when it's pitch black. But more than that, at night, I sense living things like they're on radar. There's no point asking me to explain. I don't know how it works."

"These...talents...allow you to creep up on an animal?"

"And jump," she said, and raised her clawed fingers so fast that John startled and banged his head against the wall. Laughing, she wriggled her fingers. "I sink my nails into them and they can't get away."

"What next?"

She held out the first two fingers on her right hand, curved into a hook. "I cut a hole in the neck like this," she said, with a quick jab, "and suck out the blood." She fluttered her eyelids closed. "It's fucking ambrosia, John. Do you know what ambrosia means? The drink and food of the gods."

"So, you're a god now? Is that it?"

Her eyes opened. The blue irises glittered with a bright and

157

preternatural shine. She sat between John and the doorway. The realisation clenched his stomach. Unless he broke through the window, there was no other way out of the room.

"If you drink blood," he said, "you must be a type of vampire."

"He calls us the Marked Ones," Meredith said.

"He? You mean Sebastian?"

"After I suck the blood, I skin the animal and eat the meat."

"Guts too?"

She gave a coy smile. "Oh, come on now. Can't a girl keep any secrets?"

"You bring the skeletons home."

"Yes."

"What for? Trophies?"

Amused, she ran her palms lightly across the bones on the floor, rattling them against the hardwood boards. It was an awful sound. A shiver trembled down John's back. How many dismembered skeletons did she have? There must be at least twenty boxes to a bookshelf, and four bookshelves in total. That didn't include the boxes stacked up against one wall, which must number a few dozen. Christ, she must have the remains of hundreds of bodies stashed in here, maybe even thousands.

"Hey," he said. "Are the bones trophies or what?"

"Oh, you wouldn't understand."

"Try me."

"No, I don't think I will. I don't think I want to talk about it anymore."

"Answer my goddamned question."

Her smile vanished. The bones forgotten, she tensed and glared, lowering her head. John's scalp prickled. This is what it must feel like to lock eyes with a panther, he thought, in the moment before it tears you to pieces. She stiffened her fingers against the floorboards. Her nails gouged long scratches through the varnish.

Fuck this for a joke.

He scrambled to his feet.

"What's the matter?" she said. "Tired of playing?"

He walked around her, keeping to the walls, giving her as wide a berth as possible within the tight confines of the room.

She lunged, swiping her nails.

The flesh of his ankles seemed to shrivel in anticipation of pain. Yelping, he jumped out of reach and stumbled to the doorway, unscathed, preparing to run. Her melodious, hearty laughter stopped him and brought a flush of humiliation to his cheeks. He'd packed himself, scampered like a frightened schoolgirl. He looked back. Meredith had spun around to face him.

"That wasn't funny, Merry."

"Not funny? I beg to differ. It was fucking hilarious."

"Don't scare me like that again."

"Or what?" Leaning forward, she put her hands on the floor as if preparing to crawl—or spring. "What will you do, Captain Courageous? Shit your pants?"

He walked the hallway towards his end of the house, mindful to take slow and unhurried steps to feign nonchalance, his ears straining for the slightest noise that might indicate she was following him, stalking him.

"Sook," she called. "Don't ask questions if you're afraid of the answers."

Once inside his room, he bolted the door. He desperately needed a drink, but too bad, a smoke would have to do. He took a fresh pack from the chest of drawers, sat on the edge of his bed and went through four cigarettes waiting for his pulse to slow down and his hands to stop shaking.

Christ almighty.

Meredith wasn't human.

By her own admission: inhuman, some kind of monster.

If not a vampire, what was she? Zombie, werewolf, mummy, Frankenstein's creation; he couldn't think of any other monsters, but maybe she was a type you didn't find in the movies, a type that was real. Jesus, her fingernails must be as hard as metal screws. How else could she scratch the floor? Punch holes through fur, skin and muscle and into the blood vessels beneath?

He grabbed his phone and looked up 'vampire' on Wikipedia. The page titled *List of vampires in folklore and mythology* had scores and scores of entries in alphabetical order: *Abchanchu* of Bolivia, *Abere* of Melanesia, *Adze* of Ghana... With a groan, he rubbed at his eyelids. It would take him days to read through each entry. He didn't have days to spare. Now what? Who could he ask for help? Nobody; not the police, not Nate Rossi, not Donna—

Oh, shit.

Donna.

He had to get Merry away from her, away from Cassie and Tiger, far away.

Using his mobile, he found a website for a big real estate firm. He would rent a place in Melbourne's northwest, exactly opposite as the crow flies to his current address, a place some fifty kilometres from Donna's clinker-brick shithole, too distant for Meredith who hunted on foot. Donna, Cassie and Tiger would be safe.

He pressed the number for the agency. As he listened to the ring tone, a stray notion wended through his mind: if Meredith wasn't human, would killing her be considered murder? Before he could follow this train of thought, the phone answered.

"Yeah, hi," he said. "I need to rent a three-bedroom place in the north-western suburbs, as soon as possible. Have you got anything to lease straight away?"

He kept his voice low in case Meredith was listening at the door. Then again, it seemed her powers of extra-perception only switched on at night. Maybe she couldn't hear him. Nevertheless, he whispered his way through five more phone calls to different real estate agencies. There were precious few properties available. Fuck Melbourne and its ridiculous immigration rate, he thought, as he lit another cigarette, hacking and coughing. A hundred thousand extra people a year, every year, wasn't it? Something like that. Too many people anyway, and not enough houses.

"I'll take anything," he said to the next agent. "Flat, unit, four-bedroom, one-bedroom, whatever, just get me something now."

After a couple of hours, he had lined up six potential properties. The earliest viewing was Thursday, two days away. Well, too bad about work. He dialled the office number. The receptionist picked up.

"Gail?" he said. "John Penrose from the mounting department on B-shift. Look, I've caught some kind of stomach bug… Yeah, it's coming out of me both ends… Yeah, something I ate, maybe. Could you tell the boss I won't be in for the week? I don't want to spread anything through the factory… Thanks. Catch you later."

He hung up. His phone battery had dropped to twenty-six per cent. He noticed a new text message and opened it. The text from Donna, sent about an hour ago, read: *Hope you liked brekkie. See you tonight?*

He wiped his mouth, rubbed the back of his neck.

Finally, he texted back: *Sorry but im sick. Tomorrow?*

He plugged the phone into the charger, sat on his bed, and stared out the window at the ruins of his vegie patch. Shit. What lie would he tell Donna this time?

He didn't leave his room for the rest of the day. His stomach grumbled with hunger. Stone-cold sober, his head ached and throbbed, tender as a boil. None of that mattered. Lying on the bed, he passed the hours by chain-smoking, checking his watch, staring out the windows, and thinking, planning, plotting.

Evening came. The sky lost its blue tint. A stripe of deep orange peeped over the fence as the sun went down. The bellies of tufted clouds turned dark navy. As the light faded, the yard became monochrome. The first few stars began to glitter. Crickets shirred and chirped. Birds called goodnight to one another from the trees.

John checked his watch again. Inside the rucksack by the bedroom door was a water bottle filled from his bathroom tap, smokes, a lighter, and a pair of binoculars. He had changed into black jeans, black t-shirt and black sneakers. His only jacket, however, was blue. That couldn't be helped. With the temperature dropping to ten degrees overnight, he had no intention of leaving home without a jacket. Next to him on the mattress lay his black woollen balaclava, a relic from his teenage years when he used to ride a pushbike to school and didn't want to freeze his face off in winter.

Around midnight, the front door opened.

A click—that must be Meredith pushing in the tongue of the deadlock—and the door closed. She had left to hunt. John leapt up, pulled the rolled-up balaclava over his scalp like a beanie, wrestled his arms into the straps of the rucksack, and exited his room. When his hand closed around the handle of the front door, his courage left him for a trembling moment. Then he was outside.

He dragged the balaclava down to his chin. His sneakers trod soundlessly across the front yard. The half-moon bathed the street in grey shades. The windows over the road were dark. Donna and Cassie must be sound asleep by now.

He looked up the street both ways.

Shit, had he lost Meredith already?

But no, there she was, heading towards the T-intersection, striding, poised and strong, her athletic gait so different to her usual crabbed and unsteady shuffle. If it weren't for her hair, shining white and luminous in the moonlight, he would have sworn on a stack of Bibles that it wasn't her. Fear tightened the flesh on his thighs and buttocks. Oh yes, Meredith was a creature of the night, make no mistake.

He swallowed hard and began to follow her.

She moved so swiftly he had to occasionally break into a jog. He craved a cigarette but feared giving himself away. What if she turned around and spotted the glowing orange ember? He trailed her, giving her a good fifty-metre lead, ducking behind parked cars, using the gum and wattle trees on the nature strip for cover. She never looked back. At the T-intersection, he figured she'd turn left—across the nearby highway was a reserve with plenty of bushes for possums and birds, and a pond to attract ducks—but instead, she turned right into the cul-de-sacs, crescents and squares of residential suburbia.

Ten minutes passed, twenty minutes. He shadowed her doggedly.

Where the hell was she going?

She wended through a maze of back streets, ones which he didn't know. At first, he tried to keep track of the unfamiliar surroundings, hold a mental map of the rights and lefts so he could find his way back, but her route was too circuitous. John sweated despite the cold air. Christ, the suspense was a killer. Is this how Meredith hunted every night, roaming some half an hour away from home before striking?

Or had she spotted his tail?

Was she leading him into a trap?

Finally, she slowed her pace and disappeared from the footpath. John sprinted to catch up and stopped just in time. Meredith had entered a park built on a vacant lot between two houses. He peeked around the fence of the weatherboard property.

Meredith was approaching a central playground. Two people, a man and a woman, stood up from the swing set. A third—Sebastian—rode down the slide. They all embraced Meredith. Forming a circle, the quartet crouched and howled like cats.

The sound raised the hairs on the nape of John's neck. The strange notes made by the male and female throats seesawed in a way that made him dizzy and queasy at the same time. A dog barked. The yowling stopped, but if by coincidence, John had no idea. The foursome jumped to their feet and scattered into the trees. They made no sound, even though the play equipment sat within a bed of tan bark, which should have crunched and crackled underfoot.

John wrenched off the rucksack and grabbed his binoculars. He raised the lenses to his eyes and swept the park.

The quartet was hunkered together already. John could hear ripping and rending sounds, the squawks and squeals of unseen victims. Shit, had these monsters caught their prey already? How could that be? John had taken less than half a minute to get his binoculars. Even the fastest hunters on earth—spiders, piranhas, snakes, Komodo dragons—need time to stalk.

His hands shook. To steady the view through the binoculars, John leaned an elbow on the weatherboard's letterbox. As soon as he did, his blood chilled.

The monsters had paused, motionless, noses lifted to the air.

He held his breath.

Simultaneously, they looked in his direction and stood up.

With a horrified gasp, John ducked back behind the fence. He stuffed the binoculars into the rucksack. His ears strained and heard only crickets, the distant sounds of traffic. He risked a glance. Meredith, Sebastian and the two others were hurrying towards him.

John turned and ran.

16

He ran in a blind panic. His sneakers pounded the footpath in dull thuds. The rucksack bounced against him, the binoculars smacking his shoulder blade over and over. He risked a backwards glance. Jesus, the four monsters were in pursuit. He pushed himself to go faster, faster, *faster*, his arms and legs pumping, chest heaving, heart clamouring inside his ribcage like a wild animal fighting to get out.

What would they do to him if they caught him?

Kill him with teeth and nails.

Bite him fifty-two times and convert him.

Maybe something worse.

Oh, fuck no. Oh, please.

He should never have followed Meredith. What had he hoped to achieve? Too late now for regrets. My God, he thought in a kind of dazed surprise, I'm actually running for my life. He looked back. The monsters had broken up. Sebastian and Meredith were behind him; the man and woman sprinting along the footpath on the other side of the road. They're planning ahead, he realised, getting ready to cut me off when I turn a corner. The street was deserted. If a car happened to pass by, he would run onto the road and flag the driver down, throw himself onto the goddamned bonnet if he must. But no vehicle came.

The balaclava provoked a suffocating claustrophobia—*the mask of a man on the gallows*—and he ripped it off and threw it aside. He ought to dump the rucksack too, lighten the load. But that was the least of his troubles. His pack-a-day habit and lack of exercise were catching up with him, right here and now, in the heavy wheeze of his lungs, the stitch in his side. Christ almighty, was he slowing down already?

That's when he heard their laughter, soft and tinkling, sounding for all the world like the laughing of excited children enjoying a game of chasey. The laughter swirled around him, first beside him, then in front, as if thrown by ventriloquism. He felt a pain in his chest. I'm doomed, he thought. If they wanted, they could catch me in an instant, but they are the cats and I am the mouse. *They're playing with me.*

A fresh squirt of adrenaline lengthened his stride. He coughed and hacked, spat a glob of phlegm. His breath was ragged, his windpipe burning.

"John," Meredith called, "come and meet my friends."

She didn't sound puffed in the slightest.

"Don't be daft," shouted Sebastian. "You'll give yourself a heart attack."

"Stop, John. Stop and say hello."

They were pretending to be friendly, trying to trick him. The laughter swirled around him again. How far behind were they? What if they were almost upon him? He didn't want to look. The terrifying sight would make him lose hope and impetus, drop him to the ground in a defeated heap. The fact that he couldn't hear their footfalls shredded his nerves. Yes, they were like cats, all right, padding on soft paws, ready to unsheathe their claws. Why couldn't he hear them running? He considered shouting for help. When you want help from strangers, it's important to shout FIRE to draw people's attention and inspire them to action.

"Fire," he rasped, his breath no more than a whistle. "Fire."

"It's no use," Meredith called. "You may as well give up."

"We're not going to hurt you, old chap," Sebastian added. "You're being a terrible bore."

The laughter again, that maddening laughter.

A buckle in the footpath wobbled John's foot and wrenched at his ankle, nearly tripping him. He half-expected to feel the slice of fingernails against his scalp, but a moment of clarity struck him instead. Jesus, how stupid to keep running in a straight line, illuminated by the moon and street lights! A strategy came to mind. If the monsters expected to cut him off at a corner, he'd catch them off guard.

John veered onto the nearest property, over the lawn and through the carport into the back yard. The laughter stopped. A good sign. The two-metre fence dividing this property from the next loomed ahead. He hadn't jumped a fence since his teenage years, but the step-vault technique came to him in a flood of muscle memory: a running leap, both hands on the railing, a foot planted on the top of the fence, the launch of his whole body over the other side. He dropped to the ground running.

This back yard had a pool. As he veered around it, he remembered falling into Darren Shaw's pool the night of the bonfire party. He sped up as he approached the next fence and hopped over it. He ran through the front yard, dodging a magnolia tree, and dashed onto the road. Behind him, he heard the unmistakable splash of a body falling into the pool. Hah! Please God, let it be Sebastian taking an unscheduled swim, and please God, give him pneumonia for his troubles, the sick fucking freak.

John ducked into the next-door property and scaled the fence. His footsteps woke a terrier that raised its head and yapped. John leapt another fence into the neighbouring yard, sprinted across the patio, vaulted over more wooden palings.

"John!" Meredith shouted, her voice far away. "Where are you?"

Almost home and hosed, he thought, and redoubled his efforts. The yards were fragrant with varied flowers in spring bloom—lavender, rose, gardenia, daphne, frangipani—which would help mask his own scents of fear and sweat. These monsters could sniff like bloodhounds, he felt sure of it. And if they couldn't see him or smell him, they would have the devil's own job of tracking him.

He zigzagged through one yard after another, mindlessly at first, desperate to build on his head start. The plan seemed to be going well until he noticed the barking.

Shit, he was leaving a trail of agitated dogs in his wake.

Jumping a chain-link fence, his trailing foot caught the top rail. He sprawled into the garden bed, lifting his hands at the last moment to stop himself from face-planting. A shooting pain coursed through his left arm. Panting, retching, he staggered to his feet. God, he felt ill, like throwing up. He coughed and spat. Leaning on his legs, he gasped and panted. His heart boomed in his throat. An outside light came on.

With a groan, John looked up.

A stout backlit figure appeared behind a screen door.

"Hey, you there!" bellowed an old, cracked voice. "What are you doing?"

John tried to run but couldn't. His legs felt leaden, his muscles flooded with lactic acid. Hawking and spitting, he raised his hand in what he hoped looked like a friendly, non-threatening gesture. He needed a minute to get his wind back.

"Mavis," the old voice continued, "phone the police."

"Is it a peeping Tom? Stuff the cops, I'm getting the air rifle."

Staggering, gulping for air, John scaled the fence into the next yard. He struggled over more fences, again and again, until he found himself on a street that led to a main road. Invigorated, he jogged towards it. He glanced behind: nothing. The monsters had lost his trail. When he reached the main road, he slowed down. The tyre shop, the plant nursery, the timber and hardware factory...okay, now he had his bearings. He made his way through dozens of properties, slowly, muscles shaking, each climb of a fence more arduous than the one before.

It took him close to an hour to get home. When he finally locked the door behind him, he slid to the floor and wept for a few seconds, in relief and shock. The pain in his left arm caught his attention. Carefully, he made a fist, palpated his wrist bones, felt along his forearm. No, he hadn't broken anything in his fall; just a sprain. He slumped against the door with his eyes closed.

Oh, Jesus, what a fucking night...

Rolling sideways, he got on his hands and knees. Grunting, holding to the door handle, he made it to his feet, head pounding, mouth tasting like copper. He hobbled towards his end of the house. Fuck leaving the door unlocked. Meredith could sleep on the porch for all he cared.

He bolted himself inside the bedroom, shucked the rucksack and jacket, and kicked off the sneakers. His skin felt tacky from drying sweat. He contemplated a shower but decided against it. What if Meredith was leading the other monsters here? He had to be ready to fight. In the bathroom, he kept a wrench to periodically tighten the hexagonal nut of the showerhead, and he took up the wrench, opened the blinds so he could see the bastards coming, and sat on his bed, tense and alert.

Despite the wheezing and crackling in his lungs, he lit a cigarette. The smoke hurt his throat. Once the coughing fit passed, he considered his options. He was in no state to take on four supernatural beings. Should he leave while the going was good? Perhaps stay at a motel? He brooded over the events of the chase, the taunting words of Meredith and Sebastian in particular:

John, come and meet my friends.

Don't be daft. You'll give yourself a heart attack.

Stop, John. Stop and say hello.

We're not going to hurt you, old chap. You're being a terrible bore.

Wait a minute...taunting? No, not really. In fact, now that John was home, among safe and familiar things, it seemed Meredith and Sebastian had sounded...well, maybe not *friendly*. But maybe not hostile, either. Not completely hostile, at any rate. What was it that had made him assume they were planning to attack?

Feeling foolish, he looked down at the wrench and considered putting it back.

But no, he would hold on to it. In the park, when the foursome had dropped to their haunches and howled like cats, the hairs had raised on John's neck, just as they were doing now at the memory of that eerie, otherworldly scene. Meredith and her 'friends' were dangerous monsters—during the night, at least. Something about day-time took the edge off them. Like vampires.

He shuddered. They could have bitten him. Turned him into... whatever the hell kind of monster that Meredith and Sebastian happened to be.

Okay, first things first. He would move house with Meredith to the other side of the city. Once he got her away from Donna—and Sebastian—she would lapse back into her harmless, semi-catatonic state. After that, he would decide what to do next.

One hurdle at a time.

He got up, wrench in hand, and snibbed the deadlock on the front door in anticipation of Meredith's return. No sense in making her break a window. After all, its replacement would come out of his own hip pocket. He went back to his room and lay down. At about four o'clock, as a false dawn brightened the sky, he heard the front door open and close, followed by the soft click of the latch to her bedroom.

Only then did John give in to his fatigue.

The soft, insistent knocking roused John from sleep. Sunlight flooded his room through the open blinds. Groggy, he squinted at the alarm clock: 8.03 a.m.

Who would be knocking at this hour?

He struggled out of bed, wincing. Beer o'clock might have to come early today. His muscles and joints ached as if he'd had the crap beaten out of him.

The knocking continued.

"Hang on," he yelled, which provoked a brief coughing fit.

He stood up, fully dressed in his black ensemble from the night before. As he reached for his smokes, he noticed he still held the wrench. He threw it on the mattress. Opening his hand made his knuckles pop and creak. God, he felt terrible, worse than any hangover. He contemplated lying down again. To hell with the visitor.

Knock, knock, knock.

Oh, for fuck's sake.

He lit a cigarette. The first drag seared his windpipe. Hacking and hawking, he limped along the hallway on bruised, tender feet. Meredith's bedroom and hobby room were shut tight, as he knew they would be. Hopefully, she would stay in isolation the entire day. He was in no mood to see her. Not now, maybe not ever.

"All right, all right," he shouted at the front door, and opened it.

He caught Cassie in mid-knock, her fist raised. Donna stood behind her. Taken aback, John blinked. God, what a sight he must be: unshaven, uncombed, sweaty, dirty, clothes rumpled and grass-stained—

"Sorry for waking you," Donna said. "I know you're unwell."

Unwell? It took him a moment to remember their last text-message exchange:

"Hope you liked brekkie. See you tonight?" "Sorry but im sick. Tomorrow?"
Well, at least he looked the part, a bag of absolute shit.

Donna was still talking. "We hate to disturb you, but this couldn't wait."

What couldn't wait?

Oh, no. Cassie's eyes were swollen and red, her lashes wet. An awful precognition shivered down John's spine. No, no, *no*... He braced himself.

"Have you seen Tiger?" Cassie said. "Mum let him out last night."

"He was yowling, I didn't have a choice. He'd keep us awake otherwise."

"But he always comes back. He meows at the kitchen window because he's hungry and wants breakfast. I feed him before school, that's one of my jobs. This morning, he wasn't at the window. I went outside, and I called and called—"

"Shush, honey," Donna said. "It's okay."

"And he wasn't there. He's gone. Have you seen him?"

He stared down at the girl's beseeching eyes. A jag of self-loathing bubbled up like hot bile from deep in his guts. He had known this day would come. And what had he done to stop it? Nothing. Not a goddamned thing. Instead of taking steps, he had closed his eyes and crossed his fingers, wishing it away like the despicable coward he was, and he hated himself with a swift and violent passion.

Cassie clutched at his hand.

"Have you seen him?" she said. "Please tell me you've seen him."

If only he could say, *Why, yes, Tiger is here with me, fine and dandy, sitting at my table, scarfing down a tin of tuna and a saucer of milk.*

John shook his head. She dropped his hand. Her face set hard.

"It's the witch," she said. "The white-haired witch killed him and ate him."

John flinched in astonishment. *Killed him and ate him.* Why would Cassie assume something like that? More to the point, she seemed to know it to be true. He felt a slew of sickly vertigo. Everything and everyone seemed connected somehow, but what did it all mean? Hold on to your sanity, he thought, you're getting paranoid. On the other hand, it's not paranoia if you're right. Jesus. If he could figure out the pattern, predict what event was coming next, he might be able to take control of this juggernaut, prevent any more bad things from happening.

"That's enough, honey," Donna was saying. "You're scaring yourself."

The girl kept her focus on John. "The witch got him, didn't she?"

John held his breath. Stay in your room, Merry, he thought. How could I explain keeping the witch in my own house? Stay in your room, stay—

"Tiger is just the start," Cassie continued, voice rising. "The witch is coming for us, one by one. First, she'll kill Mum. I'll be next. And then—"

"Stop!" Donna grabbed Cassie's shoulders. "Enough crazy talk."

"She hates us, she's out to get us."

"Stop your nonsense right now."

"Mum!" Cassie stamped her foot. "Why won't you believe me?"

"Hey!" John said.

They both startled and gaped at him. God, they looked so pale, so frightened.

He said, "No one's killing anybody, okay? There's no such thing as witches. The homeless grandma, remember? And Tiger is fine. Cats go roaming. It's what they do, it's in their nature. If you ask me, he's found himself a girlfriend."

Cassie crossed her arms. "We had his balls chopped off."

"He must be with another family. I've seen it before. A cat roams about, some neighbour starts leaving out food, and pretty soon, the cat divides its time between two households. Boom, you've got yourself a court case."

"A court case?"

"Well, sure," he continued, as he warmed to the lie. "Haven't you read about that kind of thing in the papers? Two families have to ask a judge to decide who owns the cat. It happens more often than you think."

Cassie frowned. "You mean Tiger is with another family?"

"Maybe."

"He's not dead?"

Oh, he's dead, all right. Dead and digested.

John said, "Why don't you make a missing poster? I'll photocopy it at work so you can put it around the neighbourhood…"

He trailed off, remembering Mrs Dwight from his last address, that fat old pensioner with her saggy chin swinging like a dewlap, asking about her Siamese. *Angel's a homebody. It's not like him to stay away… Cats are funny creatures, Mrs Dwight. Sometimes they wander…* Déjà vu. The memory froze his throat and dried out his mouth. Wheels within wheels. For a split second, the curtains pulled aside and he could see the clockwork springs of the universe, its cogs interlocked.

"That's a good idea, honey," Donna said. "Why don't you ask Mr Schulz if you can make a poster during recess?"

Cassie scowled but seemed to consider.

"Now hop in the car," Donna added. "Quick, we're going to be late for school."

The girl offered a wan smile and ran to the footpath. She looked both ways, crossed the road, and climbed into the red Toyota. John felt tears prick his eyes. Poor Cassie. *This is my fault*, he wanted to confess. *Everyone I love, I destroy.*

"Look at these," Donna said, scrabbling a hand inside her jeans pocket. She held out two sheets of thick and creamy notepaper, each folded twice into neat squares, the kind he recognised with a sinking stomach. Donna said, "Someone pushed them under our front door. I hid them from Cassie."

Reluctantly, he took the papers.

"Don't you want to read them?" she said.

"In a minute."

"Look, I'm scheduled for a couple of hours at the café. Can I come back after that?" she said. "I really need to talk this out. Would you mind?"

"Okay, no worries."

She hesitated for a moment. "I'm calling the police."

"What? The police?"

"This is serious enough, isn't it?"

"Well, I don't know."

Donna narrowed her eyes, briefly, and glanced at her watch. "I've got to go."

She jogged across the road. He watched her jump into the Toyota. Cassie was staring at him through the car window. He waved. The girl didn't wave back. She must know he was lying. Why not? She seemed to know everything else. The car reversed out the driveway and took off down the road at high speed.

John leaned against the door jamb. *Everything is repeating itself. Everything is coming to a head. What goes around comes around.* He closed the front door. Silence cloaked the house. He looked at Meredith's bedroom door, close enough to touch. *How much had she heard? Probably the whole conversation. How would she react? No idea.* Trembling, he opened the folded papers.

KEEP YOUR HANDS TO YOURSELF!!

YOU ARE A DIRTY WHORE!!

A cold chill moved through him. Just like the notes Meredith had sent to their previous neighbours, the Kapoors. Why had she hated their budgerigars? Who knew. The birds, in a range of pretty rainbow colours from white to blue to green to purple, chirped and whistled softly and melodically from dawn 'til dusk. Mrs Kapoor's intention to call the police had triggered John's search for a new house, for this house, the faux miner's cottage, where he had hoped for a new beginning, an end to the bad times and the bad dreams. Well, the joke was on him. *There's no such thing as a 'new beginning'. Only the old shit recycled around and around, rabbit-punching you in the head, over and over, driving you mad.*

He put the notes in his pocket, took a last, hurried drag of the smoke and flicked the butt to the lawn. Okay, Meredith was going to talk. Right now. He closed the front door and barged into her bedroom. Empty. He flung open the door to the hobby room.

Jesus.

Gagging, he staggered back, lifting a hand to his mouth.

Oh, Jesus Christ almighty.

What the hell?

Meredith paused mid-chew, looked up, and met his gaze. She was crouched on her haunches. The big silver pot sat between her knees. She held a raw and skinned carcass, beheaded, the exact size of a cat. Blood smeared her lips and dripped from her chin. She must have found his horror amusing, for she smiled. The mirthless sight shrivelled John's nut-sack into a frightened clutch. He gripped the door frame. Vomit

173

rose in his throat. He swallowed hard, again and again.

"I'm busy," she said. "Go away."

"No. I'm coming in."

"I wouldn't if I were you."

"Well," he said, "fuck what you want."

Tensing, baring her teeth, she watched him, eyes slitted, as he took one step after another. He had to see inside the pot. Oh shit, he had cooked pasta in that pot, for God's sake. And soup too. Corned beef. Meredith's whole body seemed to tighten at his approach, as if readying to spring.

The pot.

He had to see.

"Turn around," she said. "Leave. Shut the door behind you."

One more step.

John looked down.

Tiger's head lay on its face, the ginger fur unmistakable and matted with drying blood. The skin lay crumpled, inside out like a discarded glove, on top of a pile of glistening and grey intestines. The stump of the tail had clotted where Meredith must have ripped it from the body. Perhaps she always started the skinning process at the tail. Dizzy, John held both shaking hands to his mouth.

"Happy now?" Meredith said. "You can't say I didn't warn you. If you're going to chuck, don't do it in here."

17

"You killed Tiger," John whispered.

Meredith shrugged and took another bite. The gelatinous muscle tissue shone wet and dark red. A fresh dribble of blood ran down her chin and drip, drip, dripped into the pot. Black dots swirled across John's vision for a moment.

Talking around the meat, she said, "Did you really think I'd leave that cat alone? On your say-so? On your fucking authority? Hah."

"So that's it. You killed Tiger to spite me."

"And a few other reasons, namely hunger."

"Hunger?" He ran both sweating hands through his hair. "What's wrong with possums? Roosting pigeons? I don't understand, Merry. I never ask you for anything. I pay the bills, take care of the house, do your goddamned washing. I look the other way when it comes to your disgusting habits. This one thing, Merry, this one thing. I asked you to leave Tiger alone, and you went out of your way to kill him."

"It was easy too."

"Easy?"

"God, what a dumb cat. No street smarts at all. I've had dogs hit by cars and lying injured on the road that were harder to catch than this idiot," she said, waving the carcass by its shank for emphasis. "You know how I got him?"

"No idea."

"Have a guess."

Numbly, John shook his head.

"All right, I'll tell you." Reaching out her free hand, she rubbed the bloody fingertips together and made kissing sounds with her gory lips.

"Puss, puss, puss." She laughed, dropped the act, and took another bite. Her mouth full, she added, "The moron walked right on over to me, bam, just like that."

Groping, John leaned on the nearest wall to steady himself. Meredith kept eating. She seemed happy, content, a child at a picnic on a sunny day tucking into a slice of chocolate cake. Blood ran down her arms. John's stomach turned over.

"Don't you understand," he said at last, "what you've become?"

She glanced up, puzzled. "What I've become?"

"Back in the day, you were a gorgeous woman. Sophisticated, upper class. You could have been a model."

"A model? Pfft. Those girls eat nothing but cocaine and cigarettes."

"You should have lived your life in a…in a *grand* way."

"Huh? What are you talking about?"

"You had beauty, brains…everything going for you."

She raised an eyebrow. "Oh, get over yourself. We're both down here in the gutter. Or were you destined for yachts as well?"

He flushed. "I was never in your league."

"League? You've lost your mind. You know what I think? You're rambling. You blew an artery in your head with all that running last night." She sniggered. "My God, you're unfit. Join a gym already."

Embarrassed, he turned his face.

"We had you scared shitless, didn't we?" she said.

"One of you is enough. Four is too much."

"They're a nice enough crew. You should have stopped to say hello."

"I don't want to talk to monsters."

"Monsters?" she said, and her back stiffened, her smile falling away. "You think I'm a monster?"

He held her gaze for a long time. "Yes, I do."

"Fuck you," she whispered.

"No, fuck *you*. Tiger is dead. What about Cassie and Donna?"

"What about them?" She threw the carcass into the pot and wiped her mouth with the back of her hand, smearing blood across her cheeks. "I couldn't care less."

"Too bad. Now you've dropped us both in the shit. Donna wants to call the police because of those notes you shoved under her door."

Meredith pouted, sulky as a toddler.

He added, "We're moving again because of you."

"Good."

"I'm looking at units tomorrow."

She gave him three, slow claps. His temper flared.

"You're making me break the lease. You know what that means? I have to keep paying rent until the landlord finds another tenant. And what happens if he doesn't find another tenant? I'll be paying rent on two places, that's what, and I'm already living from pay-cheque to pay-cheque. I'll have to take out a loan or something, get a few credit cards, I don't know. For Christ's sake, Merry, are you even listening?"

Her face was sullen, her arms crossed. "The money doesn't matter."

"That's easy for you to say. You're not the one fronting the goddamned cash."

"It's worth any amount of money to get you away from that dirty whore."

John gritted his teeth and rubbed at his temples. "Oh, why are you doing this to me? Can't I have one friend?"

"A friend?" Her eyes flashed. "Give me a break. For years, I had to compete with Lyle for your attention. I'm not competing with that dirty whore as well."

For a moment, John's heart stopped beating. "Lyle? That's the second time you've remembered him."

"Yes, Lyle, my brother, my twin fucking brother. How could you forget that arrogant little prick?"

"Not me. You."

"What?"

"Hang on a second." John ducked into her bedroom, reached under the bed and hauled out the box of memorabilia she kept from high school. Pushing aside the paperback copy of *Oliver Twist* with its picture of Luke Skywalker taped to the cover, he grabbed the first pack of photographs. Wheels within wheels…

"Hey," Meredith called. "Get out of my room."

He hurried back to her, crouched down, and pulled the photographs from their paper jacket. "Our school trip to Central Australia, 1984, Year Eleven," he said, thumbing through each snap. "Uluru, or Ayers Rock as it was called back then; kangaroos, the tents, our bus driver and cook. Here's you sitting on the back of a camel screaming your head off. Remember this?" He flapped the photograph under her nose. "Remember?"

Quiet and pale, thoughtful, she frowned and nodded.

"Look here," he ordered, holding up the picture of himself, Meredith and Lyle linking arms in the desert twilight. "Who's that bloke?"

After a moment, she reached out a bloodied finger and murmured, "Lyle."

"Exactly."

John slapped the photograph against her chest. Scrabbling, she took hold of it with both hands and stared at it, mouth open, as if at a ghost. John stood up.

"Two weeks ago," he said, "when we were getting ready to move from the unit to this joint, you saw that photo and didn't recognise him."

Her wide, haunted eyes showed the whites all the way round. "I didn't?"

"No, you didn't. And every time we've moved house—about half a dozen times so far, maybe more—you've dragged out this box of crap and got me to go through these same goddamned pictures, and every time you haven't recognised your own brother. Now you do." He flung the remaining photographs to the floor. "What's going on, Merry? You've changed. It's like you're waking up. Why? What the fuck is going on here?"

Carefully, she studied the photograph. "Lyle…"

"Yeah, Lyle. Now tell me. Are you waking up? What's happened to end this…coma…you've been in since I found you in the park? Is it Donna? Are you jealous of her, is that it? Answer me. You've killed her cat, what's your next move? Tell me."

The memory of Cassie's words lodged like a fish bone inside his throat. *The witch is coming for us, one by one.* The surge of anger and panic felt suffocating. He had to struggle to breathe.

"Merry," he said. "Answer me, or so help me…"

Freezing, she seemed to slip into her catatonic state, but only for a moment. With a gasp, she pressed the photograph to her bloodied cheek and closed her eyes.

She moaned, "Oh, he's dead."

John's teeth shut with a click. "No. Lyle is a missing person."

"He's dead."

What would make her say something like that? Maybe she knew. Did John talk in his sleep? Oh, Christ. Now, wait a minute, were those tears squeezing out from between her lashless eyelids? Yes. Tears for Lyle. Exhausted, John slumped against the wall, slid down it, and sat on the floor.

"Don't cry, Merry," he said after a time.

"Why not? My big brother's dead. He's older than me by nine minutes, did you know that? Lyle's dead. My brother is dead."

"You don't know for sure. Nate Rossi thinks he's in Bali."

"Bali?" Her faint laugh was cryptic. "He's not in Bali. You know it. I know it."

"We know only what the police reckon, that Lyle is a missing person. End of story. If you think any different, you're fooling yourself."

She held out the photograph and gazed upon it. A hint of a smile curled her lips. John struggled to read her expression. Nostalgic? Sad? No, it was something else, something...unsettling. She took the photo in both hands and, to his surprise, tore it in half. Putting the pieces together, she tore them again, then again, and let the shreds fall into the silver pot. She laughed and dusted her hands together with a theatrical flourish. Now he could read her expression. Triumphant. Mocking. He felt uneasy.

"Let's have a smoke," she said, and got up.

He leapt to his feet and backed into the hallway. She moved past him to the bathroom. The raft of disturbed air in her wake smelled ripe and coppery. The bile rose to his tongue. Jesus, poor Tiger. Meredith must have speared him with her nails, torn open his jugular and drank his blood, drained the animal empty.

John approached the door of the bathroom. Meredith was washing her face and hands in the sink. She caught his eye in the mirror and winked.

John said, "Did you suck Tiger's blood while he was still alive?"

"Well, it's no good once the heart stops pumping."

"You're a vampire, aren't you?"

She snorted and turned off the tap. "You've got a tiny little mind. According to pin-heads like you, there are just so many things that exist in this world and no more. You couldn't be more wrong. What's the old saying? There are creatures in heaven and earth, Horatio...oh, I forget the rest."

"If you're not a vampire," he said, "what are you?"

"Who knows?"

She ran her fingers through her hair as if preening, and studied her reflection in profile, first one side and then the other. She looked ghastly—pale as wax, sunken cheeked, with heavy dark rings carved beneath her hollowed eye sockets—but she seemed pleased with what she saw in the mirror.

"Tell me the truth for once," he said.

"The truth? That's rich, coming from you." She laughed. "You think I'm a monster. Isn't that a good enough definition?"

She pushed past him. He followed her to the kitchen and grabbed himself a beer. *You're an alky if you drink before 10.45 a.m.*—but surely, this occasion didn't count, this was an emergency. Cigarettes and a lighter sat on the bench. Meredith put two smokes in her mouth and lit them both. When she held one out, he hesitated.

She arched an eyebrow. "Relax. I don't have cooties."

"I don't know what you've got. You won't tell me."

"Nothing you can catch from a ciggy."

He took the smoke and accidentally touched her fingers. They felt ice cold. A shiver of revulsion ran along his spine.

"A zombie, then," he said. "Something undead."

She rolled her eyes. "We've already had this conversation."

"You never gave me an answer."

"Fine. I'm a combination vampire-zombie-witch. Satisfied?"

"No. I don't understand."

"And you never will." She sat at the table. "Stop acting so weird. We've been living together for years. Years! Don't look at me like you don't know me."

"But I don't know you. All this time, I thought you were…mentally ill."

"Hah. Not even close."

"Then why did your parents send you to a nuthouse?"

"Because I kept telling them I'd killed Lyle."

The strength drained from him, fast, like water from a tipped bucket. Slowly, carefully, he grasped the back of a chair and lowered himself into it. He put down the stubby, jittering it against the table top.

Meredith tutted. "There you go again, looking like you want to puke."

When he didn't answer, she picked up the stubby and twisted off the top. She held it out. After a while, he took the beer and drank most of it down in a couple of long and thirsty swallows.

"Are you going to puke?" she said.

"No, I'm fine."

"Put your head between your knees."

"I told you, I'm fine."

She pointed at his cigarette. "Are you going to smoke that or let it burn out?"

With trembling fingers, he laid the cigarette in the ashtray. "Stop, Merry."

"Stop what?"

"Tormenting me," he said, his voice cracking. "I've done everything for you. Paid the bills. Taken care of you—"

"Yes, yes," she interrupted. "Washed my clothes, and all that shit.

180

I know, I know. You want me in your debt, and why not? You buried my brother for me."

He jolted. She must mean that metaphorically. Nobody knew what had happened down at the river. Nobody but himself and Lyle. Nevertheless, he couldn't meet her gaze. Instead, he stared at the table top. Waves of shame, regret and self-loathing broke over him in a cold sweat. The sounds of the river came back. He winced at the memory of Lyle's broken head, bouncing and bumping over the rocky ground as John had dragged him by the ankles deeper into the forest...

But no, wait, *Lyle* was to blame for what happened. John had approached with his hand out, ready to shake, ready to put the argument behind them.

"Hey," Meredith said. "What's the matter?"

"Nothing."

But now it was John's turn to close his eyes against a sudden onset of tears. One punch. One single, solitary punch. How many lives had John destroyed with that moment of anger? How many days, countless days, had he spent wishing it had never happened? Oh, but he knew how many. All the long and empty days of his life ever since Sunday October 19th, 1985.

Something cold touched the back of his wrist.

John's eyes flew open. Meredith had laid her hand on him. He jerked away and rubbed at his skin as if it burned. Her eyes narrowed.

"You know, for a minute there," she said, "I actually felt sorry for you."

Tired and heartsick, he pushed away from the table. Now what? A shower. He needed to freshen up, change into clean clothes, shave, get a different perspective, get a *grip*. Then breakfast. Eggs and bacon, toast, orange juice, black coffee. After that, start figuring out some kind of plan.

"Where are you going?" she said.

"To have a shower. Is that okay with you?"

From the ashtray, she took his discarded cigarette and relit it, dragging hard. As he reached the hallway, she said, "Hey, Sampson, don't forget to bolt the door behind you."

He continued into his room and bolted the door.

It was a relief to peel off the crusty, sweaty clothes, soiled from the mad chase the night before. The shower belted down in needles, a painful ablution. John lifted his face into the hot sting and wished he could wipe his mind clean.

So, Merry had told her parents that she had killed Lyle.

Why? It didn't make sense.

Unless she had felt responsible somehow for her brother's disappearance. Perhaps Lyle had threatened suicide, and Merry had believed him. But why would Lyle have reacted so badly to her loss of virginity in the first place? That didn't make sense either. A ghastly suspicion flickered through John's mind, but he dismissed it out of hand. Perhaps Lyle's jealousy made sense if you had grown up with a sibling. John had never discovered the details of the twins' argument beyond what Lyle had mentioned at the river. Well, that was going to change. Today. After he was dressed, John would quiz Merry, find out everything once and for all, and maybe get a little goddamned peace after thirty-one years.

He turned off the shower and scrubbed himself dry with a towel. When he went to the bathroom cabinet to get the deodorant, he saw Meredith in the mirror. *Shit.* Heart thumping, he spun around, holding the towel in front of him.

She was sitting on his bed, shoulders slumped, face tear-streaked.

Calm down, he thought, she doesn't appear threatening. Then he noticed the black animal pelt. She was holding it, squeezing and worrying at it with both hands. A flash of alarm raced through him. But no, a moment later he recognised the object for what it was: his balaclava. When he had ripped it off his head last night during the pursuit, he had flung it to the footpath and kept on running.

"What are you doing in here?" he said.

She lifted the balaclava. "I brought this home for you."

When he didn't react, she smiled sadly and laid the balaclava on his pillow.

"Thanks," he said, wrapping the towel about his waist. He took a t-shirt and tracksuit pants from his wardrobe. "How did you get in? I had the door bolted."

"Oh, I come in here all the time."

He paused. "All the time?"

"When you're at work. Sometimes when you're asleep."

"You watch me when I'm asleep?"

"Like a mother over her baby. Can't you understand?"

"No."

Meredith shook her head and bit at her chapped lips.

Hurriedly, he dressed in the bathroom. He felt scared, yes, but exhilarated too. Meredith was ready to talk. He would find out everything, he could feel it. Her secrets would be laid bare. When he came out from behind the dividing wall, she was holding two lit cigarettes. She proffered one to him. He took it, careful not to touch her. He leaned against the window, which was as far away from her as he could get.

"I'm going crazy," she whispered.

"How come?"

She wiped at tears with the heels of both hands. "I'm remembering things, John. Terrible things."

"Like what?"

"Things about Lyle. Stuff I haven't remembered in years." She dragged on the smoke. It shook between her trembling lips. "I always hated him. Did you know that?"

"You always gave that impression, yeah. But if you hated him so much, why are you crying?"

"God, he was such a smartarse."

John shrugged. "Actually, that was one of the things I liked about him."

"He could be cruel too. Selfish. Everything had to be his way." She closed her eyes, spilling fresh tears down her cheeks. "You weren't my first."

"Your first...?"

"Do you remember the time we made love?"

"Of course, I do."

She smiled, tears shimmering. "You were nervous. You kept apologising, and that made me laugh, and then you would laugh too. Remember? It was fun. It was innocent. While we made love, we looked at each other. You kept giving me little kisses on my nose, on my forehead. Such tender little kisses. You told me you loved me." She drew on the cigarette. "It's one of my best memories."

"One of mine too."

She brightened and laughed, pressing a hand to her chest. "Is it?"

"Definitely."

"You thought we were both virgins." Her smile crumpled.

"Hey, that doesn't matter to me, all right? So, you had a lover or two before we got together. No big deal."

"No, you don't understand." She bit her lips together, blinking hard, seeming to brace herself. "Lyle and I were young when it started. Eight or nine. I didn't know it was wrong. Maybe he did."

A slow creep of dread crawled along John's spine. "Wait, what...?"

"It was a game initially. He called it 'Like-Unlike'. We used to have baths together. Playing Like-Unlike meant pointing out where we were similar and where we were different. We had to touch each other's different places."

Breathless, his stomach heavy and churning, John groped for the mattress and sat down next to her. When she laid an icy hand on his leg, he didn't pull away. She didn't speak for a long time. The cigarette burned down between her fingers. Gently, he took the butt from her and dropped it in the ashtray.

She said, "I was twelve when Lyle fucked me."

"Oh, Christ."

"December 28th, 1979. The summer break between Grade Six and Year Seven."

John saw again that first day of high school, Meredith with her platinum-blonde hair worn in a bob, her regal stance with one hand on her hip, those model-thin limbs. And Lyle sidling over with his schoolbag full of cigarette packets: *Winnie red or blue? If you want menthol, you're a poofter, and I can't stand poofters. Anyhow have a Winfield.*

"Mum and Dad had gone out to dinner," she was saying. "It was their wedding anniversary. They figured we were old enough to be left by ourselves. We did it on a beanbag in the rumpus room."

John felt sick. The beanbags—both red vinyl, he could see them still—in the Berg-Olsen rumpus room where John would later have his sleepovers, he and Lyle watching movies on the VCR, smoking on the patio in the middle of the night, doing homework together, bitching about teachers, talking about girls.

His guts turned over. Staggering, he reached the toilet just in time. He vomited so forcefully that it seemed his innards would heave out of his mouth.

18

At last, John stopped retching. He became aware that Meredith was rubbing his back as if to comfort him. He spat into the bowl, wiped the back of his hand over his lips.

"I'm sorry," she was saying, over and over.

"For what?"

"For what happened with Lyle."

He straightened up, flushed the toilet and moved to the sink. As he washed his hands and mouth, he watched her in the mirror. She had a pleading, terrified look in her eyes.

"It wasn't your fault," he said.

"Yes, it was."

"For God's sake, Lyle raped you."

She shook her head. "I liked it just as much as him. We did it for years."

John buried his face in a towel. She touched his shoulder. He wrenched away and dropped the towel to the floor.

"I'm so sorry," she said.

He pushed past her and hurried out of the room. A beer. Good Christ almighty, he needed a beer right this instant. She followed him.

"I thought you hated him," John said.

"I did."

"But you rooted him anyway."

"Look, I know it doesn't make sense."

He flung open the refrigerator door. "Nothing about you makes sense, Merry. You do my fucking head in."

As he floundered about for a stubby, he knocked over the tomato sauce bottle, the mustard jar. He tried to straighten them but his shaking hand couldn't manage. Giving up, he shoved the sauce and mustard to the back of the shelf so they wouldn't fall out, and he shut the door. Meredith took the stubby from him and opened it. He snatched it back and drank most of the beer in a couple of gulps.

"Do you want a cigarette?" she said. "I can fetch one for you."

"Leave me alone. I need to get my head straight."

He sat at the kitchen table and lit a smoke. She took a seat opposite and stared at him with that same kicked-dog look in her eyes, a look he couldn't bear. He concentrated on finishing the stubby and the cigarette. His stomach kept flip-flopping. Every time he tried to organise his thoughts, his mind became nothing but a bright, over-exposed wasteland. Could he be in shock? Maybe. Probably. Certainly. He stood up to get another drink. Meredith leapt to her feet too.

"Don't hate me," she said.

"Go away."

"Everything changed once you became my boyfriend, I swear."

"Fuck off, would you?" he said, grabbing a beer. "I can't hear myself think."

"After you and I made love, I told Lyle I wouldn't do it with him anymore. That's why we argued on the day he disappeared."

John froze. His hand tightened reflexively around the stubby. This is what he'd been waiting for, after all these years. Some kind of explanation. He closed the fridge and sat at the table.

"I'm listening," he said.

She tapped a cigarette from the packet. As she lit it, he noticed the crusts of dried blood beneath her fingernails. Tiger's blood. The cat's dismembered and half-eaten corpse was sitting in a pot in the next room. The muscles of John's legs tensed. Don't get complacent, he warned himself. She may be crying, but perhaps they could be crocodile tears. Keep your guard up.

Meredith blew a steady stream of smoke at the ceiling.

"I'm waiting," he said.

"I don't know where to start."

"Tell me what happened on Sunday October 19th, 1985."

"Okay." She sat opposite him and gazed at the table. "We had an early breakfast, like normal. Mum and Dad went to see Little Nana at the nursing home. They did that every Sunday before church. That's when Lyle and I used to...do it. I told him that day, no, I had a boyfriend and wanted to be faithful. I told him I'd never do it with him again."

"What happened?"

"He slapped me."

"Then what?"

"He called me a dirty whore. Said I needed his permission to sleep with anybody else, and he wouldn't ever give it."

Sweating, John wiped at his lip, took a drink of beer. How could he reconcile this version of Lyle with his own? Lyle had been his best friend, his only friend, a top bloke, the kind of bloke that John had wished himself to be.

"He punched me in the belly," she continued, "and called me a cheater."

"A cheater?"

"Fucking weird, right? Like I was his wife or something."

John's stomach roiled. He put his hand over his mouth, fighting the urge to retch. Meredith tapped the cigarette against the ashtray until the flaming tip fell out. John picked up the lighter. She put the cigarette stump to her lips and he relit it.

"What happened when you told him your boyfriend was me?" John said.

"He freaked out. Started crying. Called me a traitor. Said I'd stolen the one person he cared about in the whole world."

Tears pricked John's eyes. "He said that? Exactly those words?"

She nodded. "He loved you."

"He did?"

"More than anybody else."

"Oh, God." John rubbed at his temples. "Oh, dear God."

He saw himself packing the dirt, one handful at a time, around Lyle's blank and waxy face, remembered Lyle's half-open eye that had stared, unfocused, into the far reaches of infinity. John's body shook and the maddening urge to rip out his hair tore through him. Instead, he ground his teeth. His foot jittered against the floor.

"He told me he would break us up," Meredith went on. "That he would tell you I'd been fucking him. You'd be so disgusted you'd never speak to me again. Guess what I said?" She waited. "John?"

"What?"

"Guess what I said to him."

John gave a weak shrug. "No idea."

"That if you found out, you'd never speak to him again either."

Would that have been true? If John had known the truth about his best friend and the love of his life, how would he have reacted? His mind went blank, snap, a tripped fuse. He drank his beer instead. Crisp, fizzy and bitter on his tongue, it became a flowering warmth in his stomach. Glorious. A few more stubbies, and he would get the buzz, the relaxation, the feeling that things were okay in the world.

Nate Rossi came to mind, slurping his spilled whisky off the bench in that dingy caravan. John's heart cramped into a ball. Nate, he thought, I shouldn't have judged you, mate. Sometimes, life offers poor bastards like us plenty of reasons to drink. Too many reasons. You're an alky, Nate. Guess what? Me, too.

I'm an alcoholic.

It was an invigorating kind of relief to admit it to himself, like exhaling a long-held breath.

"I begged Lyle not to tell," Meredith was saying.

"Huh?"

"John, are you even listening?"

"Yeah, you begged him not to tell. What did he do?"

"Kept hitting me. In places where clothes would hide the bruises. My belly, my back, my chest." She crushed out her cigarette and sat in silence. At last, fidgeting, picking at her fingernails, she said, "Well? Say something. What are you thinking?"

"I don't know."

"How are you feeling?"

"I don't know."

Tears spilled onto his cheeks. He stood and walked over to the window. The sun shone over the back yard, the sparse lawn, the broken-down fence, the ruins of his vegie patch. Everything was ruined. His whole life. Ruined.

From behind, Meredith's arms closed about his waist. She was cold, as if made from clay.

"Don't cry," she whispered. "It's all right. I love you, John. I love you."

He turned around. For the first time in thirty years, he held her in his arms. He closed his eyes. Her hair smelled fruity, like the shampoo he bought for her, yet there was a faint odour of rot beneath it. She rubbed her face against his shoulder, over and over as if drying her own tears, and the sleeve of his t-shirt rolled up. Her icy lips pressed against his bicep in a gentle kiss.

An endless vista of burnt orange soil appeared.

Surprised, John looked around.

There was grevillea, mulga and bloodwood trees. Wildflowers, daisies and mulla mulla formed a patchy blanket over the dunes. A rocky outcrop sat on the horizon. Stars were beginning to glow in the cloudless twilit sky, a billion of them, a trillion, each one as bright and clear as the tip of a soldering iron. The sounds of the desert came to him. Trilling cicadas. The call of hidden birds. He recognised a few: cockatoos, fairy wrens, zebra finches.

God, it was beautiful. His heart swelled.

A breeze rustled the leaves of nearby bloodwood trees, their barks shining red in the fading light. Spellbound, he walked between the flowers and shrubs. He ran his palms over the soft tickle of blooms. A flock of budgerigars, chirping and squawking, flew overhead. He looked up but the birds were already gone. The stars were brighter still, turning above him in a mesmerising swirl.

He had always wanted to visit the most lonely areas of the outback. Now he was here. It was more amazing than he had ever imagined. He looked behind him. The desert landscape stretched away as far as he could see. A twinge of anxiety fluttered in his chest.

Where was his car?

He tried to remember. Had he driven here? Taken a bus, a plane? He looked down at himself. Barefoot, in tracksuit pants and t-shirt. What the hell was he doing here? Alone, no water, no food, no transport. He must be dreaming.

With effort, he wrenched open his eyes.

He was standing by the window in his kitchen. Snarling noises... Meredith. She had hold of his arm. Blood ran from bite marks on his left bicep. She sank her teeth into him again and shook her head like a terrier with a rat. He tried to cry out. The glittering stars overhead bore down. The desert soil felt as silky as talcum powder between his toes. He tried to run. To where, to where?

And what for?

He couldn't recall.

A couple of butterflies zigzagged past, twirling and wheeling together in an intricate dance through the blossoms. The breeze caressed his skin and made him drowsy. For a moment, he lost himself. He considered lying down amongst the wildflowers. The small, white petals of the grevillea plants smelled like honey and caramel. Yes, a nap would be perfect. He knelt down, stopped. A familiar riffle of anxiety had moved through him. Now he remembered: something was wrong. What was it? He looked about, saw his bare feet. Turned, realised there was no car. How had he got here? The honey and caramel scents made him so tired... No, wait, he was dreaming. He clenched his fists and willed his eyelids to open. The red and gold of the sunset flickered, stuttered.

Back in his kitchen, Meredith was gnawing at the crook of his elbow.

He swung his arm with all his strength. She fell away and skidded across the tiles in an ungainly scramble of long, emaciated limbs.

"What the fuck?" he shouted, gaping down at his torn and bleeding arm. The bite marks resembled pairs of waxing and waning moons, facing each other. "Jesus, Merry, what the actual *fuck*?"

She sat up, her face bloodied and tear-streaked. "We deserve to be together."

"Like a pair of zombies? You want me to be like you?"

"There's no other way. Please, John." She began to weep. "Please."

He ran to the kitchen sink. Turning on the taps full bore, he thrust his arm under the pummel of water. The run-off swirled red. Yet the wounds didn't hurt. This frightened him more than anything else. He remembered Meredith's account of Sebastian's attack: *You want to know the funny thing? It didn't hurt until the very last bite: the fifty-second bite. Then all the bites hurt at once, and they hurt like hell.*

How many times had she bitten him? He checked his injured arm. Seven. He checked his other arm. Nothing. He wrenched up the legs of his tracksuit pants. Nothing. Thank Christ. Only seven bites, not the dreaded fifty-two. He was safe, wasn't he? Or was he?

"Have you infected me?" he yelled. "Am I infected?"

Meredith, kneeling on the tiles, had both hands clasped together as if in prayer. "I'm trying to do what's best for us both," she said. "Try to understand. It's not so bad. I swear, John, I swear. It's not so bad."

"Fuck that. Get away from me."

He turned off the taps and grabbed the Dettol from the cupboard. Opening the cap, he held his arm in the sink and poured the whole bottle of antiseptic over his wounds, staining his skin dark brown. The Dettol didn't sting. Had her bite killed his nerve endings? He prodded at his torn flesh with a forefinger. Nothing.

"Why is it numb?" he said. "Why can't I feel anything?"

"It's the saliva. It has some kind of anaesthetic. At least, that's my theory. Like the bite from a leech."

He shuddered. Good God, a *leech*…

"Will my arm get better?" he said.

"Sure. No big deal."

Goddamn her flippant tone of voice, as if he were over-reacting, as if these bites were nothing to worry about. He grabbed a tea towel from the rail. Wrapping it around the wounds, he secured it with one of the rubber bands he kept in a jar by the fridge. The tea towel turned wet with blood.

Meredith got up from the floor. Gangly arms and gangly legs, face as sharp as a hatchet, dead-white skin. She had stopped crying. Her gaze was intent, unblinking, guarded. She lowered her head, tensed her shoulders. John grabbed the cleaver from the knife block and held it out.

"Really?" she said, and tutted. "Come on. Don't be so dramatic."

Her moods were changing so fast he couldn't keep track, couldn't predict her behaviour. He realised he was breathing fast and heavy. He was scared. Scared out of his mind. And angry, confused.

Meredith sat at the table. He put the cleaver on the bench.

"Pass me the smokes," he said.

"Fuck you."

"Chuck me the goddamned smokes."

She threw the packet. He caught it. She hurled the lighter at his head, and he caught that too. He lit a cigarette and took a beer from the fridge. The tea towel was soaked. He covered it with another tea towel, using a half-dozen rubber bands to keep the material in place. Maybe the rubber bands would staunch the bleeding. Maybe he needed medical help. Stitches. A tetanus shot. Meredith was an animal, wasn't she?

He drew on his cigarette. She regarded him, scowling, eyebrows knitted.

"Why did you bite me?" he said.

"I told you already. I'm not sharing you again."

"This is about Donna?"

Meredith curled her lip.

"You and me aren't an item," he said. "We have, literally, nothing to do with each other. And you're jealous? I don't get it. What do you care?"

"If I wouldn't share you with my own fucking brother, there's no way I'm sharing you with that dirty whore." She began to chuckle but it was a hollow, joyless sound. "Lyle thought he could win? Hah. Well, I sure taught him a lesson, didn't I? And I'll teach her too, if it comes to that, believe me."

John forgot about his arm and the beer. "What are you talking about?"

"Donna, naturally. Ugh, you're such a dickhead."

"No, I mean about Lyle."

"Huh?"

"You taught him a lesson. What lesson, Merry?"

She looked puzzled, lost, her face going slack. He thought she might slip away into a fugue state. But no. Her eyes narrowed in concentration, then opened so wide that the whites showed all the way around. She clapped a hand to her mouth.

"Oh, fuck," she said. "Oh, no."

"What is it? Tell me."

She put her hands in her hair. "I don't like this. I don't like remembering."

"Neither do I. Now tell me what you meant. How did you teach him a lesson?"

She shook her head, over and over. When she stopped at last, she gazed at John in wonder, as if seeing him for the first time. Then she began to laugh. It was a wild and crazy screeching, a cackling, like a witch. *Holy shit.* John's fingers inched across the bench towards the cleaver. Just in case, just in case.

Meredith gained control of herself. With a tilt of her chin, she glared at him with triumphant, glittering eyes.

"Sunday October 19th, 1985," she announced, "was my liberation day."

"What does that mean?"

"The day I freed myself from servitude. The day I won, and my brother lost."

"Go on," John said, his body breaking into a cold sweat. "Keep talking."

She put her heels on the chair and hugged her knees in both scarred arms. "After he beat me, he took his schoolbag and left to go to Aaron's house. It was my turn to have Mum's car that weekend." She sniggered. "Lyle was brave enough to bash the shit out of me, but not brave enough to go against Mum and Dad. If he'd taken the car, there'd have been hell to pay."

"When he left, what did you do?"

"For a while, I cried. Then I felt panicked. I had to reach you first, you see? Had to tell you my side of the story before Lyle got in your ear and twisted the facts around. So, I left the house and I drove and I drove and I drove..."

Smiling, she trailed off, gazing blindly into the mid-distance at nothing, as if watching an invisible movie-reel of memories spooling inside her mind.

"Where did you go?" he said.

"To find you."

"And where was I?"

"Fishing, of course."

John's legs trembled. Leaning against the bench, he felt his way to the table and sat down opposite her. His cigarette had gone out. He dropped it into the ashtray and lit another.

"You'd told me about that spot in the Yarra Ranges, near Warburton," she said, "and how it was great for trout. You showed me on the map, remember? Marked it out in my Melways with a little x." She giggled. "X marks the spot."

He nodded.

It came back to him.

One weekend, he had caught so many fish that he had brought a couple of fat rainbow trout to the Berg-Olsen's house. Mrs Berg-Olsen had fussed and made a show of going through her cookbooks for trout recipes—in fact, he could recall the recipe she had chosen, a dish with flaked almonds—while Mr Berg-Olsen had talked about big game fishing and how he had once caught a marlin off the shores of Cairns in Queensland. I belong here, John had thought. These people are like family. Lyle had picked up a fish and wobbled its dead head at Meredith, saying in a high-pitched voice, "Give us a smooch, sweetheart!" and Merry had rolled her eyes and said, "Piss off," which made everyone laugh, including John. He had caught Merry's eye. They'd kissed for the first time at the bonfire party a few weeks before, made out a few times since. Once Mrs Berg-Olsen had decided on the trout recipe, Merry had brought him a pencil and the Melways map book and asked him to show the fishing spot.

X marks the spot...

It was a warm and pleasant memory. One of the few that didn't hurt.

He had a feeling that was about to change.

"Stop," he said. "I don't want to hear any more."

There was a pain in his chest. Was he having a heart attack? He sucked hard on the cigarette and coughed. God, he should never have left Devonport. The carpet factory had closed down—so what? There would have been other job opportunities for an unskilled labourer such as himself, a position on the docks, perhaps. He had his forklift license. Why had he turned his back on the security of that Tasmanian town? To get away from Cheryl, the only girlfriend he'd ever had apart from Meredith? Was Cheryl the reason? Or had he come back in the hope of finding Meredith, of picking up where they had left off?

"I feel pretty rotten," John muttered. "I'd better call an ambulance."

Now, he reached for the mobile in his pocket. It wasn't there. It must be in his room, perhaps on the bedside table. He didn't know if he had the strength to get up. The chest pains scared him. He felt clammy, dizzy, unable to catch his breath.

"Don't you want to hear the rest of my story?" Meredith said.

"No."

"But you'll like it, John, I promise. It's a good story."

He shook his head.

"I drove and I drove and I drove," she said. "On a winding road with trees on both sides, I saw your car up ahead. Can you believe it? Your dad's Commodore. There was another car between us, but on the bends, I could see the back of your head and the back of Lyle's." Meredith frowned and bit at a bloodied cuticle. "I thought I was too late. That he was already spilling his guts to you. I've never been so mad."

"Don't," John said. "No more."

"You took the turnoffs to the river. I parked back in the trees and walked the rest of the way. I spied on you both, saw your stupid argument, saw you hit him, saw him fall."

John clutched at his chest.

"You drove away," she said. "Then I did what I had to do. What I'd wanted to do for such a long, long time."

There was colour in her pallid cheeks, a rare flush of blood. Unshed tears stood in her eyes. Her expression spoke of regret and shame. But only for a second. She smirked and began to tap her long, manicured fingers on the table top.

"You killed him," John said.

"Damn right, I did."

John swallowed. A thudding pulse started up in his guts somewhere. "You picked up a rock and smashed in his skull."

"Yep."

John put his face in his hands. He was falling head-first into a yawning chasm, a dark and bottomless pit. This is where I lose my mind, he thought. He only had to resign himself, give up, and keep falling.

Instead, he looked at Meredith.

Pensive, she was gnawing on the inside of her cheek.

"Was he conscious?" he said. "Was Lyle awake when you killed him?"

"Groggy, but awake. Lying on his back, but half-raised on his elbows. I asked him if he'd told you about us, about our 'Like-Unlike' game. He told me you'd knocked him out before he'd had the chance." She giggled. "I kicked him in the ribs. He rolled onto his stomach. I grabbed a rock. You want to know his last words?"

Nauseated, John shook his head.

"What the fuck do you think you're doing, bitch?"

19

Every muscle in John's body quivered. His bare heels jittered against the kitchen tiles.

"For thirty-one years," he said, his voice a hoarse croak, "I thought I'd done it."

Meredith lit a cigarette. "I'm not the villain. Lyle wrecked both of our lives, and his own too."

Groaning, breaking down and weeping, John dug his fingers into his chest. His heart cramped like a charley horse. He could picture the cardiac tissue withering and turning grey. It was for the best. Death—oblivion—wouldn't be so bad, would have to be better than this living nightmare.

"You buried him, didn't you?" she said.

"What?"

"Up there in the Yarra Ranges. You dug a hole and buried him. Right?"

He took a last drag of his cigarette and dropped it into the ashtray.

"No one ever found his body," she went on. "You must have buried him."

"I'm calling an ambulance. This is a heart attack."

She reached out and laid her hand on his. "A few more bites, John, and you won't have to worry about shit like that."

"Don't touch me." He pulled away. "Wait, are you saying you can't die?"

"Well, not from a heart attack, at least."

"Why not?"

She winked and offered a coy smile.

It came to him in a rush. Feeling sick, he said, "I know why."

"Enlighten me."

"Because you don't have a beating heart. It stopped beating when Sebastian bit you that fifty-second time. Am I right?"

She crossed her arms. "Fuck you."

"I need my phone," he said, and found he couldn't stand. "I think it's in my room. Get me the phone."

"Get it yourself."

"I don't understand you, Merry. I don't understand you one bit."

"For fuck's sake, dopey, it's a panic attack. Breathe into a paper bag."

Tap, tap, tap.

The knock at the front door jolted them both. Frantic, John checked his watch.

Oh, no.

Donna.

She had finished her two hours at The Brunch Corner and had returned to speak with him about Tiger, the anonymous notes, the waggle-tongued witch. He had a wild desire to run through the back yard and jump the fence.

"Tell the dirty whore to fuck off," Meredith said.

"Hey, I've got to handle this Donna situation with care, don't you get it? Jesus, she wants to call the police because of you."

"Let her, I don't give a damn."

Adrenaline strengthened his legs. He stood, clattering the chair, wiping the tears from his cheeks. Shit, he couldn't talk to Donna *now*. He was a sweating, gibbering mess. "Okay, give me a second," he said. "I'll turn her away. Hurry up, Merry. Get to your room."

She sneered and wouldn't budge. Shocked, he could only gape at her. She made a show of studying her fingernails.

"What if Donna happens to see you?" he said. "Quick. Get going."

She poked out her tongue.

Tap, tap, tap.

"You will go to your fucking room," he said, grabbing her arm. "Right now."

He dragged her through the kitchen, down the hallway, and shoved her into her bedroom. Rubbing her wrist, she glowered at him, teeth bared.

"Don't come out," he whispered. "You hear me?"

She flipped her middle finger.

He closed the bedroom door, gently, in case the sound might carry. Donna knocked again, louder this time. John smoothed his hair, straightened the waistband of his tracksuit pants, arranged his face into what he hoped resembled a mild and neutral expression, and opened the door.

Donna's jaw dropped in alarm.

"Good Lord!" she said.

"Huh?"

"Your *arm*."

With a sinking feeling, he looked down at his bicep, at the bloodied tea towels secured with rubber bands. Oh, fuck. That's the problem when you don't feel pain, he thought. You forget about injuries. But he should have remembered this one.

Donna clapped both hands to her cheeks. "What the hell happened?"

"What happened? Well, it's a long story…"

He ducked the couple of metres down the hallway to the linen cupboard and took out a bath towel. As he wrapped it around his arm, the front door clicked shut. He spun around. Uh-oh. Donna had come inside. He hadn't figured on that. He figured she would have stayed on the porch. Meredith's doorknob didn't move, thank Christ. Stay in your room, he silently begged. Please.

"Listen, Donna, this is a bad time," he said.

"Where's your first aid kit?"

"I don't think I've got one. Can we have this conversation later?"

Donna took him by the elbow and walked him down the hallway and into the kitchen. There, she began opening and closing cupboards, hunting for the non-existent first aid kit. At least his chest pain had gone. Maybe it had been a panic attack after all. Shaking, he lit a cigarette.

"Hey, I should go to the doctor's," he said. "I'll drop in afterwards, okay?"

"Tell me what happened to your arm."

He went to answer. Nothing came to mind. Momentary panic. Usually, a lie popped out of its own accord. How could he explain an injury like this? So much blood…

"I was…" he began, "mowing the lawns…"

"You did that on Monday."

"Yeah, okay. I was changing the mower blades, and I…"

Christ, why couldn't he think of anything to say? Donna paused, closed the cupboard doors, and turned to face him. Hot beads of sweat were running down his forehead, he could feel them. A big, fat drip gathered at the tip of his nose. As nonchalantly as he could, he wiped it away.

"You were changing blades," she said, "while the mower was running?"

"Of course not."

"So, you missed the mower and shoved the blades into your arm?"

Oh, he recognised that look she was giving him. If you're with a woman long enough, any woman, she will eventually give you the look which says: *one more false move, buddy, and you're falling straight through the ice.*

"Okay," he said. "I'll tell you the truth. I just didn't want to scare you."

"Scare me? About what?"

"Considering Tiger is missing…"

She flinched. Good. He was on firmer ground already.

"It was a dog," he said. "Some kind of big bastard, like a pit bull. I was in the front yard, and it bit me."

"It bit you?"

"Yeah." He indicated his bicep, clamped against his body to keep the towel in place. "Right here."

"And what were you doing in your front yard?"

"Huh?"

"What were you doing when the dog bit you?"

Wait a second. Donna had that look again. He felt a fresh prickle of sweat in his hairline. Stalling, he sat at the table and worked on his cigarette.

"Gee," he said. "Thanks for your concern."

"Were you changing the mower blades?" she said. "Is that what you were doing in your front yard when this dog bit you?"

The question was a trap. He could see it in her eyes. There was only one correct answer—*yes* or *no*—but he wasn't sure which one it could be.

"Well?" she said.

He took a punt.

"Yeah, I was changing the mower blades. And then, out of nowhere, this bloody big bastard of a pit bull—maybe it was a Rhodesian Ridgeback, it had these stripes on its back—this big bastard comes racing along the—"

"Stop."

He dragged on his smoke, tried to smile. "What?"

She put her hands on her hips.

"Anyway," he continued, "it latched onto my arm—"

"You're a liar, John. A born liar."

He wiped perspiration from his forehead. "What are you talking about?"

"A natural born liar." She pressed her lips together. "From the get-go, something felt a little off about you. Oh, I tried to ignore it because I fancied you. Desperation, probably. I hadn't been laid in a while. But the signs were there. And, by the way, you squint whenever you spout a line of bullshit."

"Wait, what, I squint?"

She wagged a finger. "This isn't my first rodeo, mate. I've been with bullshit artists before. My ex-husband, Graeme, was the king of bullshit artists. You're not even close to his level of expertise."

"This is crazy."

"You don't have any kids, do you? Grown or otherwise?"

That took him by surprise. He tried to snort out a derisive laugh and coughed.

"What are their names?" she said. "I'll give you a clue: they're both daughters."

Frozen, he stared at her.

"Okay, here's an easy one," she continued. "What's your grandson called?"

Damn it. Her eyes bored into him.

"Well?" she said.

Finally, he muttered, "Jake."

"Close, but no kewpie doll, thanks for playing. It's *Jack*, you arsehole. Your make-believe grandson is called Jack."

"Yeah, nah, but we call him Jake too."

"Oh, man. What a piece of work you are."

A headache clamped his skull. He pinched at the bridge of his nose.

"I've got no idea of the kind of person you really are, mate," she went on, "but you know what? I don't even care. And I don't care what happened to your arm, either. Keep your dumb secrets. You're nothing to me, understand? We're finished. If you see me on the street, don't bother to wave. Look the other way." She jabbed a finger close to his face. "And you keep away from my daughter," she hissed. "Is that clear? Or so help me God, I'll fuck you up."

"Look, I can explain—"

"With more lies?"

"No," he said, feeling weak, beaten down and defeated with nothing left to lose. "I'm ready to tell you the whole goddamned thing, I swear."

Maybe Donna would understand. If he laid it out, fact by awful fact, she might see the situation through his eyes and understand. Confession. Yes, he would confess. It would feel like lancing an abscess. Corruption and pus filled his soul, and he just had to...he only had to *tell* somebody, somebody who cared—

"One last thing," Donna said. "Where's Tiger?"

John's breath caught. "What?"

"You heard me. Where's my fucking cat?"

In the spare room, he wanted to say, in the big silver pot I use to cook pasta and corned beef. Your cat is beheaded, skinned, disembowelled, half-eaten. I can give you his tail to hang from your rear-view mirror as a good luck charm. The gallows humour made him groan. His cigarette had burnt down to the butt. He shook out a fresh smoke and lit it from the ember.

"Well?" she said. "I thought you were ready to tell me the truth."

"Yeah, but...only from the start. If I tell it out of order—"

She slapped the cigarette from his mouth. It landed in a brief shower of sparks on the tiles, bouncing twice. He stared at it in disbelief.

"Tell me what you did to my cat."

He looked at her, his eyes wet with fresh tears. "Jesus, you think *I* hurt him?"

"I think you know what happened."

"No, come on. I wouldn't hurt Tiger. I love animals."

"Give it a rest. You hated Tiger. You couldn't stand being on the same couch. Where is he? My little girl is breaking her heart. Answer me. Answer me right now."

John shook his head. Sweat trickled down the small of his back and gathered in the band of his tracksuit pants.

"You wrote those notes, didn't you?" she said.

He gaped at her, speechless.

"Don't give me that innocent look. You kidnapped my cat. You wrote those notes and pushed them under my door to scare me. *Keep your hands to yourself. You are a dirty whore.* What was the plan, John? To control me through fear?"

"No. Jesus, no, I didn't—"

"I've read about sick fuckers like you."

"Read about...? I don't know what—"

"Fuckers like you make up a stalker to force a woman to want your protection. Pretty soon, she can't even take a crap without checking in first with her guardian." She leaned over him, eyes flashing. "Well, to hell with you, John Penrose, if that's even your real name. I'm wise to your bullshit."

He put his hands to his temples and squeezed. "No. That's not what happened."

"Where's my cat?"

"Please, you have to believe me."

"Tell me where he is."

John clenched his jaw and closed his eyes. His breath came shallow, ragged. The chest pain returned. Good, he thought. Let me die of a heart attack. After a time, he realised that Donna had fallen quiet. Uneasily, he opened his eyes. She was staring at him, face stony, her arms crossed.

"We're done here," she said. "Expect a visit from the cops, arsehole."

"Donna, please. Wait. I can explain."

Her boots stamped across the tiles. When she turned down the hallway, a door creaked on its hinges.

Oh, no.

John leapt to his feet.

Donna screamed. Rigid, she backed at speed into the kitchen.

A few seconds later, Meredith sauntered to the doorway and paused there, grinning, admiring her captive audience.

There was blood smeared over her teeth, her face, her hands, through the wild and crazy tufts of her hair. She must have sneaked into the hobby room while Donna and I were arguing, John thought, and further desecrated Tiger's poor, wretched body in order to put on this freak show.

The breath left him.

For the first time, he saw Merry as a stranger would see her.

As Donna must see her.

A skeleton with mummified and papery skin, an undead thing with sunken eyes that glinted with an eerie, supernatural sheen. This monster wasn't Meredith Berg-Olsen. A creeping horror tightened his flesh into goosebumps. No, Meredith Berg-Olsen had died a long time ago. On the fifty-second bite.

Donna backed up until she hit the sink.

"It's the witch," she gasped. "Do something! How did she get in? For God's sake, it's the witch!"

"And you're the dirty whore," Meredith said. "Nice to meet you. Strictly speaking, we've already met. You opened your bedroom curtains and told me, if I recall correctly, to fuck off."

Donna blanched. "You're the one who wrote those awful notes."

"Awful? No, just a couple of pleasant warnings, that's all, from one woman to another." Meredith stretched her lips across her teeth. "Stay away from John."

"John?" Donna rocked on her heels. "Don't tell me you know this woman?"

"Better than that," Meredith said. "I've been his de facto for close to a decade."

"De facto...?"

"That's not true," John said. "Look, I knew her from high school. She got sick, lived on the streets. I've been looking after her. Taking care of her. Out of mercy."

"See?" Meredith said. "He's quite the hero. Did he tell you I killed your cat?"

Laughing, she waggled her tongue and slurped at the palm of one gory hand. John felt pinned, unable to move. If only he could have told Donna everything in the strict order of events, from the beginning, she would have understood.

Donna lifted a trembling finger. "Is that...is that Tiger's blood?"

"Yes, and it's delicious. Tell her, John. Go ahead and tell your dirty whore what happened to her cat. I'm sure she'll forgive you once you explain the circumstances. Or shall I bring out the silver pot and show her the remains?"

Stiffly, eyes bulging with fear, Donna turned towards him. He could see dozens of micro-expressions flitting across her face as her mind worked to put the pieces of this bizarre and unexpected puzzle together. Please, he wanted to say. I never meant to hurt you. We could have been a family: you and me, Cassie, Tiger—

The flash of raw hatred in her eyes tore at his heart.

Too late, too late. He'd had a chance at love and Merry had ruined it for him. The fucking *bitch*. His vision misted red. Nate's words came to mind—*forget about Meredith, all right? Donna is your future*—as he launched himself across the room.

Ducking his head like a rugby player, he slammed into Meredith's mid-section, his impetus carrying them both through the plasterboard of the hallway. Merry's spine hit a stud and her bones pop, pop, popped.

Dimly, somewhere outside of the red mist, he could hear Donna screaming.

He found his feet and grabbed Merry by the arms. She weighed next to nothing. He pulled her out of the smashed hole in the plasterboard and, as hard as he could, hurled her at the kitchen table. She hit it like a broken marionette, limbs sprawling at impossible angles, dislocating, joints folding back on themselves. The table fell, pinning her at the hips. He leapt upon her, shoved the table aside, and put his hands around her throat, closing his fists, crushing her windpipe. Yes, yes, he could feel the cartilage crumpling, grinding and cracking, splitting. And yet...

Her *eyes*.

Shock cleared the red mist.

Merry's eyes were two intense and flaming coals. And she was laughing. Christ, she was somehow laughing while he was choking the life out of her.

She doubled up a spindly leg and kicked him flying across the room. He bounced off the kitchen bench. Agony shot through his elbow. Dazed and winded, he slumped to the floor. Who was screaming? He could hear screaming. He struggled to sit up. Donna was still backed against the kitchen sink.

"Look out!" she screamed.

Where was Meredith?

A movement overhead caught his eye. He glanced up. Meredith had the microwave in both hands. She brought it down on his head.

White kitchen tiles.

Shards of plastic and metal.

The microwave nearby, wrecked.

And blood. Spots and splashes of it everywhere.

John blinked.

Pain.

Oh, shit, so much pain. He reached up and touched his scalp. Wet. His fingers slipped into a gaping tear in his hairline. What the fuck? He looked at his hand. Bloody. He tried to move. *Ow.* What had happened?

Exhausted, he closed his eyes.

Whimpering sounds tugged at his attention.

"Hello?" he said, lifting his head.

The kitchen looked as if a cyclone had torn through it. The table and chairs lay scattered. Everything from the benches—the toaster, kettle, draining rack, knife block—strewn about, broken crockery from one side of the room to the other. A cool breeze fanned in through the shattered window. A jet of someone's blood—his own?—had sprayed over the wall. The faint whimpering sounds continued.

John struggled to sit up. Out of the corner of his eye, he saw a foot.

Bony, as white as wax, the skinny toes like talons.

"Merry?" he said.

He leaned on his arm, trying to turn, and winced at the shooting pain in his elbow. Gingerly, he got to his knees and shuffled to face her. Meredith lay on her back, limbs sprawled in awkward postures, motionless.

"Merry, are you awake?"

It came back to him in a rush. Meredith confronting Donna. His fight with Meredith. Getting cracked over the head with the goddamned microwave. Christ, she could have killed him. He would have to be careful. Slowly, he crawled towards her.

There was blood on her throat and t-shirt, blood on the floor in a halo around her, great gouts of it. At least, he figured the liquid must be blood, yet it was unnaturally thick and dark, like molasses, and its rank and mouldy smell reminded him of a stagnant pond. He shuddered.

"Merry?"

She didn't respond. John's heart boomed. He crawled as close to her as he could, being careful to avoid the puddle of blood, and reached out, grabbed her by the hair. Merry's head bobbled without resistance, as if barely tethered to her body. Uh-oh. Carefully, he tipped her head back, and gasped.

The laceration across her throat yawned open. Muscle, tendon, windpipe, the exposed tissues a pale, cooked-mutton brown.

Dry heaving, he let go and scooted backwards across the tiles until he hit the wall and could retreat no further.

Meredith was dead.

Not undead-dead, not zombie- or vampire-dead, but honest to God *dead*.

He couldn't remember doing it. Next to her body was the cleaver, the same knife he had taken earlier from the block and laid on the bench, just in case. After she had smashed the microwave over his head, John must have...what? Rallied...how? Snatched up the cleaver and... Yeah, well, who could blame him? Theirs had been a fight to the death. He waited to feel grief, remorse. Instead, he felt nothing.

Now what?

Well, shit, he had to figure out how to dispose of the body.

That's when he realised he could still hear whimpering.

And since it wasn't coming from Meredith... Oh, Jesus. The whimpering was coming from the other side of the kitchen bench.

Oh, no.

No, no, no, no, no, no, no, no, no, no—

"Donna?" he said. "Is that you?"

The whimpering continued. He jumped to his feet, swooned, and almost fell. The head injury, shit, maybe his skull was fractured. Stepping over Meredith's corpse, wincing as his feet crunched over broken ceramic, he approached the bench. Then stopped. Unable go any further. He couldn't bear to look.

The whimpering went on and on.

Faltering, legs trembling, he tried again to walk around the end of the bench. Found that he still couldn't move. Fuck. Donna needs you, he told himself. Man up. Help her. Taking a breath, he stepped around the bench.

And screamed.

20

Donna sat on the kitchen floor, curled up with her knees at her chest, cowering, face pressed against the cupboard doors, naked except for her underwear, her bare arms and legs streaming with blood.

John dropped down beside her.

"Let me see," he said. "How many times did she bite you? How many?"

When he hauled Donna from her crouched position, she moaned and her eyes rolled as if she were close to losing consciousness. As if she were entering some kind of fugue state. *Oh, no, no, no—*

"Donna, can you hear me? It's John. Say something."

Her eyes focused on him and opened wide in terror. Her mouth dropped as if preparing to let out a long, loud shriek. Panicked, John put his forefinger to her lips and shushed her. She recoiled and began whimpering again. God, how much had the neighbours heard already? What if somebody had called the cops?

"It's all right," he whispered, fast and urgent, "everything's going to be okay. I'm not going to hurt you. Donna, please, I'm here to help you. Can you hear me?"

She gaped at him for a few seconds and nodded.

"Let me see your arms," he said.

Shaking, she held them out. And there was the characteristic wound pattern, waxing and waning moons facing each other, in a long column down the inside of both her arms. He wiped sweat and blood from his eyes, grabbed her left arm to begin, and tried to count the wounds. One, two, three—

"She bit you too, didn't she?" Donna said, teeth chattering.

"Yeah."

Four, five, six—

"On the arm."

"Yeah."

Seven, eight—

"Not mower blades, not a dog. The witch."

"Yeah."

Nine, ten, eleven—

"Is she dead?" Donna said.

"And then some. Her head is virtually cut off."

Damn, he'd lost count. Okay, start over. One, two, three, four—

"I had to do it," Donna said.

"What?"

"I *had* to do it."

He sat back on his heels. "*You* killed Meredith?"

"She came at me like an animal," Donna said. "How could a skinny old lady be so strong?"

Because she wasn't human.

"She ripped off my clothes and started biting me." Donna's wild eyes filled with tears. "And I saw strange things, weird things."

He held his breath. "You were in the outback?"

"No, on a boat. A huge, beautiful boat with white sails, some kind of yacht. The ocean was deep blue; nearly purple." Her gaze became faraway. "The sun shone. I could smell salt on the wind. And dolphins were jumping ahead of the boat." She closed her eyes. Tears coursed down her cheeks. "I felt happy. Blessed."

"What snapped you out of it?"

"I looked around for Cassie and she wasn't there. Nobody was there. I was the only one on deck. How the hell am I on a fucking boat in the middle of nowhere? I can't even steer a rowboat for the life of me."

"So, you woke up."

"Yeah. To the witch biting me. I went ballistic."

John tried to smile. "I can tell. The kitchen's a mess."

"I'm a mother, John. I'm a fucking mother. I've got my little girl to think about. I wasn't about to let that witch kill me, no way, no chance."

Meredith wasn't trying to kill you, he thought, but *change* you so we couldn't be together. Gently, he took hold of her wrist and straightened out her arm.

"I need to count the bite marks," he said. "It's important."

One, two, three, four, five, six—

"Somehow, I got the big knife," she said. "Back in high school, I used to play softball. And I was good at it, too. The lead-off batter. I swung that knife like hitting a fastball. The power comes up from the legs and into the hips. Through the twist of the hips and into the arm, like a boxer throwing a punch. I slashed her. Just once. You know what it sounded like when I cut her throat?"

"Be quiet. I'm trying to count."

"Like cutting into a pumpkin." Donna's breath seesawed into a giggle. "A giant, woody pumpkin." She shivered. "And her head fell back on her neck. It took her a second to start bleeding. You know what I saw in that second? Up inside her windpipe. It looked like a yellow hose. I've never seen inside anyone's body before. Her blood was black, John. Why would it be black?"

"Shut up for a minute."

She pushed him away and struggled to stand, gripping the cupboard handles, the benchtop.

"What are you doing?" he said. "I'm still counting the bite marks."

"We have to call the police."

"What? No."

"Where's your phone?"

He got up. "Are you insane? You'll go to prison."

"For self-defence?"

Involving the law would unravel the whole sordid mess, all the way back to Lyle's disappearance. John couldn't let that happen. Not under any circumstances. Not even for Donna. For the first time in a long time, he saw a glimmer of hope, a way out, and he intended to grab hold of it with both hands.

"Stop and think," he said, and spread his arms to indicate the gore and chaos of the kitchen. "How is this going to look to the cops?"

"Huh? No, we only have to explain—"

"You'll lose custody of Cassie."

"Lose custody? But I—"

"At least during the investigation. Maybe permanently. Graeme could petition the court. And he could win. I mean, why not? Jesus, you murdered somebody."

"Self-defence!" Donna cried in anguish. "It was self-defence."

"You reckon the Family Court will give a stuff about minor details? You killed someone, slashed their throat. An old lady, too. Almost cut her goddamned head off."

"She attacked *me*. Surely, the judge would—"

"For Christ's sake, don't kid yourself. Use common sense. Can you see the Family Court granting a killer, a savage killer, custody of a child? You'd be lucky if they allowed you custody of a ten-cent goldfish."

She gaped at him. "I can't lose Cassie."

"Exactly."

"She's my whole world."

"I know. That's why we have to avoid the cops."

Donna put both hands to her mouth. She appeared young and scared. "But what...what are we...what are we going to..."

He looked around at the floor. When he finally spotted her flannelette shirt, he picked it up and put it over her shoulders. She grabbed at the collar, trembling. Next, he righted a chair and sat her down. Finding his cigarettes and lighter amongst the debris took some time. He lit a smoke, righted another chair, and sat opposite her.

"First things first," he said. "Call Graeme. Tell him you're sick. Tell him to pick up Cassie from school and keep her overnight."

"How come?"

"We need time to sort out this shit."

"You've got a plan?"

"It's coming together, yeah," he said. "You clean up the kitchen and clean it up good. Mop the floors, the walls, the ceiling if you have to, okay? Straighten everything. The room has to pass inspection with a real estate agent on Friday."

"What about the broken window?"

"Don't worry about that. I'll arrange for it to be replaced tomorrow. The cleaning products are in the laundry. When you're done, throw the mop-head, sponges, rags, anything you've used into the bin. I'll dump it at the tip."

"Uh-huh, okay."

She was coming out of shock, he could see it on her face, in her eyes; could see her mind working again. He went and took a beer from the fridge.

"Want a stubby?" he said.

"Yes, please."

They drank in silence. At least her bleeding had stopped. The bites must have been shallow. Was that a good thing? Did the depth of the bites matter? John wasn't sure how the infection process worked. But Donna seemed okay. That was a good thing, surely?

Her gaze slid across the floor to Meredith's body.

"What about the witch?" she said.

"Let me worry about that. While you're cleaning up, I'll get rid of her."

"How?"

"The less you know the better." He drew hard on the cigarette. To his surprise, his hands weren't shaking. "Are you right to call Graeme?"

"I think so."

"Maybe you should text him instead. You can't sound scared or crazy. If he suspects anything—"

"No, I'm fine."

She retrieved her jeans from the floor by the hallway. When she sat down again, she smiled stiffly and took her phone from one of the pockets.

"Are you sure?" John said, muscles tense. "Don't bullshit me. You can do it?"

She nodded, pressed a few buttons on her phone, and waited.

John watched her carefully, sweat gathering in his armpits.

She sat up straight and put on a smile. "Graeme? Hi. Look, I've come down with gastro... Yeah, I know... The poached eggs at the café, probably... I've caught the cook before drying batch after batch with the same tea towel... Ugh, tell me about it... No, the Health Department might shut them down... Hey, it's a good job... Graeme, listen, I didn't ring to argue... Can you pick up Cassie today, have her sleep over tonight? I don't want her getting sick. She's got an excursion to the zoo on Friday, and she's really looking forward to it... Oh, that's great... Yeah, three-thirty. Fantastic, thanks so much... Bye." She hung up and looked at John. "How was that?"

He made the OK sign with thumb and forefinger.

Tears filled her eyes. "I don't understand what the fuck is going on here."

"Relax, I'll explain everything later."

"You're not going to...John, you're not going to hurt me, are you?"

He took her hands. "Trust me. I'll get us out of this shit. Do you trust me?"

"I don't have any choice."

She pulled away, stood, went to a cupboard and brought down packets of sticking plasters and adhesive dressings.

"When did you find those?" he said.

"While hunting for a first aid kit. Get cleaned up. You'll need to leave the house to get rid of her body, won't you? You can't go out looking like that. It's not Halloween. Don't worry about me. I'll dress my own wounds."

"Yeah but count them first."

"Why?"

"Jesus, like I keep saying, I'll tell you later. Let's get the business done before we start yakking and lounging about with our feet up."

"Can't you tell me quick?"

"No, I can't. It's...complicated."

He went and grabbed the doona from Meredith's bed and returned to the kitchen. Donna stopped fussing with the dressings to watch, eyes wide. He spread the doona on the floor by the window, where there was glass but no blood spatter, and approached Meredith's body. He felt a strange kind of peace, an exciting, giddy sensation that prickled the hairs on the nape of his neck. I have atoned, he thought, for everything I did—and wrongly believed that I did—to you and Lyle.

My penance is over.

The halo of blood had dried, formed a skin, and stuck her corpse fast to the floor. John gagged at the slurping sound as he dragged her by the ankles out of the black puddle. Her head rolled and lolled on her split neck. Jesus. Okay, next, to get her onto the doona, he had to pick her up.

Fuck.

He held his breath against the smell of mould and lifted her by the waist and legs to avoid touching that dark, viscous blood. Her head dangled at an unnatural angle. In his arms, Merry felt as light as a bundle of sticks. How the fuck did she kick him clear across the room? But this was no time for pondering and philosophising. He laid her on the doona and rolled her up. I'm like a gangster in a movie, he thought, except I didn't use a rug.

"There's duct tape in the drawer, second from the bottom," he said.

Donna brought it over. John wrapped the tape once, twice around the head area and once, twice around the feet.

"All right," he said, panting. "I'm off to clean up. Then I'll put her in the boot of my car. I'll be gone for a few hours, at least, maybe until evening. Don't leave. Don't put on any lights. Don't make any calls. If the phone rings or someone knocks, don't answer."

"Okay," she said.

"This is really important."

"Yes, I know."

"Because if anyone gets wind of what's going on—"

"Yes, yes, for fuck's sake, I know. Stop harping."

He went to his room. Looking in the mirror gave him a fright. So much blood! He tipped his head forward to inspect the scalp wound in the reflection. Long and ragged, seeping. Now what? He got an idea. Not a great idea, but better than nothing.

Rummaging through a drawer in his bedside table, he pushed aside envelopes, paper, pens, postage stamps, tape, paperclips. He took out the stapler and checked it. Full of staples. Returning to the mirror, he pulled the lips of the wound together with one hand and pressed the stapler into his scalp with the other, again and again and again and again, until he had closed the cut. Doing so had hardly hurt at all.

He unwrapped the blood-soaked tea towels from his bicep and inspected the wounds. They had stopped bleeding. And seemed to be healing already. Another magical property in Meredith's saliva besides the anaesthetic? Even so, the skin around the bites was turning purple. Bruised, even while the broken skin repaired itself at the rate of knots. Creepy.

After showering, he dressed in jeans and a short-sleeved shirt, heavy boots. Rolling his balaclava into a beanie, he pulled it down over his scalp to hide the staples. He inspected himself in the mirror. Perfectly normal...except for that psycho look in his eyes. Maybe he should wear sunglasses.

He went to the kitchen. Donna, wearing her jeans and torn flannelette shirt, was dropping shards of crockery into the bin.

"Did you count the bite marks?" he said.

She turned, her face red and blotchy from crying. "Forty-something."

"Forty-something?" For a moment, he felt relieved. No, come on, forty-something is vague and close to fifty-two. "Don't tell me you guessed," he said. "How many exactly?"

"Oh, for fuck's sake," she said, weeping afresh.

"Forget it. I'll count them myself when I get back."

The sticking plasters and adhesive dressings sat on the bench. He took a few minutes to carefully and thoroughly dress his arm. No doubt, the exertion he was about to undertake would open the wounds and start them bleeding again. When he finished, he surveyed his handiwork. Too conspicuous. He went to his room and changed into a long-sleeved shirt so the dressings wouldn't show.

"What's taking you so long?" Donna called.

"I'm getting ready," he shouted. "Hey, back off. I'm the one with the plan."

"Will you call me? Text me when you're done?"

"No," he said, exiting his room. "No digital trail. Don't call or text me either, no matter what happens. I'm turning off my phone."

"But how long will you be?"

"I told you, I don't know for sure. Three or four hours. Could be longer."

He hurried down the hall, grabbed the keys from the hook, and went out the front door. The day was overcast, the light a dull grey, the sky threatening showers. He reversed his sedan through the carport and around into the back yard. Parking, he popped the boot. He alighted, took a pickaxe and a shovel from the lock-up shed in the carport, and dropped them in the boot. A battery-powered lantern, to be on the safe side. A sledgehammer. He opened the laundry door and stepped inside. Donna had the mop and bucket. The house smelled of disinfectant already.

"You right?" he said.

She nodded, her face strained. "You?"

"As rain."

Hefting the rolled-up doona onto his shoulder, he took it outside and dropped it into the boot. And this is how it ends, he thought. A stray memory caught him by surprise: the patio of the Berg-Olsen house, summer, the dead of night, Lyle snoring in the rumpus room, John sitting at the outdoor table in his footy shorts having a smoke, and Merry standing at the door in baby-doll pyjamas, her hair mussed. Her first words to him: *Got a spare durry?*

He brushed away tears and stared into the boot. Did he have everything he needed? He ran into the house and took a six-pack. From experience, he knew that digging a grave was thirsty work.

"Please call me when you're done," Donna said.

"No. What for?"

"To let me know everything is okay. That you're coming back." Her teeth were clenched, the cords standing out on her throat. "What if the police pull you over for speeding? Or someone sees you getting rid of her? What if you have a prang?"

"I'll be back, don't worry. No phone calls. No texts."

"John—"

"Be strong. Think of Cassie."

She dropped her head, nodded weakly, hiccupped on a sob.

"Clean the kitchen," he said. "Spotless, okay? Don't call or text me or anybody else. Don't leave. Don't answer the phone or the door. And if I'm not back by sun-down, remember, don't turn on any lights. Promise?"

"Promise."

He smiled with one side of his mouth. "We'll be fine. Cross my heart."

"And hope to die?" She didn't smile back.

John drove towards Warburton. He knew the route by heart. Tension gripped his shoulders. Perhaps his fishing spot would be a 7-Eleven by now, or a petrol station; a collection of two-storey townhouses with rooms so small you couldn't swing a cat—

(...*Oh God, Tiger, I'm so sorry...*)

—or maybe it would still be his isolated little patch of river, untouched.

Why the compulsion to return to the same fishing spot? He didn't know, but it felt right somehow. The twins ought to be together. John had buried one and now he must bury the other. But could he find Lyle's grave? The location was thirty-one years in the past. He had dragged Lyle for about fifteen minutes uphill from the river. The shrubs and trees had been close together, the ground a carpet of leaf litter, every part of the forest looking the same. To find the grave seemed an impossible task.

Yet it seemed important to try.

The further east he travelled, the lighter the traffic. By the time the road climbed and dwindled to a single lane each way, there were only two vehicles in front of him—a ute and a station wagon—and none behind. The road began to wind.

Bump, bump.

John's heart gave a kick. What the fuck was that? The sound had come from the boot. He snapped off the radio and took another curve.

Bump, bump.

Yes, the noise was definitely coming from the boot.

Bump, bump.

Gooseflesh rose on his forearms. Could Merry be...alive?

No, out of the question. Ludicrous. She had been more or less decapitated. No matter what kind of monster she happened to be, nothing in this world could survive such a catastrophic injury. And besides, what appeared to be her entire blood supply had oozed across his kitchen tiles. The dark, sticky blood that had reeked of mould—

Bump, bump.

More than likely, the sounds were that of the shovel, pickaxe and lantern shifting around on the curves. Meredith's dried-up bones wouldn't hold enough weight. And she was wrapped, head to foot, in a cushion of feather-filled doona. No, it was the tools and the lantern. Shit, it could be his six-pack, the beer getting turned to suds. Perhaps the occy strap had come loose.

Bump, bump.

Gritting his teeth, he switched on the radio and cranked the volume. He tapped on the steering wheel in time with the music.

How might Donna be getting along? The temptation to call was strong, but he resisted. Cops do this triangulation thing with mobile phones, he knew. They use two or three towers to pinpoint your location. Relax. Donna wouldn't renege or contact the authorities, not with the threat of losing Cassie hanging over her.

Would Donna really lose custody in this kind of situation?

John hadn't the faintest idea. He smiled in grim satisfaction. So, he thought, I've got a 'tell' whenever I lie? A giveaway squint? Well, you missed it this time, sweetheart. Donna would cooperate. By the time he returned home, the kitchen would be sparkling clean and Donna would be waiting for him, docile and afraid, trusting—

Oh shit, *the turn-off—*

Braking hard, John fishtailed the back end, steered onto the gravel road.

Bump, bump.

The gravel road was exactly as he remembered. He killed the radio and opened his driver's side window.

The air smelled fresh and organic, mossy, fragrant with the honey-mint scent of eucalyptus. He wanted to hear the river. This had always been the best part of the journey; hearing the river before seeing it, listening to the rush and gurgle, imagining the sleek, silvery fish darting through cool waters. But wait, he couldn't hear the river.

Whoa, the second turn-off—

He almost missed it.

Jamming on the brake, he hesitated, looked around. Was this the right place? The dirt path was overgrown, almost obscured by branches. Cautiously, he steered onto the path and edged the car forward. Switches of leaves swiped along the car body, whispering, murmuring. Could he be lost?

The babble of the river came to him.

Unexpectedly, tears rose.

The branches parted. There it was, his fishing spot, looking the same.

He parked, switched off the engine, got out and listened. Only the call of fairy wrens, the cawing of cockatoos, the mutter of the river. He crossed the spread of grey stones on the bank and dipped his hands into the water. So very cold; cold enough to numb his fingers. He splashed his face. It made him gasp. The desire to wade into the river, to feel it close over his head, felt overwhelming. But no, he had work to do.

He looked back at the car.

The car seemed to look back at him, expectant.

21

Rubbing at his neck and rolling his tight, aching shoulders, John walked to the car and stood by the boot. Despite himself, he was listening. Maybe not for the *bump bump*, but for something else; a scratching, a clawing, the revolutions of long nails moving around and around in circles. Sweat prickled on his forehead.

"We're finished, Merry," he whispered. "You can't hurt me any-more."

He popped the boot and stepped back, fists raised. Meredith leapt at him like a bloodied jack-in-the-box—but only in his imagination. He dropped his fists. You idiot, he thought, she's *dead*. Stop scaring yourself. He stared at the doona and tools. The occy strap had held the beers in place. Grateful, he took a stubby, opened it and drank it in a few mouthfuls. Then he grabbed the pickaxe and shovel, and closed the boot, locking it. Even though this place seemed long deserted, it would be typical of John's luck if a bunch of tourists, lost, turned up and decided to start peeking and poking around the car.

He strode away from the river and into the bush. In his mind's eye, he saw the ruins of Lyle's head bouncing over the uneven ground as John had dragged him by the ankles... He shook his head and blinked away tears. This was no time to get sappy. He doubled his pace and shouldered through the foliage of eucalyptus and ferns. King parrots and crimson rosellas called from high in the canopy. Leaf litter crunched underfoot. He began to hum to himself, tunelessly.

Would he find Lyle's grave? His stomach lurched at the thought. Would some strange kind of synchronicity lead him back to the exact spot? He felt, somehow, like that would happen, must happen, as if it were preordained. He would dig into the soil and uncover Lyle's hand, the bony fingers outstretched.

Stop it, he thought. Don't lose your cool.

The handles of the pickaxe and shovel wore at his palms. Oh, shit, he should have remembered his leather gloves. He would get blisters again, followed by calluses, just like last time. Bile rose in his throat, and he spat.

"Okay," he said, out loud, to reassure himself. "This ought to be far enough."

He had come to a small, narrow clearing between the trees. Using the shovel, he scraped the leaf litter into a big pile a few metres away. He broke ground with the pickaxe. And just like last time, the top layer of soil was soft, red and volcanic.

Flies had begun to gather around Lyle's nostrils and half-open eye.

John paused, took off his beanie, and tucked it into his back pocket.

The pickaxe juddered in his hands with every strike.

Thunk. Thunk.

After some half an hour, he swapped the pickaxe for the shovel and began moving the dirt to one side, piling it neatly. When he hit a thick snarl of roots, he leaned the shovel against a tree and used the pickaxe.

Thunk. Thunk.

Rigor mortis had pulled Lyle's mouth into a rictus grin. In his dreams, John often saw that stiffened, dead smile. Not only in his dreams. Sometimes when his mind lay blank, when he was driving a familiar route, say, or shaving, washing a sink full of dishes, the image would come to him, unexpected and unbidden. Lyle's mouth had taken on a shape it had never expressed in life: that of a perfect rectangle, a letterbox slot. Every tooth in Lyle's head had been on display. In his dreams, that letterbox slot of a mouth sometimes yawned open and pulled in John's fingers, the teeth gnashing and gnawing down to the wrist.

Thunk. Thunk.

Panting, sweating, John leaned the pickaxe against a trunk, took off his long-sleeved shirt, and slung it over a branch. He sat down and lit a cigarette.

Maybe the dreams would go away now along with the guilt since he hadn't killed Lyle. Buried him, yes, but not killed him.

John pulled the cigarette smoke deep into his lungs and coughed.

It would be amazing if the nightmare went away forever. He could hardly imagine it. After thirty-one years of Lyle screaming as dirt rained down, what might John dream about instead? He had no idea.

He thought of long-term criminals, finally released after decades in prison and how bewildered they must feel, how lost and afraid, how ill-equipped to deal with a strange and unfamiliar world. He swallowed hard. Without the guilt, without the punishment, the contrition, what was left?

He butted the cigarette, checked his watch. Getting late. He stared at the fresh grave, some two metres long, one metre wide, about a half-metre deep.

"Mate, where are you?" he murmured. "I'm here to give your sister back."

He put his hand into the grave and brushed at the dirt. An electric sensation darted through his fingertips. Yes, this was the spot, he could feel it, he could sense it. He burrowed his fingers into the soil. Any second now, he would touch Lyle's bones. Any second now... Any second...

No, don't be stupid.

He still had some half-metre of soil to move before he could reach Lyle.

A kookaburra whooped and cackled in the distance. John held his knees and rocked back and forth. Squinting up through the canopy, he watched raggedy clouds drift across a clear, ice-blue sky.

"How could you root your own sister? No wonder she hated you."

He lit another smoke.

"My whole life, I figured we were mates, but I didn't know you at all, did I? You were the better liar."

Watch yourself, he thought. Don't get soft.

He threw the cigarette into the grave, stood up, grabbed the shovel, and kept digging. The muscles in his back, shoulders and arms burned, just like last time. One of Lyle's eyes had been half-open, gazing at infinity, abuzz with flies. Their skittering black legs had roved back and forth over the dusty eyeball. John hacked through a fresh tangle of roots with the pickaxe and inspected his palms. A mess of angry red welts and blisters.

Why hadn't he brought gloves?

He wiped at the sweat in his hairline and flinched at the sudden pain. Shit. He'd forgotten the staples. Gently, he ran his fingers over the repaired laceration. It seemed intact. He grabbed the shovel.

How might Donna be getting along? Please God, don't let her do anything stupid. Don't let her call the cops, or worse, a girlfriend for moral support.

Next to the grave, the pile of dirt grew bigger and bigger.

"Jeez," he said, "are you there, mate?"

He attacked the compacted, root-riddled dirt with the pickaxe.

Thunk. Thunk.

Sweat dripped into his eyes, ran down his back and chest.

"Show yourself."

Thunk. Thunk.

In a frenzy, he brought down the pickaxe, again and again. Clods of soil flew in every direction.

"Where are you?" he shouted. "Where the fuck did you go?"

Thunk. Thunk.

Exhausted, John dropped the pickaxe and allowed his legs to fold beneath him. The leaf litter provided a soft landing. Gasping, unable to catch his breath, sobbing, John turned his face into the earth and let out a long scream.

The madness left him.

Now he felt numb.

Good, he thought. I've got the panic out of my system.

Focus.

He had to focus.

Stumbling to his feet, he wiped away tears and picked up the shovel. Okay, he hadn't found Lyle's grave. Big deal. So, there wasn't some kind of mystical connection that tied him to Lyle across the years, across the veil between life and death. Of course not. Only a fool would imagine otherwise. And yet, John had felt so sure. He worked the shovel, half-expecting to discover bones, despite himself...

Focus.

What was his plan?

Once he got home, he would gather Meredith's belongings, including her hobby boxes, and pack them in his trailer for the tip. They might have CCTV cameras at the gate, but surely not in the tip itself. Perhaps he ought to first pulverise her collection of animal bones with the sledgehammer, put the remains in a garbage bag before dumping them at the tip, dispose of the boxes a few pieces at a time in the recycle bin at home, week after week, until the boxes were gone. Burn her memorabilia, the Central Australia photos, her copy of *Oliver Twist* with Luke Skywalker taped to the cover. Yes, it would be wise to scatter the evidence.

Next, the glazier for the broken window.

After that, the appointments with real estate agents for somewhere to live.

Everything would go to plan.

Everything would work out if he kept a cool head.

At last, the grave was deep enough. John dropped the shovel and lurched down the hillside. When he spotted the car, he hid behind a tree and scanned the riverbank. Nothing and no one. Thank Christ. He walked into the clearing, popped the boot, slammed down a couple of stubbies, and contemplated the doona.

Should he bury Meredith cocooned inside the doona or not?

Cops do forensic tests on things like bed linen, he knew, and can link results to the original crime scene. How they did it, John couldn't remember, even though he had watched plenty of crime shows on TV. Perhaps he ought to strip the doona first and dispose of it down the tip. Or burn it, maybe. He gnawed on his lip. The duct tape wound about the head and feet drew his eye. Could he actually unwind that tape, unwind that doona? Look again at Merry? He imagined her eyes springing open.

Relax, dickhead, she was dead. Really dead.

But he didn't want to see, ever again, that gaping wound in her throat.

Or touch her to put her into the grave.

Something worse came to mind. What if rigor mortis had taken hold? What if her mouth was pulled into the shape of a letterbox slot? The dreams, those awful dreams…how could he bear any more?

"Oh, fuck," he whispered, scrubbing at his temples, "I wish I'd never met you."

Was that true?

"Fine," he said. "I wish I'd never met you eight years ago in the park. I wish I'd never seen you sleeping under that banksia." He put his hand on the doona and felt tears rise. "I loved you, Merry. I still do, in a dumb kind of way, even though you ruined my whole fucking life. You and your shithead brother." He picked up the doona and slung it over his shoulder. "But Donna's my future now."

On unsteady legs, he trudged up the hillside. When he reached the grave, he dropped the doona. It bounced lightly. He stared at the duct tape, flexing his hands, blowing his breath in and out. Screw it, maybe he should boot her into the grave as is, doona and all. As he swung back his foot, Crimestopper adverts came to mind. He paused. On TV, cops displaying dirty t-shirts on shop dummies, laying out eiderdowns, asking the public for help. Murders get solved that way. Someone always recognises the material—but who else but he and Merry had ever seen her doona cover? What difference would it make if the cops found it?

Again, he went to kick the body into the grave. Again, he hesitated. He put his hands on his hips, walked around the grave a few times, shook his head, gazed at the canopy and at the shifting leaves as the breeze moved through the treetops.

"Shit," he said through his teeth.

Dropping to his haunches, he tore the duct tape at both ends, and stuffed the tape in his pockets for later disposal. He took hold of the doona. In one motion, he stood up and unrolled it, making a flip-flip-fluttering sound.

Something tumbled out onto the ground.

But it wasn't Meredith Berg-Olsen.

Not by a long shot.

John gagged, staggered back, both hands at his mouth. For a second, he felt faint. That *thing* lying in the leaf litter didn't move. He took a tentative step closer.

"What the fuck?" he said. "What the actual fuck is *this*?"

A skeleton shrink-wrapped in black, parched and leathery skin, that's what the fuck it was. Like an unwrapped mummy, something buried in the desert for a thousand years or dug out of Himalayan snow, dragged from a peat bog. Even the teeth were black. The gums. The tongue, too, shrivelled and pitted like a barbecue briquette. Holy Christ. John's hands shook. He dropped them to his sides, wiped his sweaty palms on his jeans. He could have sworn on a stack of Bibles that this *thing* wasn't Meredith, if not for the tufts of white hair, the familiar ice-blue eyes glaring up sightlessly at the sky. The doona nearby lay stained with dried black slime.

"Oh, God," he muttered, and groped for a cigarette. It took him six or seven attempts to light the damned thing. He smoked it down to the butt inside a minute, but still managed to drop it a few times from between his quaking fingers.

"Merry, you'd better be dead. If you so much as wink, I'll shit my pants."

He tried to laugh, but his larynx only croaked. The sound of his voice frightened him. Chilled, shivering, he tucked his hands under his perspiring armpits and gazed at the *thing*. It looked carved out of wood. How could this be Merry? How?

Witch, zombie, vampire, demon, monster.

In old and superstitious cultures, people used to perform rituals on a corpse to make sure it couldn't rise again. He had read about such rituals on Wikipedia. A stake through the heart, a stone in the mouth, burial face-down, decapitation with the head placed at the feet. He kicked the *thing* into the grave and scraped the toe of his boot again and again in the soil, fearful of contamination.

"All right, Merry," he said. "This is it."

Picking up the shovel, he stood with one foot on either side of the grave. The *thing's* ice-blue eyes glowered blindly. If he leaned over, just a bit, it was as if the eyes looked at him, which freaked him out. He straightened and raised the shovel.

"Whatever you are," he said, "I'm not going to lie awake at night, waiting for you to knock on my goddamned window. It ends here, Merry. It ends now."

With both hands tight around the handle, he brought down the shovel, fast, and with all his strength. The blade cut through the *thing's* neck with a faint crack.

John held his breath.

Nothing happened. The withered corpse lay still. Carefully, he scooped the severed head onto the shovel blade and placed it at the end of the grave, making sure not to touch it against the blackened and bony feet.

"There," he said, and wiped his brow.

Was it enough? He put the shovel against a trunk and searched the ground. After a while, he found a rock. The *thing's* mouth was already open. Panting with fear, waiting for the skull to spring to life and come snap, snap, snapping at his fingers, at his face, he wedged the rock between the long and sharp teeth. Using the shovel, he tipped the skull onto its front. He inspected his handiwork.

Nope, still not enough.

He found a stout branch and rammed it between a couple of ribs where the heart ought to be, if there had been any internal organs left.

"Goodbye," he said. "I did my best, okay? Honest."

Working quickly, he filled the grave with soil, faster and faster. His lungs burned and his pulse thudded in his head. Once the *thing* was out of sight, he slowed down. It had taken hours to dig the grave, but only minutes to fill it, and he wondered if that realisation had any deeper meaning. If so, he couldn't think of one.

He stopped for a cigarette. After finishing it, he heaved his beers into the dirt in spasm after spasm, until he felt drained and empty, lightheaded. He lost his footing and sat down hard.

Giving in to his fatigue, he lay back and stared at the canopy. A pair of crimson rosellas hung from high branches, chattering, nibbling at blossoms. Ants crawled over his fingers. He closed his eyes and smelled the eucalyptus, tuned in to the murmuring of the Yarra River, and wanted to sleep for a long, long time.

He got up.

After stamping down the soil, he scattered over the leaf litter, just as he had done with Lyle's grave, until Merry's grave looked the same as the rest of the forest.

Weary, John rolled up the doona, careful not to touch the black stain, and picked up his tools and shirt. During the walk back to the car, he kept stopping to lean against trees and catch his breath. The river sounds gave him strength. When he came out into the clearing, he began to cry.

Stop. He had to stop.

Popping the boot, he threw in the items and opened a stubby. The beer was warm, but damn, tasted good. He dropped the empty bottle into the boot and tottered to the bank. The grey river stones reminded him of Donna, with her eyes the same colour, and of Lyle, as he had fallen back and smacked his head. John squatted, put his sore and bleeding hands into the water. The freezing temperature took the sting from his blisters. He wept some more. The river gurgled and rushed. He splashed water over his face and chest.

Get a grip.

It wasn't finished yet.

He stood up, put on his shirt, pulled the beanie over his head. Time to go home, to check on Donna, to smash the bones in the hobby boxes to powder, load up Meredith's belongings in the trailer. He should also detail the car, inside and out. He would do that tomorrow at the local servo. As soon as possible, he should sell the car.

The air felt fresh and invigorating. He leaned against the sedan with his eyes closed, breathing, inhaling and exhaling, the tension and terror ebbing from his body and mind. Then he got in the car and twisted the key in the ignition. The engine roared, the radio came on, and he could no longer hear the sounds of the river.

John drove towards home, dazed. Everything looked brighter. The clarity of the sky, the bluish underbellies of clouds, the silhouette of Melbourne's city skyline on the horizon with the windows of the Rialto reflecting sunshine in a shimmering sparkle of faraway gems. Beautiful, so fucking beautiful. Even the cars around him: the whites so vibrant, the reds so vivid, the silvers like shiny new coins. When stopped at every light, he glanced around, smiling and tearful. The other drivers seemed distracted, pensive or unhappy. Not John. He was laughing, wiping at his eyes, singing along to the radio, compulsively rubbing and scrubbing the raw blisters of his palms against the steering wheel, the pain a cleansing tonic, a blessing, a relief. A blessed relief.

Too close, he passed a cyclist on the shoulder.

Oh, Jesus, fuck, he almost hit the bastard, missing him by a bee's dick.

Come on, John told himself, get your shit *together*.

Focus.

The sun, swathed in pink and orange clouds, was setting. Too late to get to the tip before closing time, but he would dump Meredith's belongings first thing tomorrow. Meredith. Soon, that name would mean nothing to him. Meredith's name and Lyle's too. John would bury those names and never think of them again. He remembered some of the last words Nate Rossi had said about Meredith: *A crazy bitch like that? What the fuck are you hanging on for?* No reason. Not anymore.

Donna, he thought, I'm coming home. You and me, baby. We're going to be a family. It's not too late. Us and Cassie. Once I explain everything from the beginning, you'll understand. You'll forgive. I'll be pleasant to Graeme during his access visits. And I'll get you a cat, as good as Tiger, maybe even better—

A car horn sounded.

John wrestled the steering wheel. Fuck, he had drifted into another lane. He squeezed his bloodied hands on the wheel, the pain clearing his head. If he stacked now, and the cops attended, then what? How would he explain the shovel, pickaxe, sledgehammer, the doona dried to a crackle with Christ knows what kind of corpse-juice? He drove the rest of the way carefully, slowly, the radio switched off, paying the utmost attention, sweating through his clothes.

When he pulled into the driveway of the faux miner's cottage, the sun was kissing the horizon. No visible lights in the windows. Good. He parked. Getting out of the car, however, felt too much to ask. Everything hurt. Exhausted, he leaned his head against the steering wheel. Somewhere in the neighbourhood, a dog barked.

You're so close to the finish line, he thought. One last push.

Legs quivering, John stepped out of the car. He expected Donna would open the door once she heard his boots on the porch, but no, she didn't. He fitted the key into the lock, turned it. The house was in darkness. He shut the door behind him and put the keys on the hook. His nerves jangled. Adrenaline pumped. It felt, he realised, like coming home to Meredith.

"Donna?" he called. "It's me. I'm back."

No answer.

"Donna, are you here?"

The house smelled of lemon and disinfectant. He started down the hallway. Donna wasn't in the lounge. The doors to Merry's bedroom and hobby room were shut and he left them that way. He couldn't imagine Donna wanting to spend time in either room. The bathroom was empty too. As he approached the kitchen, he stopped.

"Donna?" he said.

Groping, he turned on the switch to the kitchen. The glare of yellow lights hurt his eyes. He stepped through the doorway.

The kitchen was neat and gleaming, the smell of cleaning products overpowering despite the chill breezing through the smashed window. Donna sat at the table, hands in her lap, staring into the mid-distance at nothing in particular.

"Hey," he whispered. "It's done. Everything went okay, no problems."

Her grey eyes twitched, blinked. Slowly, her gaze roved over the table, climbed his body, and found his face. "You know what?" she said.

"What?"

"I don't feel so good."

EPILOGUE

A few minutes before knock-off, John parked the forklift inside its bay, lowered the forks, and killed the engine. The factory manager, a stout and ruddy-faced man called Bazza, waved and made his way over. He carried a clipboard and a pen.

"Hey, Johnno," he said. "We can order pizza for the Christmas party. What kind do you want?"

John alighted and removed his safety helmet. The summer heat had soaked his hair with sweat. The office might be air-conditioned, but the pet-supply warehouse itself always had the giant roller-door open. Supplies came and went every minute.

"I wouldn't mind a Hawaiian, thanks," John said.

"Large or family?"

"Family. Can we order anything else or just pizza?"

Bazza grinned. "Whatever you like, mate. It's the boss's dime."

"Put me down for a garlic bread too."

"No worries." Bazza made a note. "Got plans for the break?"

"Nah, not really. There's a blackberry bush in the yard I might dig out."

Bazza nodded and began to move off. "Yeah, a week's not long enough to go anywhere, is it? I'm staying home with the missus. Gonna watch cricket on the telly and suck on piss."

"Sounds good," John called. "See ya tomorrow."

Without turning around, Bazza lifted a hand in farewell.

At the car, John took off his high-vis vest and dumped it along with the helmet inside the boot. A couple of other blokes were leaving too, and John waved. They waved back. He drove out of the car park and onto the main road.

At 3 p.m., the traffic wasn't too bad. The air-con, however, struggled to force the heat soak from the cabin. John lit a smoke and cracked the window. The journey between the factory and home was pleasant and he always enjoyed it. For the majority of the twenty minutes, he drove mostly along a country road lined with trees. He lived in Melbourne's far northeast, right on the fringe of what would be considered the metropolitan area, in a suburb more eucalypt forest than anything else.

His street was a gravel track cut into a hillside. The rental property, a three-bedroom weatherboard, couldn't be seen from the road since it was built on the slope. He turned into the drive and, foot on the brake, coasted down the hill and parked under the tin-roofed carport. This was the best part: switching off the engine and listening to the birds.

They were everywhere.

Calling, singing, cawing, screeching, laughing, in the sky and in the trees.

Sulphur-crested white cockatoos, crimson rosellas, king parrots, kookaburras, olive-backed orioles, budgerigars, robins, and more.

Since moving here in late September, John had become something of a bird fancier. He had bought a book to help identify different species. About a month ago, he had hung feeders around the eaves. It soothed him to sit in the lounge or kitchen and watch the colourful, beautiful creatures eat the seeds, chatter, and interact with one another. Outside his bedroom window, he had installed a bird bath. Sometimes, he would lie on the bed, drinking, and watch the parrots bathe and splash and preen. For some reason, only parrots visited the bath. Perhaps it was a territorial issue. He had hoped to see kookaburras, but oh well, you can't have it all.

He got out of the car. The weatherboard looked about a century old, worn out and unloved, in need of repainting, but John didn't mind. Its dilapidated state seemed to complement the wild surroundings. He tramped down the hillside alongside the house. The back yard was a sprawling acre of eucalypts, ferns, weeds, and dirt. At the bottom, over a rusted wire fence, crawled a mud-brown creek. Last weekend, he had fished for yabbies and hauled in enough for a decent feed. He looked about for neighbours, just in case. The blocks were spaced far apart, and the many trees ensured privacy. However, it never hurt to be cautious.

By now, he knew the location of every trap by heart. A dozen to ensure at least three animals per night. They were 'soft jaw' rubber-lined traps of various sizes, designed to snare animals by the leg but not injure them. He caught rabbits mostly, the occasional possum or fox. And cats. Plenty of cats. The feral kind were in plague proportions throughout the north-eastern suburbs. As for the others, if cat owners didn't keep them in at night, fuck them, they got what was coming.

The first trap had a jaw spread of ten centimetres for the smaller critters. Squatting, he lifted the hinge, stood, and put one foot on each side-wing to open the trap until it lay flat. Squatting again, he clicked the hinge back in place to set the pressure plate and stepped off. The trap lay in the grass, yawning, ready for a paw to touch the pan. Some nights, the screaming of rabbits woke him.

It took about half an hour to locate and set each trap. By the time he finished, sweat from the afternoon sun had stuck his orange and blue work-shirt to his back.

He lit a smoke and made long, easy strides up the hillside towards the stairs at the rear of the weatherboard. The lawnmower and tool shed were gathering dust and spider webs beneath the deck. There was no cultivated garden to speak of, and John didn't care to make one. Trudging up the stairs, careful to avoid the rotten planks, he pulled his keys from his pocket. The deck had a clotheshorse, a Weber barbecue. He often left mincemeat or offcuts from chops on the deck's handrail for the kookaburras. After dinner, he liked to put out apple chunks for the ringtail possums. The larger brushtail possums showed up too, however, and while he disliked them because of their brute size, the way they hissed, and their stubborn refusal to be intimidated, he couldn't figure a way to scare them off that wouldn't also scare off the ringtails.

He took off his boots, opened the back door and entered the kitchen. Pausing, he listened. Nothing. The house sounded empty.

He closed the door, put down his boots, and slung the keys on the hook.

"I'm home," he called.

No response.

He walked through the kitchen and into the lounge. Donna sat on the sofa, stiff-backed and still, her face angled towards the picture window that overlooked the front patio. For all he knew, she might have been sitting like that for the whole day.

"I've got work's Christmas party tomorrow," he said, going to the fridge and taking out a beer. He opened it and drank it. The silver pot sat on the draining board, upside down. "The boss is buying us pizza. That's pretty decent, right?"

"Right," Donna said. "Pretty decent."

He grabbed another beer and sat in his customary spot, the armchair. Donna liked to look out the window, presumably at the birds, and John didn't ever want to sit next to her. He regarded her profile. From day one, he had dressed her in long-sleeved tops and trousers to hide the fifty-two pairs of waxing and waning moons on her limbs. He didn't want to see them. And she didn't seem to feel the heat anyway.

"How was your day?" he said.

She nodded.

He worked on his beer.

She must have simmered a batch of bones. She did it two or three times per week. At least, that's how often he came home from work and found the silver pot, washed and rinsed, upended on the draining board. Her hobby room held two boxes already. He still didn't know why it was important to keep the bones. Perhaps he would never find out. Most of the time, Donna behaved as if she were heavily sedated, deaf and mute, lost within a distant fog.

Could she remember what had happened? He had no idea. After that wild day when she had killed Meredith, Donna's life had fallen apart, very quickly. She lost her job. The landlord evicted her from the clinker-brick shithole for failure to pay rent. She lost custody of Cassie. And Graeme decided that Donna was not the kind of mother that should have contact with his child, under any circumstances, and the law had agreed. But she never spoke about Cassie. In fact, Donna hardly spoke at all.

"Let me ask you something," he said.

No response.

"Donna?"

"Yes."

"Let me ask you something, okay? Are you happy?"

Slowly and smoothly, as if on a flywheel, Donna turned her head to look at him. Her grey eyes shone like molten lead. Her skin was pale, very pale. She looked as if she had lost more weight. He would have to buy additional traps. Encourage her to eat. The dark rings under her eyes resembled bruises.

"Can you hear me?" he said.

"Yes."

He hesitated. "Are you happy?"

"Of course."

"Are you sure?"

"I'm sure." The corners of her chapped lips twitched into a smile. "You've made me the happiest woman in the world."

Lightning Source UK Ltd.
Milton Keynes UK
UKHW04f0630130918
328823UK00001B/239/P